House of De Vries

Dear Rachel and Ian

Thank you for your support

Enjoy your book

Love Susan Pready

First Published in 2023

ISBN 978-1-7394043-0-7 (Paperback)
978-1-7394043-1-4 (Ebook)

Cover Design and Book Layout by:
SpiffingCovers.com

Published by:
Studio 1709 Publishing

House of De Vries

SUSAN PFEIFFER

"A mysterious time-travelling tale exploring humanities darkest traits. House of De Vries is beguiling and compelling."

Emma Marlow-De Silva

This book is dedicated to
Rob Walters
Utrinque Paratus

Love never dies.

Chapter 1

On a bleak winter's day, huddled by the office radiator keeping warm amongst the pile of notes that littered my desk, I stared out the window, desperately searching for inspiration, but nothing came. Time ticked so slowly as I watched the day go by. The greyness of the sky mirrored my thoughts, overwhelmed and under pressure with another deadline to make. I anxiously tugged at my mousy brown hair and waited. My mind turned inwards as I wrestled with my past; if only Klaus was still with me, things would have been different. He knew how hard it was for me to form relationships after my turbulent past; I felt safe and loved when I was with him. Several years ago, he vanished from my life, leaving a note on my pillow with a red rose saying, 'Sorry, I had no choice but to leave; I promise, one day, I will find you.' Heartbroken, I was cautious when Paul entered my life, but desperate to leave home, to escape from my father's controlling and strict upbringing, a deep friendship was formed. I married in haste, and all was well until my nightmares returned. Heavy-hearted, I struggled daily with my inner demons. Maybe I should have seen a counsellor, but I wasn't ready to face my thoughts. I glanced at my watch, disparagingly, staring at my blank screen.

At precisely 5 pm, as always, Charles Hunter, the *Daily Record* editor, marched into my office, wearing his crisp white shirt with cufflinks to match his pleated blue trousers. Immaculately groomed, he stood, overpowering, belittling me.

"Right, Sophia, what's the story, then?" he asked bluntly, smoothing his greying hair and covering his receding hairline.

"I'm still searching for one," I mumbled.

"You have until 8 pm, now don't let me down, Sophia."

"I won't, Mr Hunter," I muttered as he walked out of the room.

Will he be disappointed yet again? For days I had sat at my desk, but nothing had stirred me to write, even knowing that my job was on the line. Feeling frustrated and lost, I pulled my comfy old beige, bobbled cardigan tightly around me.

At last, 6 pm arrived. Grabbing my hat and coat and in need of a caffeine fix, I left the chilly office and headed towards the warmth of my favourite cafe.

"Good evening, madam. Is it your usual? Flat white?" asked the waiter.

"Yes, please," I nodded.

I took a seat by the window, but rain and mist clouded my view of the outside world. Sipping my flat white, I started contemplating my future. I had just turned forty with a divorce behind me. Stuck in the monotony of London life, I sighed heavily, running my fingers through my lacklustre hair, knowing time was running out.

The cafe was unusually quiet until a group of young men entered and sat at the table next to mine. Their conversation was in Dutch. Instantly, I recalled a strong memory of a deep-red painted house along the canal in Amsterdam.

Paul, my ex, and I often visited Holland and passed this house on many trips. It stood out among the rest, looking grand and imposing. All the mismatched houses along the canal had a story to tell, but this one intrigued me. The dark crimson building with a gothic design didn't quite match the others; it looked strange, which was compelling. Taller than the rest as the gable ends protruded out over the canal, the metallic black front door contrasted with the ornate brass doorknob. Every time I passed this mysterious building, my stomach churned anxiously.

Taking another sip of coffee, I shivered, pulling my coat closer around me, as I remembered the last time we visited, seeing a womanly silhouette peering from the top attic window of the red house. Hands shaking, nausea propelled me to the ladies' room.

It was now raining heavily. Annoyed, as I had left my umbrella in the office, I quickly ran to the nearest tube station, Charing Cross. Down into the depths of the Northern Line, I descended and raced for my train.

I needed to find a story, but all I could think about was the grand house along the canal and the woman's haunting eyes as she looked through the window towards me. I closed my eyes as the train noisily bounced along the track towards home. I awoke with a jerk as it pulled into Edgware, rubbing my neck; I was eager to relax in front of the fire with a large glass of Sauvignon Blanc.

Relieved to be home at last. I sat slumped on my sofa, staring at my phone. At 8 pm precisely, Mr Hunter, of course, called me.

"Well, Sophia, have you got that story for me?"

I hesitated as my thoughts drifted back to Holland and the alluring house.

"Yes," I replied, winging it.

"It's about a grand imposing house I've seen along the canal in Amsterdam, which seems to have a dark secret within its walls. While researching for the National History Museum, Paul found some interesting facts about this property but was forbidden to tell me. I'd like to unmask its secrets."

There was a pause as I waited for his reply, expecting his answer would be no, but at least I had an idea. Glancing at my hand, I had a strong memory of a beautiful sapphire ring; it captivated me every time I visited the museum with Paul. It was alluring yet powerful; it took centre stage amongst the rare artefacts and was admired by many. I would often daydream that I was the owner of this most exquisite ring.

To my surprise, he replied, "OK Sophia, yes I do recall Paul mentioning something about this to me. Book an early flight for tomorrow, and I shall look forward to reading your journal; you've got three days max. Just one thing, make sure you seek the owner of the house," he insisted. "I believe her name is Anna; she's a hypnotherapist and has a room available for you."

"Yes," I replied, feeling perplexed. Who was Anna? And how does he know the owner of the house? Shrugging my shoulders and taking another gulp of wine, at least I was doing something different. I started to prepare for my journey. Disillusioned with my life, I was ready for an adventure.

After booking my flight, I quickly packed my small suitcase, retiring early, but sleep did not come. I lay awake, apprehensive of what I might find in Holland. The crimson house was enticing me into its web.

I reached for my notebook, and (for once) I effortlessly wrote. "Standing bold and majestic against the backdrop of the canal, steeped in history, these houses of Amsterdam play an important part in the heritage of Holland. Tomorrow I will be entering the crimson house that has haunted my dreams ever since I set eyes upon it. What secrets does it hold? I am about to find out."

Morning came at last. I arrived early at the airport with a sense of urgency; feeling slightly apprehensive, I waited for my flight.

"Boarding now, flight KLM 0011," boomed over the tannoy. Oddly, my heart sank as something felt different. With trepidation, I boarded the plane, trying not to think of things going wrong.

As we approached the landing at Schiphol, a surge of energy swept through me. Still, I clung to my seat as the other passengers departed the aircraft, leaving last.

After a smooth train journey, Amsterdam's streets were manic with a sea of bicycles flooding from all directions; the city lifted my thoughts, vibrant and full of life. I smiled as the sun made a brief appearance, warming my face on this chilly day in January. Pulling my coat tighter around me, I tentatively walked through the streets of Amsterdam, blissfully unaware of what I may find upon my quest. The Keizersgracht canal was soon in sight.

With every footstep, it brought me closer to the enticing house. It looked even more prominent than I remembered. I stood nearby, unable to move, as I surveyed the building. Old emotions resurfaced within me, feelings of guilt and remorse tugged at my heart, but I didn't know why. The light of the canal bounced back and forth with eerie reflections creating illusions of old Amsterdam. A fine hazy mist rose up from the canal, half hiding the house as I drew closer to the imposing black front door.

Heart pounding impatiently, I reached the golden brass doorknob. With a firm, yet clammy hand, I knocked hard. Strange sensations rippled through me as my hand seemed to disappear through the door, causing me to jump back as the door creaked open. A tall, elderly bearded man stood before me, looking dishevelled and dirty. Quickly, he ushered me into the building as a flash of dazzling light engulfed us.

Startled by his abrupt manner, I quickly introduced myself. "Hello, I'm Sophia Jenssen from the *Daily Record*. I'm here to see Anna," I said, hesitatingly. "You're obviously not Anna," I added.

"Hello Sophia!" he replied in his Dutch accent. "Anna, who? Welcome to the House of De Vries. I have been expecting you," he replied intriguingly.

Hearing the door slam shut behind me, an uneasy feeling grew steadily within me; unhinged, I wanted to bolt.

Chapter 2

Light-blinded, I stumbled against the door. Confused, as the light constantly flickered in front of my vision, causing an optical illusion of a different world. It felt odd, but also familiar, my heart raced as I questioned, why was I here?

"Come, dear Sophia, it's me, Julian De Jung," he replied, holding his hand out towards me.

Disoriented, through squinting eyes, my vision slowly returned. "Where's Anna?" I asked, scanning the dimly lit hallway.

"Never heard of her, but you know why you're here, Sophia?"

"Yes, I'm researching for an article."

"Hmm," he muttered under his breath.

"It's been a while since we last met, but you do seem different," said Julian, inspecting me in a suggestive manner.

His intense gaze caused me to shiver uncontrollably.

"Well, you're here now; follow me," he said sharply.

He led me to a small room in the front of the house; it was dark and dingy, with tiny lightless windows. Shabby curtains concealed damp spores in the wood, leaving a pungent smell festering in the room. Centre stage was a round table; neatly placed upon it was a red linen cloth, with a single plant, withered, drooped, all but dead. Hanging above the fireplace was an old portrait with eerie eyes following me.

"This is not what I was expecting. I don't understand; what's happening?"

"Time will tell Sophia!" he replied. "I have been waiting a lifetime for this moment to come."

Hearing a clock chime 1 pm and the sound of horse and carts outside, I anxiously tugged my hair.

"Please, where is Anna?" I asked again, "I have been informed she is the owner of the house?"

Julian walked closer to me, his face gaunt and old with his crusty fingers pointing at me. Handing me an old newspaper cutting, he shouted, "Look, I am a co-owner of this house, not Anna. Read it," he demanded.

My stomach retracted as the words leapt out at me.

"Madam De Jung flees the country."

"What has this to do with me?

"Everything," he roared angrily. "You despise me. We could have had it all, Sophia."

"But, I don't know who you are," I replied quietly.

"Speak up, Sophia. You will remember me; I'm going to make sure of that," he raged. "Look into my eyes, Sophia; what do you see," he replied harshly; grabbing my arms tightly as he held me firmly. "Look, Sophia, just look!"

His consuming brown eyes bored into my soul, repelling me with hate.

"Sophia, there is no turning back," he yelled.

Clenching my stomach tightly, I shouted: "No! this cannot be happening."

"But it is Sophia," replied Julian aggressively.

My focus turned inwards as the hazy light engulfed me. Seeing the room spinning, my oxygen depleted, I hit the floor with a thud.

Waking in a familiar bed, the scented crimson sheets invoked memories of sensual pleasures. Plush deep velvet drapes hung seductively around the four-poster bed. I laid there for some time, hugging the linen around me, shivering, absorbing the sinister energy that consumed the room. Finding courage, I slowly investigated the view from the small round window. Horrified, I stared out of the top attic window; my view was of Amsterdam many years ago.

The door to this spartan room, dominated by the huge bed was locked. I was trapped. An uneasy feeling swept through my body as cold sweat trickled down the nape of my neck.

Hearing footsteps, I retreated to my bed. Stomach-churning, choking with angst, seeing the door handle turn, I curled up into a ball as Julian entered the room.

Pouncing on me without warning, he pinned me to the bed. Twisted and bent, his dirty fingers pushed and probed my womanhood. Disgusted, I felt powerless, becoming the vulnerable child again.

Inwardly I wept as flashbacks of my younger self consumed my thoughts, sinking deeper into myself; trying desperately to block out the pain.

"I have been waiting for this, Sophia. It's time to pay the price for what you did to me," he shouted angrily.

Julian's eyes raged with malice. As he moved closer to my lips, I smelled his foul breath upon me. His slippery tongue pushed into the back of my throat. Choking, gagging profusely, I tried to push him away, but my voice was silenced as I pleaded and begged him to stop. His heavy body was now on top of mine, prising my legs wide open; he violated me as he thrust himself deep within me. Tears of misery filled my eyes. I lay there silently, waiting for him to satisfy himself. Overcome with remorse as time became irrelevant in the vapour of delusions.

Eventually, he left, locking the door behind him. Pulling the bedclothes tighter around my naked body, a deep searing pain throbbed in my heart; there was no way out. Heart racing, I noticed a small golden mirror on the wall nearest the door. Looking at my reflection, a different face glared at me, an elderly grey-haired lady stared back at me through the mirror, with her ageing eyes.

"What's happening to me?" I cried out, as I tugged and pulled my face in disbelief.

Pinching myself hard to wake from this nightmare, sweating copiously, I clung to the bed, not wanting to move or see the truth. Breathless, gulping for air, I fearfully wept.

Hearing the grand clock in the hall tick louder and louder, agitated, I paced up and down, not knowing what was real. Cold dark brick walls encased my freedom. The clock struck 3 pm, and a deathly silence filled the room.

I began to search the room, feeling the walls like a caged animal, noticing a small gap between the decaying wooden window frame. I squeezed my hand in and pulled out a neatly folded newspaper cutting.

Shockingly it read:

"Wanted Madam De Jung."

"The search for the missing babies continues. The House of De Vries is under investigation. Madam De Jung ran a house of ill-repute, where sex and gambling were rife. Rumours of death and betrayal pervaded the streets of Amsterdam."

I turned the paper over, and disturbingly I saw a photograph of the elderly lady in the mirror – it was Madam De Jung. My heart sank with heaviness, realising she was me and I am her!

Sickened to the core, horrified, my body stiffened, crouching to the floor, hiding my face in shame. Darkness engulfed me. I retreated to the comfort of my bed, not knowing what else to do.

Hearing footsteps again outside my door, I shuddered fearfully, clutching myself tightly.

Silence came at last as the clock chimed six times.

Petrified, my body shook with cold, as I clung to the hope that this nightmare would end soon.

'Tick-tock.' The haunting rhythm played in my mind, cupping my ears to stop the intrusive thoughts that protruded into my awareness.

Screaming out loud, intuitively, words fell from my mouth, as the coldness raged within my body. The words were cold and hostile, causing me to wince painfully.

"Babies in my arms, I will have you, boy or girl, you decide. Hand me your silver, and I will pay the price."

Gut-wrenching with guilt, head in my hands, pitiful, I lay there wide awake. A lightning bolt filled the room with brightness, and a hazy fine mist dimmed my view, consuming me in a void of no return; sleep came with a vengeance as I entered an unearthly world.

Chapter 3

Aroused, yet flustered as flickering candlelight cast dark images upon the walls, I breathed deeply, hiding under the bedsheets that concealed my anguish; anxious thoughts filled my mind. Clasping my head, I found the courage to leave the bed.

Shocked and alarmed, finding myself fully dressed in a purple and black velvet gown, by the side of my bed was a small pair of black, laced shoes which fitted my tiny feet. Checking myself in the mirror, Madam De Jung in all her finery stared back at me. My tawny brown hair was tied neatly into a bun with a black lacy veil covering my head. Horrified, I screamed. "No! What's happening to me?"

The door was now unlocked. Quietly, I walked along the dark, dismal corridor towards the stairs, passing many rooms reeking of stale musky sex. Walking slowly down the spiral steps that led to the ground floor, evil energy penetrated my thoughts.

Startled by a brown-hooded man lurking in the shadows, his voice caught my attention as I watched him talk to a group of ladies.

"Come, young women, I will help you." He then turned to face me, concealing his identity with his robe.

"Good evening, madam. I have some new ladies of the night awaiting your inspection."

Aghast, I followed him gingerly along a candlelit hall; the flock velvet walls were covered in mould and grime. He guided me down another flight of stairs, passing an open door, revealing lurid fornicating. I looked on with disgust, seeing a very heavily pregnant lady, legs pushed apart much to the delight of the overpowering tall man as he shouted, "more, more!"

"This way, madam," he said, pointing to a room at the end of the corridor. It was small, damp, with no daylight, as shutters concealed the window; I held my breath. A single candle flickered upon a wooden table. Noticing another door at the rear, in walked six women, all wearing black and red lace gowns, their bodices pulled tightly revealing their ample breasts.

"Madam, here are the recruits, fresh-faced and eager to learn the trade," he cackled, flashing his teeth at me.

Failing to get a glimpse of him, he pulled his hood to conceal himself and addressed all of us.

"Remember, virgins bring a higher value to us. Babies are worth their weight in gold. Madam Sophia is here to show you the way, so abide by the rules," he said firmly.

"Madam, are these to your liking?" he asked.

"Yes," I murmured.

Leaving the ladies in the room, he escorted me upstairs, ordering me to wait for Julian, then vanished quickly.

"So you've met him now, the Hooded Man," said Julian.

Surprisingly he looked younger, and his voice was softer. Agitated and flustered, he took my hand and ushered me into the study.

"Come, Sophia, we have much work to do."

A pair of brass candles in front of the fire brought life to the dreary room, blazing the room with a golden light. The study was crammed high with tall cabinets, whilst faded wallpaper looked tired and torn. A musky scent of wood-burning brought some warmth to the chilled room.

"I don't understand, what work?"

"You know full well," he replied sternly, looking at the many documents that strewed the desk.

"Sophia, please read these," waving them in front of me.

"OK, if I must."

Reading the papers, I became increasingly appalled by what I was seeing. It was a list of young children's names, ages, and payments for each child.

"No, surely not?" I replied flabbergasted.

"Yes, Sophia, you know we are bound together. You must obey me; I am your brother!"

"What!" I yelled, horrified.

Unable to move, faltering, my heart raced as violent images tormented my soul from his torturous behaviour that ripped through me like a tidal wave.

"No! How could you, Julian! This is wrong; why?" I asked apprehensively.

"Times are hard, Sophia; we took an oath that pledged our pathway here in Amsterdam. Babies are born; we have orders that we have to keep."

Appalled, I became transfixed with fear.

"No," I quivered despairingly.

"There is no way out, Sophia."

Feeling the full force of his hand on my face, he shouted, "Dare you disobey me? Now go and attend to those new ladies," he growled angrily. "They are new blood for us to make a killing."

Walking out the door, I noticed a striking portrait of a young man, his deep dark eyes clawed into my soul.

"Who is he," I inquired timidly.

"You don't need to know yet, you will find out soon. Time is not on your side," he screeched.

"You will pay for this, Julian!"

"Oh, will I, Sophia? You don't know everything," he said, pushing me to the floor.

Stunned, I lay there for some time, witnessing a shaft of bright light, causing a surge of pulsating energy throughout my body. Fine mist tainted my view as time evaporated into the abyss; I fell deeply into the unknown whilst the light constantly flickered around me.

Moments later, I stood up, brushing myself down, and with firm footsteps, I marched to the waiting ladies. Feeling youthful, I was pleasantly surprised when I caught sight of my reflection. This time a young Madam Sophia De Jung mirrored me. Dressed impeccably in a bright blue velvet gown, revealing my slender figure; my waist was tiny. My brown hair loosely curled around my face, I was now ready to seek the truth within the fabric of these walls.

My mind spun with lucid images as strange sensations rippled through my body. Rubbing my eyes, I saw three young ladies walking towards me. The tallest stepped forward. Speaking softly, she whispered, "Madam, we are here at your service and eager to learn."

Taken aback by their beauty. I feared for their safety.

"Madam, let me introduce myself. I am Catalina; these are my sisters, Martha and Rosa. We have come to seek your help. We have nowhere to go and seek employment within your establishment."

Catalina's tall frame silhouetted her shapely body, her long flaxen hair pulled tightly back, revealing her slender neck. Martha looked intently towards me with her familiar hazel eyes, she reminded me of someone, but I couldn't recall who. Her pale complexion and mousy hair exaggerated her small, defined face. Rosa was the youngest and smallest of the sisters. Her flowing tangled blonde hair tousled around her child-like face, prickling my conscience.

"I will do my best to help you, but I can't make any promises. Now run along with the other ladies and prepare for the eager men. We open for business in a few hours. Quick, quick, no time for tittle-tattle," I replied assertively.

Chapter 4

Panic-stricken, alone, I desperately searched the room, noticing a small intricately carved chest of drawers made of mahogany, tucked out of sight. A tiny key on each drawer enticed me to investigate. Hurriedly, unlocking the drawers, I happened upon a letter tucked right at the back. Hearing a knock, I quickly hid it in my bodice.

"Who is it?" I enquired.

"It is Sir Lucien De Vries."

"Enter," I replied, imperiously.

A tall, elegantly dressed man marched through the door, his manner arrogant. Charisma poured from his hypnotic aquamarine eyes. Instantly, I felt a deep connection between us. Mesmerised, I was lured into the depths of his soul by his dashing looks, with a hint of danger; I was hooked.

"What can I do for you?" I enquired tentatively.

"I am at your service, Madam Sophia."

He spoke clearly and deeply; his husky tone resonating with my soul as his words vibrated through my body.

"I'm looking for some delight," he smiled, winking at me. "A fresh virgin will do me nicely; remember, I pay well. If it wasn't for my business, you would be out with the rest of the riff-raff in the cold."

Laughing raucously, he teased his black shoulder-length hair with his slender hand, revealing an exquisite, dazzling sapphire ring on his wedding finger.

"Do you like the ring, madam?" His transparent eyes glistened as he spoke.

"Of course, I do," smiling at the gleaming gemstone.

Walking towards me, he whispered softly in my ear, "One day, this ring will be yours."

Holding me in a firm embrace, our eyes locked, and my heart leapt as our lips met. We kissed passionately long and hard, his tongue probing my mouth seductively. The fire was lit as I rose to his bait.

"Madam Sophia, you need to act now before the end of the day. I need an answer."

"Answer to what?" I replied.

"You know very well what it is, Sophia!"

"Indeed I do. I will give you an answer at midnight Sir De Vries."

"Please call me Lucien; the pleasure is all mine," he replied, flashing his gleaming teeth in my direction, and he bid me farewell, raising his hat. "I will be waiting for you, Sophia. Now fetch me a young virgin so I can be pleasured," he said, leaving the room.

"Sophia, Sophia, where are you?" I heard Julian calling me.

"It's time to open up. Hope you have got the new ladies ready for the impatient men waiting at the door."

"Yes," I responded.

Hastily, I left the room, making my way to inspect the ladies, who were now waiting for me in the front parlour.

"I hope you are all ready; let's commence this evening and greet the men with smiles that warm their hearts and fill our pockets with gold."

"Madam Sophia, we are all willing and ready," said Catalina.

She was the eldest of the new recruits. Her voluptuous body revealed her womanly figure; her complexion paled as she held her stomach tightly.

"Are you OK?"

"Yes, of course," replied Catalina, hiding her pregnancy.

"Then follow me into the main hall." I smiled as I walked, feeling Lucien would be pleased.

Julian stood at the doorway, his thin fingers wrapped around the brass door handle. I instantly moaned inwards, reliving the pain of his brutal violation of me.

"At last, Sophia, you have done well; this is just the beginning. I may have to deflower you later, Sophia."

Julian's voice echoed around the hall as his eyes lecherously devoured the women.

I heaved. "No! Please, no, Julian."

"Time will tell; now open the door, sister," he commanded.

Turning to address the women, I spoke with authority. "Ladies, work hard tonight and earn your keep."

"Yes, madam, we will."

Opening the door, breathing deeply, a surge of energy rippled through my body as I greeted the waiting men one by one.

"Good evening, sir; what takes your fancy? Blonde? Red, brunette? Or would you prefer a young virgin to satisfy your needs? Let me see your weight in gold, then take your pick."

Velvet drapes hung from the ceiling, concealing the women dressed provocatively as they sprawled across the room, pouting, waiting for their trade. A roaring fire blazed with the smell of opium; light dimmed with a red glow infusing the sexual ambience. Tables were placed around the room with coins for gambling. Women, breasts on display, were draping themselves around the men erotically. Sensuous, intoxicating feelings aroused my inner woman. I caressed my ample bosom, feeling the heat rise within me.

"Welcome to the House of De Vries, it's a place of lechery and desire," smirked Julian.

"Let the evening begin with a bang!" He then produced a gun, firing a single shot.

Startled, I jumped backwards.

The evening flowed freely with plenty of wine, contributing to a frenzy of debauchery. Men of every age, shape and status were dazzled by the opportunities before them. Every room was occupied, as men satisfied their sexual appetites. Virgins were in high demand for a lucrative price; and some women were well practised at this.

The grand clock chimed 11 pm. Sighing heavily, I knew I had to give Lucien his answer soon. Clutching my bodice, I remembered the letter concealed inside.

"Sophia, time is running out. You have until midnight," said Julian.

"What! How do you know about that?"

"Nothing gets past me," he replied curtly.

"Julian, I need to take care of something, don't worry; I will be there."

Desperately wanting to read the letter, I speedily made my way towards the basement. It was cold and dismal, with only a few candles lighting my path. Huddled by the flickering light, I held the letter in my hand.

"Sophia, Sophia, Sophia," I heard.

Turning around, no one was there.

"Sophia," I heard again.

Agitated, losing my balance, I fell hard against the cold stone slab. Dazed and confused, I stood up carefully, noticing an old wooden door. Gingerly turning the handle, I prised it open. Bright golden light dazzled my view, mesmerised by the glossy glow dancing upon the coloured walls compelling me to take a closer look.

"Sophia, oh Sophia," I heard again.

"Who's there?" I called out.

Trembling, I turned around seeing the Hooded Man.

"Sophia, you must undo the past and make amends," he said firmly.

"Read the letter!" he demanded.

My chest tightened, breathing sharply. My heart raced rapidly; taking another look, I was surprised to find myself back in the dark basement. A hint of the golden glow was just visible as it faded into the damp wall. Eagerly reading the letter, revealing Lucien's real identity, aghast and shocked! Instinctively, I knew what to do. Leaving the basement quickly, I ran up the stairs to be greeted by Julian.

"Come sister, it's nearly midnight; time for you to meet Sir Lucien De Vries, he is waiting by the canal. I will escort you to the oak tree."

"OK," I shouted, leaving through a side door and towards the canal.

Chapter 5

Lucien was waiting by the gas lamp, his tall silhouette glowing eerily against the shimmering light. His allure tugged at my heart; pensive, I slowly walked towards him.

"You are cutting it fine, Sophia," said Lucien, sneering. "Come quickly to our waiting horses, for I believe Julian is meeting us there."

"Yes," I replied hastily; my heart quickened, hearing Lucien's rich, husky voice.

Walking in unfamiliar territory, I let Lucien lead the way. Tentatively, I silently followed him as the moon shone between the trees, casting ghostly shadows. An icy wind chilled my bones. Rubbing my arms, I looked on ahead.

"Where are we going, Lucien?"

"Just follow me," he replied.

Approaching a dark, dismal alley, I gagged, trying not to inhale the foul stench of excrement. Becoming increasingly anxious, I was relieved to see the horses tethered at the end.

"So, have you got your answer for me, Sophia?" said Lucien turning to face me.

His bewitching eyes fixated on mine, drawing me in under his spell yet again. Losing myself, I surrendered to his needs. He placed his fingers over my lips as I tried to speak.

"Patience, Sophia," he commanded, mounting his horse, "you must ride with me now."

Together we rode through the many cobbled streets with Lucien at the reins. We gathered speed, becoming one with the horse. Clinging tightly, my arms were firmly around his waist.

Eventually, we arrived at the paddock; the moon was now fully visible, guiding us towards a tall old oak tree. Shivering and tired, my stomach in knots, an owl screeched in the distance, causing an eerie silence and fuelling my imagination. No words were needed.

Moments later, Julian joined us, and dismounting from our

horses, Lucien leant against the big old oak, grinning gleefully as he teased his black hair from his eyes. Julian stood by his black mare, his gaze firmly fixed towards me, it was intimidating.

"Well, Sophia or shall I call you madam? It's now time for your answer."

"Gulping nervously, I whispered, "Yes."

"Speak up," he insisted.

"Yes, I will do what is necessary."

"You have made the right choice, sister. From this moment onwards, you must obey us, do you understand?" said Julian aggressively."

"Yes," I replied.

Holding me tightly, Lucien embraced me, pushing me firmly against the tree.

"You have been waiting for this, haven't you Sophia?"

"Yes," I muttered as he grabbed my hand and quickly placed it on his hard erection, arousing my senses as the heat intensified between us both. Breathing heavily, I let out a moan of pleasure whilst Julian sniggered from behind the tree.

"Where many men are asking for sex, we will make a killing," said Lucien, teasing me with his tongue.

Lucien's grip was firm and forceful, his hands tearing at my bodice. Impatiently lifting my gown and groping at my groin, he then pulled himself towards me. I was powerless; his hand was now over my mouth as he spoke forcefully.

"Hush now, Sophia; you cannot escape me. By the light of the moon we have made a contract, the three of us are bound together."

"No," I squirmed. "I will do anything for you, Lucien, but please not with Julian."

"It's too late, Sophia. Look at the tree."

The slivery light of the moon flickered upon the tree, showing clearly an engraved heart within a symbol with the initials (L.S.J) surrounded by Lucien's coat of arms.

"The deed is already done. Welcome to the dark side Sophia; now I will have you," mocked Lucien.

Fooled by his devilish ways, he looked deep into my soul. Our lips met hungrily, seducing me into submission. He entered me forcefully while crudely caressing me; my inner pain diminished, misplacing lust for love. Whilst Julian watched, engrossed in the moment, squirming with delight.

"You know what you must do," said Lucien, biting my ears provocatively.

"Yes," I murmured as shivers of toxic electric energy rippled throughout my body. Lust, fuelled with danger, our flame ignited; letting go of fear, I was lost in wild abandonment.

Drawing breath, I said softly, "Yes, I will do as you asked, your wishes are my desires."

"Good girl Sophia," said Lucien.

"It's my turn now," shouted Julian.

"No!" I pleaded.

"Your allegiance is now with us, now bend over," demanded Julian.

Resisting his advances, I squirmed in anguish trying to push Julian away but his strong arms held me down firmly.

"You can't run, Sophia, we own you now," said Julian.

Searing pain engulfed my being as he took me forcefully from behind. Lucien stared intently, watching every move Julian made. Lucien's eyes glazed over, pushing my mouth around his throbbing penis as the energy intensified. Coming to a climactic end, relieved, we fell in a heap upon the damp grass. Looking up at the full moon, feelings of anger arose within me. Agitated, Lucien quickly placed a small mask over my mouth. I tried to resist, but the strong vapours of laudanum swept through me, leading me into an altered state of consciousness.

Hours later, I croaked trying to speak. "What's happened, Lucien?"

My question was not answered as he carried me towards the horse. Hearing gunfire in the distance, I glanced at my hands, appalled and horrified; they were covered in fresh blood.

"Hold tight," said Lucien as we both mounted the horse, galloping through the many fields.

"Where's Julian?" I shouted.

"He's gone on ahead; the deed is done, until the next time. We have made a killing tonight. Good work Sophia."

Stopping abruptly, I gasped seeing Catalina's body lying motionless in the field.

"No! This cannot be happening," I yelled, staring at my blood-stained hands. "This is not right; I don't understand."

"It had to be done," said Lucien arrogantly.

"But she was with child, do you know?"

"Yes," he replied flippantly.

"Julian went to fetch her, as her labour had started; we were informed," said Lucien.

"By whom?" I enquired tentatively.

"I cannot say, but we can trust him as we pay him well," replied Lucien, his teeth gleaming as he spoke. "Come now, hurry, we must dispose of her body," he said, pulling me off the horse.

Mortified, my hands were covered in Catalina's blood. Gathering her body, we draped her over the horse. Lucien trotted slowly whilst I walked on solemnly behind.

Stopping at last, Julian had dug a shallow grave in the thick pine forest. There we laid to rest Catalina's body. Looking at her lifeless form, distraught, I cried out in dismay.

"But what happened to her baby?"

"Her baby is safe; that's all you need to know," replied Lucien.

"We must rest before dawn. Julian will keep the first watch."

Making our way to a small clearing amongst the shrubbery bush provided us with some shelter from the cold easterly wind. Lying next to Lucien, quivering, feeling the warmth of his hand over my mouth, I succumbed, yet again, to the intoxicating vapours engulfing me in a world of obscurity.

Chapter 6

Dawn was breaking; crimson light drifted through the clouds as soft raindrops fell from the sky. Touching my cheek, I noticed my blood-stained hands. Disgusted, I sat up. Feeling the wet grass under me, I shivered uncontrollably. I crept silently away whilst Lucien slept and made my way to Catalina's shallow grave; it was empty.

"What have you done with her body?" I shouted angrily.

Julian emerged dishevelled from the bushes. Looking down at the grave, he replied sheepishly, "I kept watch all night."

His face ashen and pale, he then turned towards me.

"Sophia, don't you remember?"

"No." I stared vacantly.

"Well, you didn't do a good job, did you, Julian?" shouted Lucien, running towards us both.

We stood by the empty grave. Dumbfounded and deeply threatened, I sensed impending danger. Running for shelter as a storm broke, we took cover under the bare branches of an elm tree, giving us a little protection from the easterly wind, which chilled us to the bone.

Distant horses galloped towards us, the sound carrying on the blustery wind.

"Run now!" shouted Lucien. "We must get to our horse."

Panting, without stopping, the horses were gaining speed. Jumping quickly on our steeds, we made our escape. I clung to Lucien like a limpet with my blood-stained hands as we rode through many fields and over the endless dykes.

"Hold on tight," said Lucien, jumping over a hedge towards safety, leaving behind the trail.

Eventually, we arrived in a small hamlet, with just a few dwellings, taking shelter in a ramshackled hut.

Catching my breath, dazed and ashamed, I spoke up at last.

"Lucien, why did you kill Catalina?"

"I didn't. You did," replied Lucien sternly.

"No, this cannot be true; I could never hurt anyone."

"Well, you did last night!"

My stomach tightened, choking with remorse, denying any responsibility, not allowing his words to fall upon me.

"But I don't remember anything, Lucien, after meeting you at midnight."

Staring in disbelief at my crimson-blooded fingernails, I screamed at him, "No! You are lying."

"Shh, Sophia."

Smiling, Lucien sauntered towards me, clasping me with his strong arms around my shoulders; he stared intensely at me, pressing himself between my legs. I was weakened by his need as the energy intensified; teasing me with his moist lips, I quivered.

"You gave me your answer, sealing our deal with crime and passion," he said crudely. "Sophia, you were eager, just like me!"

Smirking, he pushed his straight black hair from his eyes, revealing the dark side of his soul.

Aghast, pushing him away, I crumbled to the floor, crying hysterically.

Grabbing my hand, Julian pulled me up, slapping me hard on the face.

He said harshly, "Sister, this is all part of our plan; the money was there for the taking."

"Why cannot I recall?" I cried fearfully. "What have I done?"

Lucien and Julian looked at me directly and said brusquely, "Good work, Sophia."

My mind spun in a turmoil. "Stop!" I shouted. "None of this is making sense."

"But it does, Sophia. You will remember soon; Catalina was always part of the plan."

My head pounding, I paced up and down in the hut, crying silently.

"Listen," said Lucien, hearing gunfire coming towards us, "we need to make haste."

"You must run to your horse," shouted Julian. "We will cover you. Now go, Sophia!"

31

Pulling out pistols from their tunic pockets, Julian and Lucien defended my escape.

The deafening sound of gunfire drew closer to me. Petrified, I ran towards the tethered horse. Relieved, climbing upon the warm-blooded animal, I let the horse lead the way. Wiping sweat from my brow, with blood on my hands, I held the reins tightly, fearing for my life. Gunshots ricocheted above my head, startling the horse as we jumped over a hedge, throwing me to the ground, landing with a thud as the horse galloped away.

I laid there motionless for some time, feeling my life draining away with every cell in my body. Drifting in and out of consciousness, I became aware that I was being carried. Peering out of my weary eyes, all I could see was a veil of mist dimming my view.

"Madam, madam, wake up," a gentle whisper caressed my ear.

My vision returned enough to see a vague figure of a man carrying me. His strong arms supported me with a faint smell of patchouli oil that lingered in the air. Clouds drifted in the sky as the sound of birds echoed down the valley. Time had no meaning, no past, no present, no future; I was hanging in an empty void. Clinging to life, like a flower in the wind, caught in a moment of desperation, my body cold as ice, darkness then came.

"Madam Sophia," I heard again, "please wake up."

Gently opening my eyes, I saw the Hooded Man.

"Sophia, rest here for the night. This is a place of sanctuary, tomorrow you must continue your journey."

The Hooded Man handed me some food and water, then quickly faded into the mist before I could ask him any questions, leaving no trace of his presence. Gradually, I started to take in my surroundings. In front of me was an altar encased in a walled stone dwelling. Now feeling more sure of finding my feet, I investigated. The room was sparse with an eerie feel, but at the same time, it felt calm. Becoming increasingly at ease with the place, I rested for a while until I noticed above the altar was a symbol within a coat of arms. Cold shivers cascaded through my whole being as I read the inscription out loud.

"All that enter this place must keep the oath. Your choice is yours, but dare you to break the oath, then hell has no fury."

Quaking fearfully, I realised I was standing in a witch's

pentagram. Shivering as coldness entered my body, finding a fur skin on a slab of rock, cradling it, I wrapped it around myself, trying to keep warm. A distant, flickering light intrigued me, drawing me towards it. Tucked away in an alcove sat a big leather-bound book. Carefully brushing off the dust revealed another symbol; this was Lucien's. Palpitations thudded in my chest. Hearing footsteps, I held my breath, stepping back into the shadows. The light grew nearer, causing Lucien's silhouette to glow through the darkness.

"Dear Sophia, don't look so surprised. I was told I would find you here. Come out of the shadows and let me see you."

"Where is Julian?" I quivered, looking all forlorn.

"He's gone back to the house," he said, laughing with malice.

"Welcome to my lair, Sophia." He pushed his hair behind his ears. "You are all mine," he said crudely.

Hypnotised by his presence, not willing to hear the truth, I crumbled towards him, eager for his touch.

"Did I really kill Catalina, Lucien?"

"Yes, you did," he growled menacingly.

"No," I whimpered in disbelief, "then I pray for forgiveness; please I beg of you, sir."

"That's not going to help you now," said Lucien, embracing me. "Sophia, this is the beginning of the end."

He murmured as our lips met once more. Tasting his sweet breath, I became lost in the oblivion of sexual gratification. Drawing breath, his tongue slipped into my mouth. We kissed passionately. Caught in his lair, like an animal, I was his prey. Ripping my gown off in a frenzy, he gorged upon me whilst running his hands along my naked body, sending ripples of erotic pleasure that I could not deny. Led by Lucien, we played dangerous games to quench his bondage fetish obsessions. I was consumed with lust, arousing my sexual appetite; it dulled the hidden pain I carried within me as he initiated me into his coven.

Chapter 7

The moment had passed. Exhausted; we lay naked, our bodies contentedly warm, drifting in and out of sleep. I awoke startled as a wave of acute anxiety swept through me, realising Lucien had found the letter.

"Well, you won't be needing this anymore," said Lucien angrily, picking it up from the floor and tearing it into shreds.

Shrinking deep inside of myself, I cried inwardly. My freedom faded like a wilting rose, knowing I had entered a dark night of my soul.

Tentatively, Lucien reached out to me, placing a silver chain around my neck; attached was a phial.

"Did I really kill Catalina?" I cried pitifully.

"Hush now, Sophia, I am all you need, and so it is."

Kissing me softly, we embraced once more; his strong presence filled every part of my body. I bore witness to his seed as our limbs entwined, awakening my sexuality; adrenalin fed my appetite as the heavy scent of dewdrops consumed my whole being. My secret was stolen as I was lost in nirvana.

Stirring, Lucien had gone, leaving his musky scent upon the fur skin that kept me warm. Tossing my tangled hair from my face, I felt agitated seeing my blood-stained hands. Gathering my gown, I retreated, out of the cavern, towards daylight, clutching the chain around my neck.

The early morning mist lifted, revealing a vast meadow; clouds raced ahead as the sky turned cerise pink. Daybreak had begun with the sound of the dawn chorus. Unaware of my location, walking barefoot upon the grass, shafts of sunlight warmed my body. Hugging myself tightly, I marched onwards towards a distant tree. Seeing my horse tethered, waiting for my return, I silently rode, smiling inwardly, knowing I had the upper hand with Lucien. Through many fields and thick forests, I travelled far until I came to a natural stream to bathe and to quench my thirst. The cold water felt refreshing, washing away the evidence on my hands. Staring deep into the water, I grew entranced by my reflection. An elderly lady glared back: it was me!

"What?" I shrieked, "this cannot be happening again!"

Glaring intently, the old lady seemed to be pointing to the chain as I played with the phial. Intrigued, I took a closer look. Amazed, I found a secret compartment; on opening it, a strong aroma of opium hit my senses. Finding a small lock of hair bound in fine thread, tucked neatly around the rim, a cold shiver tingled down my spine as I tugged at my matted hair.

Sunlight shimmered on the stream as waders ducked and dived, causing many ripples of illusions of myself, old and young. Hearing faint voices in the distance, I quickly ran to my horse, hiding us both from view behind a large pine tree, seeing Julian with another man and a young woman. Money was being exchanged freely between them. Julian's voice raised as he spoke aggressively to her.

"Take this money as part payment; the rest you will have when you have completed your deed."

They then forcefully pushed her to the ground, lifting up her gown. Taking turns to fornicate her, she willingly obliged their needs. I stared impassively until they had finished with her.

"Now be off with you, and come back when you are with child," said Julian abruptly.

Trying to get a better view of the other man, a branch behind me snapped. Startled, I turned around sharply, but no one was there, just a brooch lying on the ground amongst the leaves. It was gold and very ornate; engraved on the back was a five-pointed star. Clasping it with both hands, I immediately felt a surge of immense power that gravitated me between two worlds. Causing me to stumble, I leaned against a tree, but my ankle gave way; excruciating pain shot through me as I let out a cry.

"Who's there?" said Julian.

"It's me, Sophia. Please help me. I'm in pain."

Turning to the other man, he whispered something. The stranger then took flight upon his horse.

"There you are, sister; I have been looking for you, Sophia. We have a long journey ahead. We need to get back before nightfall, as I have an important meeting to attend, which will be very fruitful for us both," he grinned.

"Who was that man?" I enquired.

"No one of any importance, so don't ask me again," he said harshly. "Let me see to your leg, then we must go."

"Ouch." I winced as he tended to my sprained ankle.

We rode through many valleys and over neatly placed dykes, eventually arriving in a small hamlet. Seeing a tavern, we tethered our horses, entering the dark, dismal building. Both weak with hunger and exhaustion, we were led to a table in the far corner.

"Hello," said the bartender abruptly with a Flemish accent.

He looked pensive. It was hard to see the man behind his creased folds of aged skin. Wisps of silvery hair were lightly swept to one side, covering his protruding eye. Offering some food and ale, he looked directly at me.

"Madam, you took your time getting here."

I didn't reply. I just stared blankly at him, clutching my brooch. I asked, "Please excuse me. Can you direct me to the powder room."

"It's out the back," he replied curtly.

Alone, at last, refreshing my face, I breathed a long sigh, then safely secured the brooch inside my bodice. Noticing the Hooded Man, from the corner of my eye, I called out to him.

"Hey, please help me."

"Sophia, you have to get it right. There is no turning back. Look at what you see. Is it real, or is it an illusion?" asked the Hooded Man benignly.

Making my way back to Julian, I glanced back to see where the Hooded Man had gone, but he had vanished. Puzzled, I scraped my hair from my heated brow.

"Did you see the Hooded Man?"

"No, why would we? We are miles away from the House of De Vries."

"Julian, please tell me, what is going on? Did I really kill Catalina?"

"All you need to remember is that we are under oath, Sophia. Now be quiet, eat up; we are being watched."

Chapter 8

Dusk was fast approaching as we arrived back at the House of De Vries. The long journey had taken its toll on my body; weak with exhaustion, I longed for my bed, observing glimpses of the silvery moon as its watery reflections muddled my view over the murky canal.

We tended to our horses and entered the house. Increasingly unsettled, sensing a hostile environment, silently I prayed. Turning to speak to Julian, he had already entered the main lobby, closing the door behind him. Hearing muffled voices, trying to listen through the door, I was alerted by the sound of footsteps. Creeping to a place of safety, I watched closely as Julian left the room, followed by the unknown man I had seen in the field earlier. His thick, dark brown hair curled loosely around his small features; he walked with an arrogant air. Glancing at his shoes, a golden buckle with a royal seal caught my attention.

"You know the deal is tomorrow, as planned," he said to Julian.

"Yes, your Majesty."

"Then I bid you goodnight," replied Julian as he escorted him off the premises.

Hastily, I made my way to the attic without Julian knowing. Closing the door firmly shut, I laid on my bed fully clothed, my gown in tatters; retrieving my brooch, I held it tightly, sinking deeper and deeper into my body, as I drifted into a deep sleep of bewilderedness.

Daylight streamed through the small round window. Looking out, there was a stillness in the air; sounds of silence echoed my thoughts. I stood motionless as the oppressive energy raged through my body.

Roused from my thoughts, hearing a knock on my door, I was relieved.

"Who is it, please?"

"It's Catalina's sister, Martha; I need to speak to you, madam; it's urgent."

Composing myself, "Please enter," I replied.

Seeing Martha in distress, her eyes red-rimmed from crying, sunk deep into her pale complexion, moved me. Thinner and smaller than her sister, Catalina, she looked gaunt and fragile.

"What is it, Martha?"

"It's Catalina. She's dead; her body was found in a dyke. I feel she was murdered and now I fear for my life, madam, please help me," pleaded Martha.

Smothered with guilt, avoiding eye contact, I reached out to her, touching her hand.

"I'm so sorry for your loss, we must work together to find out what happened to her. Now please leave and be on your guard. We will speak again at the end of the day."

"Thank you, madam."

Crumbling behind the door as she left, ashamed, my tears blurred the view in the mirror. Seeing myself through different eyes, shaken with grief, I was lost in a void of no return. Tucked behind the door was a crushed cerise velvet gown with a tight bodice. Quickly dressing, I clasped the brooch as I made my way to the front parlour.

The room overlooked the canal. Peering out of the window, a delicate veil of mist shrouded my view. I saw a strange figure of a woman walking slowly towards the house, then stopping abruptly. Rubbing my eyes in disbelief, she was still there. Spooked, I shut the shutters tight and paced the floor, as time stood still. Holding my brooch over my heart for comfort, faltering, I sat quietly on a chair. The bereft house felt utterly empty, and silent, even Martha had vanished. Opening the shutters again, the figure was closer; breathless, I closed my eyes to avert the vision.

"Sophia, Sophia, wake up," said Julian.

Feeling the sharpness of the chair piercing my back brought me closer to the sounds of the house.

"Julian, please look out the window. I saw a strange figure coming towards the house," I replied, trembling.

"Come, now, dear sister, look, it's a bright fine morning. Can't you hear the call of the birds?" asked Julian opening the shutters wide, allowing the sun to flood the room with warmth.

"But I did see someone, I really did," I pleaded.

"You must be having one of your funny turns. You had them as a child, don't you remember?"

"No," I said faintly.

"You must rest, my dear; we have a busy evening of many guests. There will be much merry making which will fulfil our needs," he smirked. "Now, back to your bed," he demanded.

I obeyed, disgruntled, scurrying to my room.

Feeling cold as I touched my cheeks, shivering, I hid under my bed linen and waited for sleep to come. Dreaming vividly, I sweated profusely. The heat intensified as flames burned around me, twisting and swirling, painfully consuming my whole body. Immersing myself in the fire, trying to scream, I awoke in shock, deluded, trying to cling to my past, but instead, deceit and crime stared me in my face. Grabbing my brooch for comfort, feeling its power, my strength returned; as I touched each point of the five-pointed star, I intuitively recited:

"We are ladies of the night, brave and bold, are we. Fear us, and you will know. Together we are one. Oh, gracious, one of the night, we believe in the magic of life. Time is now to unlock the past to reveal the future."

Energy sparked within my hands, becoming hot and powerful; I was ready for the evening's entertainment of many men. Sighing heavily and securing my brooch into my gown, I left the attic's safety, making my way towards the main reception room.

I was greeted by many desirable men, each looking for a woman to satisfy their cravings. I was amazed that the room was now lavishly decorated with golden crimson drapes, the sweet scent of geranium masking the smell of opium. Scantily dressed, voluptuous women sprawled across the tables, enticing the men. Wine flowed freely while gambling fuelled the energy of the evening.

"We've been waiting for you, Sophia," said Julian.

"How did this happen?" I enquired suspiciously.

"Dear sister, I cannot say, just trust me, now please just make sure the ladies are ready," he sneered.

"Madam, I'm so pleased you are here," said Martha, running towards me.

She looked subdued, then quietly said. "Madam, things are not what they seem; there are other ladies with child. I fear for their lives; I only know this because ..."

She was stopped abruptly as the room fell silent. All eyes were upon a man of royalty who entered the room. His small, framed body stood out amongst the rest. Neatly dressed and well-groomed with his thick dark brown hair tied neatly back, I instantly recognised him.

"Let me introduce you to Prince Lavin of Prussia," said Julian as he reappeared.

"This is my sister, Sophia; she will escort you today."

Solemnly, I had no choice but to obey.

"Madam Sophia, I believe this is part of our agreement. You help me, and I will greatly enhance you with wealth on all levels," said the Prince in his broken accent.

"I have already spoken to Lucien, who will be joining us later."

I nodded graciously; the money was there for the taking.

"Prince Lavin, let me pleasure you," I teased, licking his ear lobe with my tongue.

"Come, this way Madam Sophia," grinned the Prince.

"The pleasure will be all yours, madam."

He smirked, laughing candidly as he gave me powders to fuel my addiction for greed and unbridled shameless behaviour.

I sniffed eagerly. Martha hurriedly rushed to my aid, but was pulled away by Julian. Instantly, I had a rush of adrenalin; light-headed, I grew dizzy. Taking my hand, Prince Lavin escorted me to his waiting carriage. Glancing back towards the canal, a hazy mist rolled in, which soon disappeared under a blanket of thick fog.

The carriage was comfortably dressed, with plush velvet cushions for comfort, and adorned with red and golden drapes to protect our privacy. Feeling the persuasive touch of the Prince's hand running up my thigh, I quivered in anticipation as he gently stroked me, tending to my vulva. Opening my legs wide, I was ready.

Abruptly, the carriage stopped and Lucien climbed on board. Aroused, flushed, I quickly closed my legs.

"Good evening, Sophia," said Lucien.

His eyes shone so brightly, dazzling me with his dangerous aura. Heat arose within me as he took his seat next to me, placing his hand on my other thigh and making his way to my moist quim.

"Prince Lavin is now ready for you," mumbled Lucien. Producing a scarf, he blindfolded me.

"This is for your own safety, Sophia," said Lucien, holding his hand over my mouth and nose.

Again, the heavy scent of laudanum engulfed me into the realm of obscurity, numbing my senses into oblivion.

Chapter 9

Distant church bells woke me from my slumber; they sounded heavy, reverberating throughout my body. Quivering, still blindfolded, Lucien led me from the carriage.

"Where are we going, Lucien?" My apprehension caught me off guard as I involuntarily shuddered.

"You will see for yourself soon," he replied curtly.

Walking on an unstable path, I stumbled as a cool breeze flowed around my legs. Stopping at last, Lucien untied the scarf, revealing a deep crypt in the underworld. Claustrophobically small, with delicate ornate windows, only a small amount of light was allowed into the room. Painted with deep shades of russet, hints of gold glinted in the sunlight upon the high ceiling.

My vision adjusted, noting an elaborate red banner of a distinctive pentagram hanging above the altar. The words boldly stood out in golden/red twine. 'As above, so below.' Clenching my knuckles, I immediately began to doubt myself.

Two candles burned brightly upon the altar, in between them stood a golden chalice. One by one, a multitude of people dressed in black hooded robes entered the chamber. Around their waists were purple twisted ropes. Intimidated, I froze as they formed a circle around the altar.

The air was musky, mixed with the scent of incense and powders. A magnificent golden statue of a man stood prominently to the left of the altar. He was draped in a rich velvet red robe and wore a crown of precious rubies. Eyes of steel stabbed my heart.

A deep voice bellowed behind the effigy, bringing a deathly silence to the crypt. Gulping as a tall man appeared, identical to the statue but with a black veil covering his face, I cringed as my anxiety rose within.

"Welcome, dear brothers and sisters, to the order of the Occult."

His powerful voice echoed, ricocheting around the cold chamber.

Lucien pushed me towards the front. His towering presence descended on me; petrified, I quivered internally.

"Sophia, welcome dear sister. I am the Lord of the Occult. You will witness much this evening, things that you will not understand, but you must obey! We have all made a sacrifice to be here. All have taken the oath."

Standing tall, he then addressed everyone. His voice echoed menacingly. Alarmed, my anxiety grew.

"Dear brothers and sisters, please repeat after me. For now and forever, we are attuned to the ritual that binds us together. We are all one; therefore, it cannot break. I obey and accept on all levels, in mind, body and spirit."

Speaking in Latin, he recited.

"Spiritu mundo, sed etiam Spiritus interpellat, pro nobis incessanter gemitibus inenarrabilibus. Fiat voluntas tua."

(Spirit of the world, but the same spirit intercedes incessantly for us with inexpressible groans. Thy will be done.)

"Sophia, you must now bare your soul and become one of us. Now stand before me naked," he commanded.

I undressed nervously as he drew me into his tangle of desires. Powerless, with clammy hands, I stood naked, exposed and fragile. I was his victim.

"Come closer, Sophia! Let me see you," he demanded menacingly.

His eyes fixated on my exposed body. With apprehension, I tentatively moved forward, heart racing, trying to avoid his glare.

"You are a fine specimen, Sophia! Put this on," he demanded, handing me a white robe, pointing to a stone slab lined with deerskin. "Lie down!" he instructed.

Quivering, I lay on the cold stone, stroking the fur for comfort, shivering uncontrollably.

"You have been waiting for this, Sophia. This is your destiny," spoke the Lord.

Choking, I recoiled from his words, refusing to hear him, staring blankly as a blast of cold wind blew out the light, then darkness came. Paralysed with fear, my blood curdling, I clung to life. Blinking, growing aware of a dim light, my peripheral vision heightened, seeing a large gathering around me. Horrified, I cried silently, transfixing on the high vaulted ceiling decorated with intricate carvings of gold, as I succumbed to my outcome.

"Today, we are gathered here to remind us of our oath and witness the birthing of our sister, Sophia, into our Occult, with the blood from a wild boar mixed with the blood of man will embody us in the ways of the old," said the Lord, masterfully.

I quivered as he produced a knife. Taking hold of my hand, he proceeded to cut my little finger sharply. Rich plasma seeped out into the golden chalice before he stemmed the bleed. Furiously, the Lord whipped my gown open for all to see. Submissive and defenceless, I awaited my fate.

"Step forward, Lucien, Julian and Prince Lavin," commanded the Lord.

"Now, take your rightful place."

Slicing their fingers, watching crimson blood as it flowed freely into the goblet, the Lord then lacerated his own, bleeding it into the mix.

Speaking in incantations, he drew a symbol of the Occult on my brow with his blood-stained finger. My body stiffened as raw energy pulsated throughout me.

"*Numerus summamque potestatem dominii ius imperiumque. A caelo usque ad centrum. Pacta esse servanda.*"

(Total, supreme power, dominion, ownership and sovereignty. From the sky to the centre. Agreements must be kept.)

Standing behind me, the Lord's menacing presence overshadowed me. Lucien was at my feet, Julian to my left and Prince Lavin to my right.

"Before you all lies my mistress. With the blood of five, we now represent the pentagram; spirit, air, water, earth and fire. I hereby decree we are now bound together. The blood of life runs deep, the blood of lust, the blood of greed and the blood of death," bellowed the Lord.

Towering over me, the Lord smeared the rest of the blood onto my naked breasts, I was condemned to silence. Humiliated, lowering my head in shame as he tied my wrists and feet, securing them to the slab. Distressed and disturbed, I clung to hope, biting my lip tightly, remembering my childhood.

"Sophia, you belong to me, and what is mine belongs to you all. The way of the Occult is decreed within your soul. You are now bound to us through time and space," ordered the Lord.

Muffled voices started to murmur around the crypt as the energy heightened, growing with anticipation.

"Silence!" shouted the Lord.

"Lucien, take your position and cover Sophia."

Gasping for breath, Lucien mounted me, whispering in my ear.

"The pleasure is all mine, Sophia."

His dulcet tone soothed my soul, hooking me under his spell. I was lost in desire, becoming as one with Lucien. Excitedly my body instinctively responded to his sensual touch, bringing me alive; I became addicted to him. Tantalising and teasing me with his tongue, Lucien licked the blood from my breasts, sending ripples of euphoria as he caressed my naked body. We were both riding high on adrenalin until he climaxed. Exhausted, opening my eyes, shockingly, a mass orgy had begun. The powerful aroma of sex infused the chamber, licking the metallic taste of blood from my mouth, relishing the moment as we kissed feverishly. Caught in his lair, my past quickly faded into obscurity. Breathlessly Lucien dismounted, leaving me bereft; I lay in anticipation, fearful of what may come next.

"Prince Lavin! It's now your turn to deflower Sophia," ordered the Lord.

"No! Please no! I beg of you," I was pleading to the Prince.

"It's too late," he replied as he straddled me.

More gore was smeared upon me. Eyes wide open, I watched the Prince satisfy his desires. I was merely his subject to be violated at whim. His firm grip held me down, crudely opening my legs; he penetrated me hard and fast. Resisting his touch, I crumbled under his weight, submitting to his seduction. Sweet juices ran freely as he pounded me deeply.

Rising to a crescendo, he shouted, "Your taste is divine; with the smell of blood, I am in complete ecstasy!"

Numb of all emotion, a searing pain swept through me; catching my breath, I urged and pleaded with the Prince to dismount. Relieved, at last, he had finished with me. I was now caught in a web of dangerous games. It was unrelenting, becoming a frenzy of debauchery.

"Julian, the time is yours to do as you please," beckoned the Lord.

"No, please no," I cried in dismay, but Julian silenced my voice as he harshly feasted upon me, attacking me with his vile words. Raging with anger, slapping me hard, too weak to defend myself, I became his sisterly whore.

"This is the way it is, sister, and no amount of pleading will stop me!" he roared.

Crying pitifully as his grubby hand penetrated me, his eyes filled with lust, he succumbed to the moment, licking his fingers before filling me. Mass hysteria fuelled his ego, bringing him to a climactic end, pushing his engorged organ into my mouth and allowing his seed to pump hideously. Defenceless and shamefully abused, I swallowed, gulping hard. Sickened to the core, my body weak with exhaustion, sobbing hysterically. I could not take any more.

"That's enough, Julian!" commanded the Lord.

Crippled in pain, tormented, I screamed inwardly.

"Silence," ordered the Lord.

Chapter 10

A deathly silence filled the chamber, and an eerie shadow loomed towards me. Compelled to look, the Lord's eyes locked with mine. Now unmasked, seeing his truth, I glared, horrified!

"It's time to witness your Lord in the act, dear brothers and sisters, as I feast myself upon our sister Sophia!" bellowed the Lord.

All eyes were transfixed on us, I was incapable of speaking, petrified, as he silently approached me. Quickly he mounted me. I was helpless with the full force of his weight and power crushing me. Breathless, I watched him produce a sword, causing ripples of gasps amongst the gathering. His brooding eyes bored into my soul, his face twisted with torment, with a deep scar from his right eye to his mouth. I prayed for my sanity. The sword, inches from my throat, dripped with blood from the chalice as he salivated over my body. Swiftly he swung his dagger high in the air before throwing it to the ground.

Excitement rifled through the crypt as the energy magnified with a deafening roar. Closing my eyes tight, the Lord's long thin tongue slithered up and down my body, violating my womanhood as he pummelled me hard with his fist.

"Enough!" he shouted as the crowd erupted into mass hysteria.

Ripping his gown off. Frozen with fear, I saw his strapped phallus; pulling my legs wide open, he plunged himself deep into me. Excruciating pain shot through my body as his animalistic act of fornication violently tore my labia. Throwing the phallus off, he reached the point of no return, allowing his seed to seep deep within me.

Moaning wickedly, he sneered. "Welcome, Sophia, you have passed my test, and now you've become my mistress."

The test completed, every cell in my body ached as I lay there in complete misery. Staring into oblivion, I saw myself rise above the slab, floating towards a bright light, it was warm and comforting. A sharp slap around my cheek brought me back into my body.

"Sophia, you have satisfied my thirst, so now you will be rewarded," he said gleefully. I could not contemplate what that would be, fearing to ask.

Untying me, he handed me a robe. Trembling, I tried to stand, seeing blood running down my legs. Lightheaded, I started to sway. Supporting me, he gave me the golden chalice of blood and wine to fortify me.

"Now drink our offering. Through time and space, you have smelt and drank our blood and tasted our seed of nectar. You have sealed it with your body, and your soul is now ours," he sneered malevolently.

"From whence we came, we came no more; before we were here, we were bound by the Universal Law. The Occult is now your family, Sophia. We are all one," he said masterfully.

Wearily, making my through the crowd, I was desperately looking for Lucien; eventually, we met.

Alone, crumbling into his arms, he whispered, "Come, dear Sophia, you must regain your strength and dignity; here is your gown, now dress yourself quickly."

Wiping my tear-stained face, he was my only salvation. His voice calmed my soul. Quickly dressing, I was relieved to feel the comfort of my brooch, holding it close to my heart as a warm glow soothed my body.

"Order! Order!" demanded the Lord. "Let us all retire to the chamber of the feast, taking your seat for the magic of the night."

Lucien led the way down a path of steps leading to a smaller enclosed dark catacomb, lit by red candles placed neatly on a large table laden with food and vats of wine. We were all given a red robe to wear before we were seated by the Lord's slaves. Upon my cloak was Lucien's coat of arms. Prince Lavin was to my right and Julian to my left. Was more to come my way?

"Dear Sophia, now we eat, drink and gamble with our lives. Tomorrow, I wish to introduce you to my beautiful betrothed, Princess Gabriella of France," said the Prince.

Wine flowed freely. I eagerly drank to numb the searing pain between my legs. The Lord looked on with contentment. Sitting on his throne, he spoke loudly, clapping his hands, calling all to attention.

"Let the magic begin!"

Enthralled and seduced by all that I witnessed, bound by the oath, temptation drew me into the web of deceit as coldness stabbed my heart. Julian seized my hand as the energy intensified; leaning forward, he spoke coldly.

"Sister, we now have to find many young women of the night, to harvest our desire and impregnate them to feed our wealth."

Shuddering with fever, trying to compose myself, remembering Catalina, I prayed silently for her sister Martha. The commotion grew insufferable with drunken behaviour and wild abandonment. I had shamelessly laid my soul to all. Slumping in the chair, inebriated in a drunken stupor, lost between two worlds, I buried my head in my arms.

The familiar erotic scent of patchouli oil aroused my senses as it lingered in the air. A gentle tap on my shoulder brought me back, turning to see the Hooded Man. His face still concealed, he spoke urgently.

"Sophia, this a warning of what may come; behold your light as it's always within you. What may seem real is all just an illusion. You have the power within you to change your path."

Turning away quickly, he soon disappeared into the mayhem.

Despite his encouraging words, I cried despairingly, overwhelmed with a sense of helplessness, not understanding his concept. If it's all an illusion, then why am I here? I repeatedly asked myself.

"Drink up," shouted Lucien as he sat next to me.

My vision blurred, confused with images of the past mixed with the future. Trying to stand, my legs buckled, exhausted, I gave in to sleep; there I slept amongst the realms of dishonour and disbelief.

"Madam, madam, come quickly; you have to leave now! Wake up!" said a familiar voice.

Stirring with a searing pain deep inside my groin, clutching my stomach, and holding onto the chair, I pulled myself up. Staggering over many sleeping bodies, Lucien was slouched in a corner whilst Martha propped him up.

"Martha, how did you get here?"

"I followed you, madam," she replied softly.

"We don't have much time until dawn; we need to make our escape now, madam, before Lucien wakes."

"It's too late, Sophia; you're not going anywhere," said Lucien, tugging at my leg and pulling me to the ground.

"Martha, just go now!" I shouted.

"We have been summoned by the Lord," said Lucien.

"No more," I pleaded to Lucien, quaking nervously. The rawness of my violation clung to me in a heavy mist, entwining my heart in a cage of blackthorns.

"When the Lord speaks, we must obey him. Come, Sophia, the Lord is waiting for us. Prince Lavin and Julian have also been summoned," said Lucien helping me to stand, brushing my tangled hair from my eyes. "This way."

In trepidation, silently, we hurried along a tiny passage with just a faint glow of candlelight to guide us. Our sticky hands glued us together, walking the clammy path of the Lord. We descended into the underworld down a deep spiral staircase; terror gripped me as I clung to Lucien. Delving deeper into the depths of the crypt, I shivered profusely as the sound of dripping water echoed through the tunnel; pungent smells of decay engulfed my stomach with a heavy dread.

"Sophia, remember you must obey the Lord. Our lives depend on it."

"Yes," I said feebly.

Reaching the last step, I shrieked as a mischief of rats converged around us.

"Not far now; you will be pleasantly surprised," said Lucien. I sighed with relief.

My gown tattered and torn, finding ourselves in a smaller tunnel surrounded by gushing water, sodden, numb with cold, we made our way to the light. It grew sharper and brighter until we were both surrounded by a golden glow. Shrouded by the haze, Lucien held me firmly.

"This way," he shouted, "hold on tightly!" He pulled me through an archway into the realms of the supreme Lord.

My distrust grew as the scene unfolded around us. The Lord's presence engulfed the small chamber of vivid colours. He stood proud against the rich dark tapestry that hung luxuriously from the ceiling. Alarmed, as the Lord's black eyes connected with mine, devoid of any emotions, anaesthetised by his stare, becoming curious, I was lured into his den.

"Madam Sophia, Welcome; you are now one of us. Within these walls are many dark secrets that must never be told. Your life depends on your loyalty to the Occult. Do you understand?" commanded the Lord.

"Yes," I stuttered.

"Very well, then let's commence, Prince Lavin and Julian, please reveal yourselves," ordered the Lord.

Within the shadows, they emerged into his sanctum of greed and power.

"Greetings, dear brothers and sister, each of us represents the five elements of the pentagram, now get into position," he instructed.

Cocooned in his web of darkness, standing in the pentagram, we became one. On the walls surrounding us were the words carved in Latin, illuminated by candlelight; I doubted my path.

"Fiat voluntas quaecumque igni ferroque maiori bono Occulta."

(*I will do whatever it takes with fire and iron for the greater good of the Occult.*)

Looking down at my feet, I became aware of swirls of energy encircling us as my throat tightened.

"It's started," said the Lord. "Now, all join hands."

"The almighty power of air make your presence felt," commanded the Lord.

Instinctively, I walked towards the Lord, bowing as he placed his hands upon my head; immediately, I felt a shift of energy engulfing me into his supreme power.

"The almighty power of Earth, please show yourself," ordered the Lord.

Lucien took his place in front of the Lord, bowing; the Lord's hands firmly pressed on his head. Instantly his eyes glowed menacingly with evil. I stood terrorised as beads of cold sweat trickled down the nape of my neck.

"The almighty power of water reveal yourself," ordered the Lord.

Prince Lavin knelt before the Lord; gushing water rose from the ground moments after the Lord touched his head. Aghast, I watched in awe.

"The almighty power of fire, please ignite our path with the flame of the Occult."

Julian stood before the Lord; a magical flame appeared from the centre of the pentagram as the Lord cupped his palms over his head. I responded nervously.

"I am the mighty power of spirit," said the Lord magnificently.

A dark shadow manifested within the flames, conveying the magic of the Occult. Rigid with fear, spellbound, I viewed my fate through the fire. Horrified, I clutched my heart as blades of ice penetrated my soul.

"Rise," the Lord bellowed, "as we turn to face the four quarters."

Turning to the East, hearing his instructions, I had no choice but to obey.

Facing the South, a surge of magnetic energy swept throughout my body, hands burning with heat. Feeling the power, I bathed in its glory.

Turning to the West, engulfed by the icy cold wind as it funnelled around us. Trembling as malevolent energy shivered down my spine.

Facing North, I was shocked to hear my words. "Oh gracious Lord of the Occult, I will obey you."

The Lord's brooding gaze haunted me, mortified, mirroring myself within the Lord. I shrivelled with disgust, seeing the darkness of Madam Sophia De Jung.

"Sophia, there are many obstacles in front of you, but now you are part of the Occult, you will be protected. There is much you can do to secure your future," said the Lord.

"Your life is with us now, Sophia; your journey has only just begun," said Lucien. His crystal-blue eyes danced as he spoke, inviting me into his wickedness.

"Sophia, please accompany me to France to meet my betrothed with Lucien," said Prince Lavin, pushing his soft wavy hair behind his ear, revealing a symbol of the Occult.

"There is much one can do in the Royal Palace to entice virgins to our lair," he smirked.

"I will return to the House of De Vries, Sophia and await your return," said Julian.

"Sophia, you will find suitable clothes for a lady through the arched doorway. Once dressed, Prince Lavin and Lucien will escort you to Paris. You now have a duty to us, to serve the Occult," instructed the Lord.

"Yes, my Lord," I said willingly.

"Before we all depart," the Lord declared, "repeat after me. To the power of the Occult and to the Lord, we all obey. Five become one, a mighty strength of fire and magic."

A red hue of dazzling light appeared around the Lord and then he was gone. Dumbfounded, I stared into empty space. "Where did he go?" I asked nervously.

"I cannot say," said Lucien sharply. "Come, Sophia, it's time for us to take our leave."

Following Lucien through the archway, I was overwhelmed by seeing a large wooden chest laden with wealth. The small alcove was awash with delicate fabrics of every colour. A plush velvet, crimson gown with a tight bodice stood out. Eagerly I dressed, my hair now neatly tied back, finding a delicate diamond necklace; I embraced the passion within me. Remembering my brooch, securing it to my red cloak, I was now ready to embark, standing in Sophia's footsteps. A time when life was cheap, and women were slaves to a man's desires.

"Sophia, you have been warned!" said a voice in the wind as a waft of patchouli oil lingered in the breeze. I laughed nervously, leaving the crypt with Lucien and the Prince to our awaiting carriage.

Chapter 11

The vast sweeping drive, with its magnificent water features and sweet-scented gardens of white gardenias, painted a picture of grandeur. Surrounding the palace in decadent wealth, the evening sun danced upon the palatial facade, beguiling me with its charm.

It had been a long, tiresome journey. Relieved, we were quickly ushered into the main lobby. Pillars of light shafted through the expansive glass windows, bringing to life the many marbled statues that graced the vestibule. Erotic paintings hung seductively, evoking passion and desire. Princess Gabriella stood elegantly, awaiting us in the grand hall.

"Welcome to my palace," said Princess Gabriella.

Gabriella's delicate soft voice pacified my soul. Her small-framed body was dressed delectably in a bewitching golden gown with crimson inserts, revealing her bare shoulders. Her long flaxen hair curled loosely around her delicate features. Mesmerised by her dignified disposition, exchanging a kiss, her soft, moist lips warmed my heart.

"Madam Sophia, I'm so pleased to make your acquaintance; we will have fun. I'm sure," she said, laughing, teasing her hair over her mouth.

"My dear, you need rest and food. Lucien and Prince Lavin. We meet again; hello! Valet, please show them to their room; I will escort Sophia. We will all meet later," said Gabriella smiling affectionately at me.

Clutching my stomach, trying to ignore the nagging pain, I followed the Princess eagerly into her exquisite palace of wealth. Sumptuous fabrics upon the walls hung with grandeur, touching the red velvet wall hangings, leading me into another realm. I became consumed with the exquisite art's richness in golden frames that embellished the walls. Walking upon the luxurious beaded twine rugs, I paused, savouring the moment.

"Come, Sophia, rest, my dear and tomorrow we will walk the streets of Paris. My personal dame d'honneur will bring you food and a change of clothing. Sleep well, my dear."

Opening the door to my exceptionally tasteful boudoir, regal shades of purple wall-covering exploded before my eyes. At the same time, velvet drapes surrounded the four-poster bed. Painted ceiling mirrors decorated with roses of many hues hung above. Eager to rest, I laid my head upon the pristine linen sheets. Staring at my reflection, dazed, I soon fell into a deep, peaceful sleep.

Searing pain in my stomach awoke me. Delirious, trying to stand, I immediately fell backwards. The pain intensified, gripping my whole body. Looking down, deep pools of blood seeped from my womb. Shocked, surrendering to the pain, I drifted between the veil of life and death. Seeing strange visions of a future I could not comprehend, death felt like an easy escape. Voices in my mind tormented me as I lay in my own blood, knowing this was my downfall.

"Sophia, remember, you have been warned. Now you have to pay the price. Suffer those poor souls, babies of the light that have been taken by the dark ones. You have a choice; do you wish to walk that path, Sophia?" said a voice in the air.

"No," I muttered, and then blackness came.

Thunderous rain pelted on the leaded windows as the light returned once more. Opening my eyes, I saw Gabriella staring at me with affection; my heart fluttered.

"My dear Sophia, welcome back; you have been in and out of consciousness for three days. I'm afraid you have miscarried."

"What do you mean, miscarry?"

"My dear, you didn't know? We thought we were going to lose you."

Feeling her arms embracing me, she kissed me softly on my cheek.

"Lucien and Prince Lavin have been called away on urgent business; this gives us time to be better acquainted," said Gabriella affectionately.

"Let me bathe you, my dear," she said, clapping her hands to her lady in waiting. "Bring me one of my ballgowns for Sophia and some food."

Alone in Gabriella's arms, I felt safe as she tenderly washed my bruised body. The passing storm gave way to golden light caressing the Princess in a heavenly glow. Watching tentatively, gazing at her hazel eyes, I was overcome with desire; her kindness captivated my heart. Eagerly she tended to all of my needs, lastly dressing me in clean undergarments made of pure cotton.

"Come, you must eat, dear Sophia, to regain your strength; together, we dine and enjoy," she said gleefully, brushing my hair from my face. Our connection intensified, charged with sexual chemistry.

"I feel it, too, Sophia, but I am to marry Prince Lavin," she said remorsefully. "I was praying by your side each night, my dear Sophia."

"Thank you for your kindness; you have a good heart, unlike mine," I replied.

"I don't believe that, Sophia. I need to confide in you, but you must promise this will not go any further."

"Of course, my Princess, your secret will be safe with me."

"Good, now please rest for this evening's entertainment; my dame d'honneur, will help you dress into your ballgown later."

Surrounded by luxurious comforts wrapped in satin sheets, Princess Gabriella had stolen my heart. Blissfully I closed my eyes contentedly as her fragrant scent lingered in the room.

"Madam, wake up," called the Princess's maid. "It's time to get ready for the ball."

She quickly dressed me in an exquisite silk and satin ballgown, embroidered pearls and ivory lace in soft, delicate pastel colours. The bodice pulled tightly around my breasts, and my auburn hair was now set in curls, framing my small face. Lastly, pinning my brooch into my gown, ghastly images of the Lord came flooding back, reminding me of my oath. Inwardly, I wept.

"Madam, you must wear this all evening," she said, handing me a black and scarlet feathered eye mask.

"Come, let me escort you. Princess Gabriella is waiting for you."

Delicate soft furnishings adorned the many corridors. I looked on in awe, captivated by the fine art, bringing an abundance of colour and saturating the walls with warmth and light.

"This way, madam," said the valet.

The door was opened to a palatial ballroom, where many people had gathered wearing their alluring masks. Gold and brass ornaments reflected the mirrored panels magnificently upon the wall, fuelling the electrifying energy of the musicians. Catching my reflection, I smiled inwardly. It turned quickly to rage, coming face to face with the Lord again.

His black eyes penetrated me, crushing my ego; deflated, I was in his power once more.

"Sophia, you have a task to do now, don't let me down." His deep, menacing voice penetrated my soul.

"Yes, my Lord," I replied nervously.

Seeing Gabriella approach me, I was averted from the Lord. She looked radiant; her golden hair complemented her divine beauty, captivating me completely.

"Sophia, come this way," said Gabriella, taking my hand, leading me through the crowded room away from the clutches of the Lord.

"Thank you, dear Princess; do you know who that was?"

"Yes, of course, I do," she replied sternly.

An uneasy feeling started to swell in my stomach, hearing her reply, but I was smitten. I followed her blindly, blissfully unaware of what was about to unfold. Out of view, she led me to a small alcove. It was brightly lit with red candles. A large red velvet chaise longue looked inviting, evoking a deep passion for Gabriella as she offered powders of opium; I accepted gracefully. I was enthralled by her charm as she seduced me into her world of fantasia. Delirious, feeling liberated, leaving the company of Gabriella, I gladly danced amongst the masses wearing provocative masks and elegant garments made of silk and satin. Caught in the moment, oblivious to the world, I became lost in the mayhem of the ball.

Chapter 12

Standing in the courtyard, shivering as the cold wind whipped around me, twilight was approaching. Among the shades of light, I noticed a silhouette walking towards me; intrigued, I stared, transfixed.

"Who are you?" I called out, but all was silent.

"Sophia, there you are. I have been looking for you," said Gabriella.

"Look, Gabriella! There is someone in the shadows."

"Sophia, don't be silly; there's no one there."

"But there is!"

"Now, do hurry along; we must dance together."

I was averted by her eyes as they radiated joy through her golden, feathered mask, enticing me into her world. Clutching Gabriella's hand, we walked back to the warmth of the palace. The grand ballroom was alive with colour and music; together, we danced in the magical energy of the night.

"How are you, my dear Sophia? You look rather pale; follow me. I have a secret room where we won't be disturbed," said Gabriella, smiling warmly. "Follow me," she insisted.

We walked through a long corridor of majestic tapestries, depicting vivid and bold copious religious scenes; fascinated, I looked on in awe.

"No time for that, Sophia; this way, hurry," said Gabriella, pushing me into the library.

A bounty of books was stacked high to the ceiling, and a musky scent hung in the air. Daylight filtered through a small window, bringing a hint of colour to the room. Gabriella eagerly took a red leather-bound book from the shelf behind us, exposing a lever. She pulled it hard, and to my astonishment, the wall slid open, revealing a wondrous bedchamber full of rare artefacts. Speechless, I gawped with amazement, taking in the splendid view of the many portraits of Gabriella, capturing her sexuality, inviting me to indulge in the pleasures of a woman.

Our lips met tentatively, embracing each other as we kissed passionately. Captivated by Gabriella's beauty, my heart started to melt as the sexual chemistry grew, engulfing me in her majestic aura.

"We don't have much time," she whispered softly.

Placing her hand inside my bodice, intensifying the moment, I wanted more as the heat within mounted. I begged her, "Please don't stop."

"We will have our time, Sophia, but not now," said Gabriella, handing me a letter.

"You must not open this. Please don't ask any questions. Tomorrow, you will be escorted by one of the ladies, who will show you where to take it."

"If you insist, my dear Princess."

"If we do not follow orders, there will be many causalities," she replied, regretfully.

"Life here is not what it seems; always be on your guard. Our past is in the fabric of time. Soon we can share our love, but not yet. Now we must hurry back to the ball before we are missed."

"There you are, Sophia," said a familiar voice as we entered the ballroom.

"I thought you were away on business, Lucien?"

His golden mask exaggerated his arrogance. Charming many women as he strutted toward us, Gabriella quickly discarded me as Lucien stood before us, seeding jealousy within me. His flamboyant charisma oozed sexuality as he smoothed his shoulder-length black hair away from his face.

"I have returned with news for you both. The stakes are even higher now," replied Lucien.

"What do you mean?"

"Sophia, you must now start to build your empire. The price of virgins is very profitable. Many men want to take their virtue. This will be our commodity, and thus we can continue taking payment for our other lucrative venture. There is always a price to pay for baby trafficking," smirked Lucien.

"What happens to the infants?" I enquired.

"You need not know."

"Sophia, Lucien, hush, I feel we are being watched," said Gabriella, glancing to her left.

"May I have this dance, Sophia?" asked Lucien, gracelessly taking my hand. Caught in the moment, I quickly became immersed in the headiness of the festivities as the music propelled me forward into the realms of dishonour.

Embraced by Lucien's strong masculinity, I was easy prey for his needs. Dancing through the crowded ballroom, Lucien led me back to the small, secluded alcove.

"Listen, Sophia, whatever you do, you must not cross the Princess. She is very cunning and deceptive. If you know anything about her plans, you must speak up now, as the Lord is here waiting for answers."

Hesitating, I grew rigid as Lucien glared at me.

"Oh Sophia, you know something. I can see it in your eyes."

Trying to pull away, Lucien held me firmly in his grasp. Reluctantly, I gave him the letter. Opening it quickly, he was shocked to see it was a blank piece of paper.

"The Princess has outwitted us both! You must return to the Princess and fulfil her orders to gain her loyalty. She will reward you with many treasures. Now run along, Sophia, remember the Lord is always watching."

The evening flowed slowly, as if time had ceased. I took solace in a cocktail of powders, then noticed Gabriella leave the ballroom. As she entered a small lobby, I followed her out of sight, where a tall, stern woman greeted her. Recognising her voice, my heart thumped heavily as I listened intently, hearing Gabriella speaking to the woman.

"Madam Sophia will play our host."

"As you wish, your grace," she replied.

"Tomorrow, she will start to build our empire from the seedy side of Paris. Madam Sophia has much to offer us both," said the Princess as they walked out of view.

Agitated and alarmed, I quickly ran towards them, but Lucien blocked my way. Wearing his tight-fitting dark blue breeches and fine golden tunic, matching his black and golden feather eye mask, I was easily charmed as he stared at my ample cleavage.

"Who is that woman, Lucien?"

"You will find out soon. The Lord is summoning us."

"No, please, no," I replied, clutching my heart.

"Dear Sophia, this is your destiny," said Lucien taking his mask off.

His crystal-ball eyes bored into my soul; instantly, I felt calmer. As he held me close, smouldering passion ignited as our lips met lustfully. His devilish ways enticed me into his world of debauchery.

"Tomorrow, you must work, but for now, you are the guest of honour at the Lord's bedchamber," said Lucien as he drew breath.

"No, Lucien, not the Lord again!" I replied warily.

"Shh, Sophia, I will be with you. Fear no more. Into the fire of the Lord's reality you must go and experience the heat within us both. Trust me, Sophia, I'm on your side."

"Really, Lucien?" I replied anxiously as cold sweat trickled down the nape of my neck.

"It's OK, Sophia. Come the Lord has spoken. We have to obey him."

Standing by the door, the fire burned brightly in the Lord's chamber. Mesmerised, it glowed fearlessly with erotic fiery energy, encircling the Lord's bed, captivating me into his world. His naked body rippled harmoniously amongst the flames of shadows.

"Welcome, dear Sophia. You have suffered much; now is the time for you to enjoy the ride," said the Lord, through his veil of deceit.

The Lord's brooding eyes invited me into his bed. My resistance quickly left as he purged his body upon mine with his firm touch of fire and lust. Our naked bodies moulded together; magic had begun as the flames temporarily flickered around us. Smiling quietly, I was high on adrenaline; briefly, I felt contented as it blocked painful memories.

Through the vapours of opium, I dreamt vividly, seeing myself standing alone in the courtyard. Hazy light muddled my vision as a horse and carriage arrived in front of me.

"Step this way, Madam Sophia," said a deep masculine voice.

Baffled, rubbing my arms to keep warm, I was surprised to find I was still wearing my ballgown; my body stiffened, and my eyes sharpened, trying to focus my mind.

"Madam Sophia, step this way, please."

A hand extended towards me through the crimson velvet drapes of the carriage.

"Madam, Sophia! Please join me."

Shivering gingerly, I climbed on board the elegant carriage. A faint aroma of patchouli wafted around me, bringing me some calmness amongst the mayhem. The carriage was decorated with golden petals of crimson roses; vibrant velvet hues lined the inside.

"Hello, Sophia, we meet again," spoke the Hooded Man.

"Oh, you again! Who are you?" I enquired nervously.

"One day, you may learn the truth. I am the voice of reason. That's all you need to know. Please give me the brooch; in return, you will receive a small old pocket watch," demanded the Hooded Man.

"I can't seem to find it!" I replied fumbling in my deep pocket, as he gave me the delicate watch. "I may have lost it in the ballroom."

"You must find it, and don't lose this. Choose wisely, Sophia. Only time will tell. Tick-tock. The clock is ticking!"

"But I don't understand."

"You will, Sophia," he whispered softly as I fell into a deep sleep.

"Sophia, Sophia, wake up," said Lucien.

"What's going on," I slurred, half asleep, hearing the constant sound of tick-tock repetitively playing in my mind.

Sitting bolt upright, strange sensations surged through my body, sending my mind in a spin. Shockingly and alarmed I found myself lying naked between Lucien and the Lord.

"What has just happened? Surely I was in the courtyard just now."

"You were in a deep sleep Sophia," replied the Lord, disapproving of my reaction.

"But it felt so real," I whispered anxiously.

"Hm, interesting," said Lucien, brushing my matted hair from my face. "Come and lay with us again. You know you cannot resist the temptation," he smirked, rubbing his penis with his other hand. My energy was depleted, and I was too weak to defend myself; our naked bodies became erotically embroiled. As I turned my attention towards the Lord, revealing his face, his jet-black hair swept over the deep scar on his right cheek. His eyes of glass, devoid of emotion, seeped into my soul as deep penetrative sex locked the three of us together; embracing the darkness of my soul, I became a victim of their fetish desires.

The sweet fragrant scent of jasmine filled the room with a rich bouquet as morning light filtered through the small arch window into the Lord's bedchamber.

"We will bath and dress you, my dear," purred Lucien.

"As long as you obey us, we will keep our promise to you," said the Lord masterfully.

Clasping hands, we recited our seal of sovereignty in Latin.

"Hodie nobis sacramentum habuerit occulto. Et non ab intra nos sunt, ut unum. Ita fiat, factum est."

(On this day, we pledge our oath to the occult. From within and without, we are as one. So be it, it is done.)

"Now you must go, Sophia, to the streets of Paris to build our empire, to feed our desires," commanded the Lord.

"Yes," I replied assertively, impregnated with the energy of the Lord and Lucien; I was now ready to make my killing.

Chapter 13

The streets of Paris were awash with torrential rain. Alone, I ran for cover, shivering as I sheltered in a nearby doorway. Pulling my purple hooded gown tightly around me, I reached inside the deep pockets and was surprised to find a shiny pocket watch. Holding it close to my ear, I heard a faint tick-tock that was in tune with the rhythm of my heartbeat. Breathing lightly, I grew aware of a bright golden light that glowed within the watch. As the light became stronger, it lit the night sky, flickering and dancing with the rain. Noticing warmth that rose up from my feet, captivated, I watched, enthralled, caught in a moment of mystical energy.

A strong gust of wind alerted me to the sound of music from a distant building; eagerly, I felt compelled to investigate as I followed the sounds leading me further into the depth of the night.

Now in the back streets of Paris, with many barely lit alleys, a passing black cat ran in front of me. His gaze stared long and hard at me with a knowing look; I shivered. Finding at last the source of the music, I entered the premises down some deep wrought iron steps into a grand music hall. It was stupendous and breathtaking; giant crystal chandeliers hung from the ceiling, creating many colours that reflected upon the dance floor. Many dancers, dressed magnificently in vivid costumes, were swinging and swirling with the sound of the orchestra. Swept along with the positive energy, I forgot my instructions, as the musicians played loudly until I was approached by an elegant, tall, well-dressed lady.

"Madam Sophia, how wonderful to make your acquaintance; I believe you have something for me?"

"Yes," I replied.

"Just exquisite, don't you think?" stroking her green velvet gown with her slender hands.

"Yes, it is indeed," I replied admiring her elegance stance.

"Follow me," she said authoritatively.

We walked through the many dancers to a small private room at the back of the hall. A warm fire glowed in the corner; her personality swiftly changed as she forcefully pinned me to the wall.

"Now, hand me the letter. You will be rewarded. Be quick; where is it?"

Carefully I reached inside my tight bodice, retrieving the letter. Cautiously, I gave it to her.

Snatching it from my fingers, she opened it quickly. Finding the letter was blank, she gasped, exasperated.

"You will both pay for this," she shouted, storming out of the room as she threw the paper on the fire in disgust.

Watching the flames engulf the letter as it burnt to ashes, coldness took over me as words from the fire tumbled from my mouth.

"Whence you came, you came no more, the dark light will fall, and then there were none."

A shiver ran down my spine as the room turned cold, enveloping me in a chilly breeze. Images of ladies of the night flashed before my eyes; I was not alone!

Hurriedly, I made my way through the crowds but was dragged back by the surge of dancers, pushing me further towards the stage.

"Hey! Come this way, madam," shouted a young woman with bright red curly hair and painted red lips. Her tiny waist was made even smaller by her tight crimson bodice.

"Scarlet is my name, and Scarlet is my nature," she laughed, sweeping her flaming hair from her piercing emerald eyes.

"I believe you're looking to recruit delectable women that have not been touched by a man."

"Yes, I am; how do you know?" I replied hesitantly.

"I have my ways," she smiled candidly, revealing a dimple on her left cheek.

"Follow me," instructed Scarlet.

Grabbing my hand, she quickly led me through the stage door and into Paris's dimly lit back streets. Mysterious, eerie shadows of the night constantly grew as the fog rolled in. Flustered, I clung to Scarlet for support.

"This way," she ordered. "There are many secret passageways that hold many stories, freezing them in time, Sophia, but you already know that."

"Do I?" I said, shrugging my shoulders.

"Yes," she replied, clicking her fingers impatiently.

The sound of the ticking watch grew louder and louder. Tick-tock, it echoed in my thoughts. A familiar musky, intoxicating scent wafted in the breeze, stopping me from going any further.

"Sophia, you must now journey deep into the shadowlands to find your truth," said a voice in the wind.

"Did you hear that, Scarlet?"

"Hear what? No," she replied, looking bemused at me. "Now come on, hurry, there will be plenty of women for you to choose," she laughed, sinisterly.

"We are nearly there, just down this alley," said Scarlet pulling my arm.

"But it's a dead end," I replied as we reached a brick wall ahead of us.

"Don't be fooled by that; this is our way in."

"Way into what?"

"Shh … listen, can you hear them?"

"No, I can only hear the sound of rats rustling amongst the leaves."

"You will, follow my lead, quick, no time like the present."

Scrambling over the wall, I was surprised to see many women huddled around a small fire. Hot ashes spat upon the stone pavement. It warmed the coldness of the night as it flickered and glowed intensely.

"Ladies, who would like to travel to Amsterdam with Madam Sophia De Jung? Please step forward and be seen, she pays well," said Scarlet brazenly, approaching the women.

In the shadowy flicker of the firelight stepped a young woman, her face I recognised.

"Is that you, Martha?"

"Yes, madam, we meet again."

"We haven't got time for chatter," said Scarlet pushing me towards the glow of the fire. "Come on, ladies, this is an opportunity. See how fine madam looks; you, too, can be just like her."

Within the crowd, a petite young woman emerged from the back. Her youthful, fresh complexion would do well in my business. I recognised Martha's sister; it was Rosa.

"I'm Rosa, we have met before. Please may I accompany you both? I promise you I will work hard for my keep."

"Yes, I do recall, very well, you will be an asset," I replied, eyeing her youthfulness.

She stood all of five feet tall. Her slender body complemented her wavy long, blonde hair; she would bring in the money to help the Lord. As the fire burned brightly, my vision became clearer, seeing many women young and old. Scarlet, Martha and Rosa were in their prime and would make an excellent addition to the House of De Vries.

"Scarlet, Rosa and Martha, welcome. I will keep you well as long as you all follow my orders."

"Yes," replied Rosa and Martha.

Scarlet defiantly shrugged her shoulders. "If needs must, madam. It's been a while since I had a gentleman titillating my fanny," she laughed raucously.

"Madam Sophia, you only have a few days to gather more women. I have been instructed by Princess Gabriella that we must return to her palace and claim your reward," said Martha.

As the fire diminished, the night became bitterly cold. The women retreated into the darkness, leaving us four huddled by the fire's dying embers. A sudden gust of wind caused many leaves to fall on the deserted cobbled streets. Vacant buildings stood derelict, with no sign of life, just an empty space of darkness hidden from sight. I was eager to return to the warmth of the grand palace.

"Don't worry, madam, our carriage will be here soon," said Martha reassuringly.

Looking up into the night sky, I searched for answers, watching the moon's reflection hide behind a blanket of clouds. I shivered anxiously, clinging to hope as conflicting emotions raced through my body. Would this night ever end?

Chapter 14

Despairingly, time ticked slowly. A layer of frost was all I could see. My hands, blue with cold, were tucked deep inside my bodice to keep warm. Remembering the warmth of Gabriella's touch, so comforting and reassuring; if only she was with me now, things would be different. Scarlet, Rosa and Martha walked solemnly side by side, four of us, numb in the cold air, as we waited by the kerbside. The sky turned black as trees rustled menacingly in the wind. My body stiffened as the energy changed dramatically, we clung together for support as fear consumed me.

"How long must we wait?" I muttered, exasperated.

"It will be here soon," reassured Martha.

The sound of horses in the distance gave a glimmer of hope. The prevailing wind grew relentless as the driving rain drenched us to the core. At last, the carriage arrived, revealing the golden seal of royalty, with four beautiful stallions at the front and a royal horseman taking the reins. He greeted us warmly in his finery as we entered the sumptuous carriage. It was lavishly dressed with deep blue velvet cushions adorned with delicate crimson flowers. Seated, I started to thaw from the rawness of the night, feeling the luxuriousness comfort of this grand carriage. I smiled inwardly as my thoughts drifted back to Gabriella.

"Thank you, ladies, for joining me. You all will be taken care of when we return to the House of De Vries. I will teach you well to gain your power and to engage with men, in return for their wealth."

I smiled candidly.

We travelled silently to the palace with an air of anticipation. I pondered on my future as the wheels quickly turned. Our carriage swiftly led us through the streets of Paris, heading towards the countryside of many valleys. The night became dawn as the morning sun rose in the east, parting the clouds with streams of light. Martha looked serene as she spoke softly to me.

"Madam Sophia, I will always be with you."

"Thank you for your kindness, but that won't be necessary," I replied, agitated.

The carriage stopped abruptly with a thud, catapulting us from our seats. Peering out of the smashed window, I heard shouts of abuse from three highwaymen as they waved a pistol at us. They were dressed in black, with pointed tricorn hats. Their faces were concealed with masks. My heart quickened as my anxiety soared, fearing they had come for me.

"Get out!" they demanded angrily.

The door violently swung open as they pulled Scarlet, Martha and Rosa into the dusty undergrowth of sodden fields.

"Not you, madam; you are coming with us," shouted the tallest of the men.

His voice was commanding and masterful; trembling, I shuddered inside as he spoke.

"You are our reward," he sneered menacingly. "Madam Sophia, you are now our prisoner."

"But, why?" I pleaded. "Surely there are more women wealthy than me? I haven't got much."

"But you have, now be quiet," he roared, slapping me hard on my face, tugging at my silver chain, smashing the small phial to the floor. He then briskly tied my hands together behind my back. Powerless, my light was diminishing as they alighted the carriage, clambering all over me with their brusque behaviour. As the wheels started turning, I heard Scarlet, Martha and Rosa calling, "We will find you, madam."

"Where are we going?" I enquired anxiously.

They glared, intimidating me with their frosty dark stares. Aghast and troubled, I dreaded what was to come. Fretful and flustered, I placed my hands in my gown's deep pockets, I felt instantly calmer clasping the small and delicate pocket watch.

It ticked rhythmically with my heartbeat. Tick-tock, tick-tock, feeling the vibration in my hands as soft energy rippled up my arms, giving me some comfort. We travelled far over many bumpy roads that led us away from Paris into a deep, dense forest. It looked foreboding as I stared from the cracked carriage window, riding into the thick of it; gulping hard, the tension started to mount. Overwrought with emotion, my heart sank, not knowing when I would see Princess Gabriella again. At last, the carriage halted as they aggressively tugged at my hair, dragging me into a ditch richly covered with many dead leaves.

"We will stay here for a while," said the tall, burly man, sneering behind his mask, revealing his brooding eyes.

"Hum," he muttered under his breath. "You will do me fine and serve my immediate needs," he sneered as he groped me under my gown, prodding his dirty fingers into my vagina. Loathing every second, I cunningly played his game.

"Yes, sir, I believe I can relieve you," I said, pulling him closer, "but you will have to untie me, so I can run my fingers up and down your throbbing manliness." Teasing him with my tongue, he quickly obliged and led me away from the watchful eye of the other highwaymen.

"This will do," he said, pinning me against a tree and pulling my gown up high. He quickly dropped his trousers, penetrating me hard and ferociously with his hard erection. The friction of the thick tree bark rubbed painfully into my back. Thinking fast, I responded to his needs. His foul breath stank of stale ale as he pushed his tongue deep into my mouth.

"Sir," I whispered as he took a breath. "If you let me take the lead, I will promise you I will take you to the place of nirvana with an electrifying climax."

He breathed deeply with anticipation, eager for his craving; he held me firmly.

"Very well, madam, you are indeed a lady of the night. I am ready," he replied, pushing his penis towards my mouth.

"Yes, sir, I am indeed. I will pleasure you, sir, but you must set me free."

"Why would I do that?" he groaned excitedly. "What do I get in return?"

"Freedom, sir, and wealth. We need a strong man to help us build our empire; you will be most welcome at the House of De Vries."

"We have a deal," he replied hastily as his desire took hold of him. "Now suck me!" he shouted.

Gagging profusely, he pushed his manhood deep into the back of my mouth. Tasting his semen, he shuddered excitedly, reaching his climax. I tried hard not to swallow any as it oozed from my mouth.

"Well, madam, you have a gift, that's for sure," he said, pulling his breeches up.

"You have only a few minutes to make your escape."

"Thank you, sir; I will keep my promise. What is your name?"

"Tobias. I've been wanting to leave this tiresome life for a while now. I shall look forward to working for you. Now, make haste before the others see you," he replied urgently.

I turned and fled, running through the dense woodland. Blackness engulfed the sky, with only the stars and nature guiding me. I blindly carried on; I was lost and alone in unfamiliar territory. A passing owl screeched above; its chilling shrill terrorised the night sky. Clinging to a tree for support, I misplaced my footing. Falling into a shaft, I braced myself for the landing, hitting my head hard. Lying on the stony ground, I drifted between two worlds, hearing the Lord speak to me in my subconscious, seeping into my soul; I searched desperately for the light. Clinging on to life, I eventually scrambled to my knees, yelling for help, but my voice was not heard in the dead of night. Despairingly, remembering the watch, I clasped it tightly in my pocket and prayed.

"Sophia, Sophia, oh Sophia," I heard alarmingly in my thoughts.

"Who's there," I asked nervously.

"The voice of reason. Remember your true path; you are the light, do not sway from it. This is all an illusion, Sophia."

My mind raced rapidly with powerful images of frightened young women leaving their babies at the mercy of the Lord. "No!" I yelled in vain. The harsh voice of the Lord replaced reason.

"Sophia, you must obey me or pay with your life," I heard repetitively.

My head throbbed loudly as I wept fearfully, tormented with my thoughts. I anxiously waited alone, trapped and lost. Grieving for myself and for those that would suffer at the hands of the Lord. Silence came at last as my eyes became heavy and weary. Time had no meaning as my fate hung in the balance. Drifting between realities, I became aware of a soft, gentle voice; she spoke to my soul, awakening me to my truth.

"Sophia, do not be fooled by the way of the dark."

Looking up at the stars, I saw glimpses of another dimension, a world I did not understand. It was strange and alien to me. Uncannily, a woman appeared in the hazy light, she looked similar to me but differently dressed. "Sophia, you must follow your heart to allow the light to return," she whispered.

Her words gave me strength as I pushed myself forward towards a tunnel of trees. With every step, I grew weaker and weaker; seeing daylight flickering in the far distance gave me the strength to continue. Relieved, at last I had found my path back to freedom; I was surprised to see Scarlet was waiting for me in the field.

"Sophia, so glad you made it through; we have been waiting for you," she said as she wrapped her arms around my cold body, planting a kiss on my cheek with her seductive crimson lips.

"Where's Martha and Rosa?" I inquired.

"We are behind you; turn around, Sophia."

They stood side by side, holding hands as they walked wearily towards me. Martha smiled warmly; her kindness touched my heart.

"But how did you know where to meet me?" I tentatively asked.

"There are some things you will never understand, Sophia, but remember we will always follow the path to the light. The clock is ticking, and you are needed back at the palace. Princess Gabriella is eager to see you again," said Martha.

"Then why do I feel the heaviness of the darkness, Martha?"

"Only you can work that out. Come on now, hurry," replied Martha.

Scarlet flicked her red hair from her face. Screwing up her nose, she cackled, "We are at your service, madam, and we will find our way back. Are you ready, sisters?"

"Yes," we replied, linking hands as we walked the many paths that led us back towards the palace of our dreams and desires.

Chapter 15

She laid all in white, waiting,
longing for her lover to return.

Chapel de Royal stood on a hill, looking grand and regal. Its tall steeple towered high in the skyline, its gothic designs including many gargoyles. The thick arched wooden door was wide open, inviting me to delve into the unknown. With trepidation, I entered the building alone, whilst Scarlet, Martha and Rosa waited outside. A dove swiftly flew in through a small open window, catching my attention as it landed near the altar. Mesmerised by the many giant, arched, stained glasses windows, I stared in awe at their beauty. Light filled the chapel as the sun's shadow radiated many colours, giving me a sense of inner peace. Kneeling before the altar, I prayed for guidance, seeing clearly in my mind Princess Gabriella in an exquisite golden satin gown, her delicate shoulders laid bare. A silk ivory shawl was loosely draped seductively, around her arms whilst her hands nestled to one side of her face. She looked radiant and beautiful as she spoke softly to me in my mind. Startled by the dove, I walked towards the back of the chapel, fixated upon the high vaulted intricate carved roof, not wanting to leave this peaceful place. As the light grew intensely with shades of magenta red, giving depth to the many tapestries that hung on the walls, I stood still, feeling disoriented.

"It's OK," whispered Scarlet, as she tapped me on my shoulders, whilst Martha and Rosa stood by her side.

"I thought you were all waiting for me outside."

"No, we needed to stay close to you," replied Martha, looking serene in the magenta light.

"Why?"

"Because the chapel is a place of visions. It has an intoxicating energy, which leads you into another dimension," replied Scarlet.

Confused, I rubbed my eyes, trying to erase the vision, but it was still clearly in my sight.

"But I heard Gabriella talking to me; she was here, and still is," I replied, gazing at the shimmering altar. It glowed mysteriously with a hazy aura, warming my heart.

"Yes, she is always here, in this reality. She comes in your dreams to guide you back to her world."

"It happened to me," said Scarlet, frowning deeply, revealing a slight scar on her forehead.

"Now look again. What do you see? Sophia."

"Just you three," I replied, baffled.

The vision had dispersed, bringing a lightness to the chapel, as the wall tapestries gently swayed from a gust of wind blowing in from the expansive stained-glass window. Walking back towards the aisle, to my left now hung a fascinating portrait of the Princess. It was precisely the vision I had seen. Her alluring hazel eyes drew me into her soul. I was utterly mesmerised by her magnetic presence as she called to me again.

"Madam Sophia, come to me," she whispered softly, as the white dove flew out of the chapel, beckoning me to her Grand Palace. Silently, I left the chapel alone.

I could just see Martha, Scarlet and Rosa walking swiftly down the hill and into the valley beyond, leading to the palace on the distant horizon. My heart still bathing in the warmth of the chapel, I rested for a while by the grassy banks, watching the sun fade and dance between the trees, leaving a trail of golden light. Sighing heavily, I bathed in the liquid sun. The sound of a horse galloping towards me brought me back to the present moment. My fate was sealed; Lucien was upon his stallion.

"Madam Sophia, I am at your service to take you back to the palace," he called out. "I shall be leaving in the morning for Amsterdam to tend to some business before returning to the House of De Vries."

Lucien was elegantly dressed in a dashing mosaic red coat and blue, golden tunic with matching breeches, his black wavy hair nestled neatly upon his shoulders, complementing his red velvet cravat. His hypnotic piercing blue eyes bored into my soul. I was easily fooled by his compelling composure and charisma.

"Sophia, you know you must seduce the Princess to uncover her secret."

"Yes," I replied, distracted by his physique as he leant forward and kissed me erotically, while his hands gently slid up my thighs under my gown, teasing me with his tongue, tantalising me into submission.

"Welcome to the dark side," he laughed, flicking his hair behind his ears, then licked his lips in anticipation.

"You only have until morning light, Sophia, to become her mistress. She has already been visiting you in your mind. She is an extremely powerful princess and cannot be trusted. She has betrayed the Lord! He seeks his revenge."

"How do you know she has been visiting me?" I replied stunned.

"Because I can see it in your eyes."

"But surely this cannot be true."

"Believe me, it is. Remember your oath, Sophia. This is the way of the occult," he replied, pulling me closer into his chest before giving me some powders from his silver snuffbox.

Glassy-eyed, I was yet again lured into Lucien's world. We kissed seductively as our tongues met eagerly, locking us together in the desire of sexual fantasy. Pushing me onto the grass, he quickly thrust his manhood deep into my moist quim as we both gyrated ecstatically. Exhausted and breathless, we lay side by side as the sun dipped behind the skyline.

"Come Sophia, we must get you back to the palace. Remember, you are one of us now," he smirked broadly as he kissed my hand.

"Yes," I replied submissively.

"Don't forget your orders to recruit more ladies of the night; the Lord is getting impatient. The clock is ticking, Sophia, tick-tock."

"Yes, I know, I don't need reminding," I replied, irritated.

Through the valley, we rode upon Lucien's horse towards the Grand Palace. The sky was clear, with many stars lighting our pathway. I held Lucien firmly around his waist as his horse gathered speed, catching a glimpse of the full moon; it beamed brightly, casting shadows upon my mind. I shuddered fearfully as my insecurity grew with each step. The palace was now in sight.

"Sophia, you can only go forward; there is no turning back," said

Lucien commandingly as we both dismounted from his horse.

Flustered, I nodded silently; his words spoke the truth. Gabriella's call was hard to ignore. Tethering his horse in the stables, we crept quietly through the cobbled courtyard and into the lavish gardens.

"This way," commanded Lucien.

"Princess Gabriella is waiting for you in her private summer house. Remember where your loyalty lies. Enter through the archway; she is waiting for you. I will be there for you at dawn; please do not disappoint me, Sophia."

"I won't," I replied as he swaggered towards the palace.

Alone, I gazed at the endless sky, looking for hope in the starry night. Remembering the watch, I clasped it tightly in my deep pocket, feeling the vibration of time gently ticking. Breathing deeply, I knew what had to be done.

Gabriella was in her luxurious summer house. Every inch of the building was adorned with lavish gold and red décor, whilst the candles flickered and glowed, arousing me. She was lying on a scarlet velvet chaise longue, looking serene and radiant, just as I had seen her in my vision. Her golden satin dress complemented her womanly body, whilst her delicate shoulders were bare, enticing me. Temptation grew within.

"My dear Sophia. Welcome to my love nest," she laughed charmingly, pushing her long flowing flaxen hair away from her shoulders, sensing my passion.

"You shouldn't look surprised Sophia; after all, we are both ladies that crave affection and wealth,"

said Gabriella smiling warmly towards me, awakening my sexual appetite. I was ready for her.

Gazing into my soul, she beckoned me to lay with her. Our soft lips met seductively, with tenderness. Her delicate perfume intoxicated my senses, overcome with elation as she gently caressed my body, as we slowly undressed each other. Kissing passionately, our bodies entwined, erotically. Becoming as one, my climax, sent waves of electric energy throughout my body; it was heavenly, leaving me spellbound by her ravishing beauty.

"My dear Sophia, we are lovers for only a short time," she whispered tenderly.

"My dear Gabriella, this saddens me much. To see you and not be with you in my heart and body," I replied, disheartened.

"I know, my dear Sophia, but I am to be married by the autumn. We still have time now, and I promise to seek you whenever I can."

Smiling broadly, she tentatively kissed my forehead as she stroked my arm, sending euphoric waves throughout my body. Feeling the warmth of Gabriella's nakedness next to mine, I drifted off to sleep, contented.

The temptress finally has
her lover in the palms of her hands.

I awoke with a sense of urgency, hearing tick-tock loudly in my mind. Daybreak had begun with the dawn chorus; morning light filtered through the undressed windows. Gabriella was still asleep, looking serene and graceful as pangs of guilt swept through me. Remembering Lucien's instructions, I quickly dressed, leaving the warmth of our love nest behind. Holding the small pocket watch for comfort, I ran my fingers over the intricate patterns, feeling the grooves as time slipped by. Sensing the watch's vibration ticking loudly, it alerted me that all was not well.

Lucien was waiting impatiently by his stallion, looking cavalier and handsome in the morning rays that shafted through the clouds. Shivering, I wrapped my velvet hooded cloak tightly around me and walked towards him across the courtyard. Our eyes connected alarmingly; I instantly responded to his unspoken words.

"Morning, Sophia. Well, have you found Gabriella's secret?" said Lucien, grooming himself.

"No, I need more time to gain her trust, but I do believe she has feelings for me."

"The Lord will not be happy; he will be waiting for you Sophia, you have been warned. I will be expecting you to return to the House of De Vries with your new recruits soon," he replied sternly.

"I promise I will have news for you in three days."

"That's not good enough," he snapped, stamping his feet on the cobbled path. "The Lord will be waiting! You are playing with your life. Do I make myself clear?"

"Yes," I replied nervously, clasping my watch tighter as time ticked loudly in my mind.

"Good. You cannot fool me, Sophia," he smirked crudely. "Your brother is expecting me to return with you. You don't have much time. I will make your excuses for now. Take this phial, seeing you have lost the one I gave you earlier; you know what to do next," he said callously.

"Yes, sir," I replied, as he slipped the small glass phial into my pocket. I sighed heavily, staring intensely at Lucien as my stomach anxiously churned. Torn between the devil and the Princess, I had no option but to obey his orders. Flicking his hair behind his ears, placing his wide brim hat upon his head, he arrogantly rode off in the hazy light of dawn. A passing raven stooped low, perching on the gatepost. His black eyes revealed the darkness within as he revealed his prey to me. Immediately I knew I would outwit them all. Hastily, I returned to the sleeping princess. Lying naked, I prayed for forgiveness for the crime I was about to commit on my beloved Gabriella as the clock ticked silently. Gracefully she aroused, as the sunlight flooded her bed, bathing us in warmth. Caressing her tenderly, I plotted my next move.

"My dear beautiful Princess, your scent is divinely heavenly. Let me taste your sweet nectar," I whispered seductively, prising her legs wide open, revealing her tantalising womanhood. I gorged upon her juices as my tongue flicked quickly over her clitoris. Arousing her into a crescendo of gratifying orgasmic waves, she purred with pleasure. Hearing the faint sound of the chapel clock chiming for morning prayers, I knew it was time. Without being seen, I carefully slipped the contents of the phial into her goblet of port. Presuming it was opium, we toasted our love, as she gulped it thirstily.

"Sophia, we are made of the same breed. Justice always comes at a price," said Gabriella as her eyes became heavy induced by the intoxicating liquid; she soon slipped into oblivion.

The fire is ignited, and long may it reign!

Chapter 16

Clutching my pocket watch close to my chest, I felt the momentum of time. A wave of deep sadness hung heavy in my heart as I looked lovingly at Gabriella. She looked so peaceful that I began to question my motives. Quietly, I left the summer house, along with my guilt. Exploring the palace's expansive gardens, full of vibrant roses of many colours, each rose had its own unique scent evoking memories from my past. Standing among the heady bouquet, a distorted vision blurred my sight as the morning sunlight beamed down. Sensing a figure silhouetted in the rays, I blinked several times. The ghostly figure walked slowly by; it was me! Fearfully, I saw my older self moving towards a waiting henchman. Mortified, the squawk of a passing crow awoke me from my transfixion as it flapped its wings rapidly above my head, before flying swiftly towards the palace. I retreated hastily to the comfort of this magnificent building.

Entering through a side door, I was surprised by how quiet it was. Not a soul to be seen, just emptiness. Hearing the grand clock striking eleven times, I hastily walked towards the Princess's private suite sensing eyes following me. Still, there was no one, just the constant sound of tick-tock playing repetitively in my thoughts. The silent palace became a place of trickery as I was engulfed in a sea of mist and a world of illusion.

"Sophia," I heard through the veils of time. "You are the master of your destiny."

"Who's there?" I yelled alarmingly, catching a familiar scent of patchouli.

"Sophia. Hold on to your watch, and don't let time slip away," commanded the voice.

Entangled between two worlds, the mist lured me from my path. I fell to the floor, confused and bewildered, clinging to my watch as time passed me by. Faster and faster it spun, twisting me in a vortex of electrifying energy until it stopped abruptly. Life was once again normal in the palace corridors where many people went about their day.

"Can I help you, madam? You seem lost," asked a valet.

Recognising his calm composure and distinguished uniform of a deep blue velvet coat, matching breeches and starched frilly shirt, I was pleased to see him again.

"Yes, I am looking for Princess Gabriella's private bedchamber."

"Follow me," he instructed. "It's this way." He pointed towards a white door embossed in gold with the Princess's coat of arms.

"I don't recall seeing that before," I replied perturbed.

"Your eyes deceive you, madam. Enter through the door and turn right into the library; you will seek what you need to see."

"But I don't understand?"

"You will," he replied. "You have to enter to unlock your future."

"Is everyone talking in riddles, as nothing makes sense to me?" I questioned flippantly, staring at the door in disbelief.

"The clock is ticking," he replied, as he walked out of view.

The door opened smoothly to an airy and elegantly furnished room, with delicate wall art and comfortable chairs to enjoy the view from the windows overlooking the gardens. Celestial shades of soft, subtle lighting led me towards the library.

I gasped in awe at its vastness; it was not the library I had visited before. Rows upon rows of leather-bound books stacked high towards the intricate curved ceiling, it was never-ending. Mesmerised by its magnificence, I followed the light as it travelled around the room, bringing life to the marbled Roman statues that graced the athenaeum. Stopping directly in front of a book, it compelled me to take a closer look. It seemed different to all the others as it stood prominently out upon the shelf. Flicking the dust off with my fingers, I curiously held it in my hands, feeling its magnetic energy. The gold/blue embossed title caught my attention; it was called *The Knowing*. Turning the pages carefully, my hands started to vibrate; it immediately jumped to page 212, revealing a small delicate sliver key which fell to the floor. Retrieving it quickly, I held it tightly. My silence was interrupted by a gentleman's voice.

"Excuse me, madam, do you have permission to be here?" asked a tall, elegantly dressed man.

"Yes, sir, but I thought I was alone."

"Ah, the mystery of our minds is a book itself," he laughed, patting his forehead, revealing his fair hair and soft blue kind eyes. "You may think you are alone, but in reality, you are not."

"I'm sorry, this is nonsense to me," I replied indignantly.

"But let me assure you, you are here for a reason. Let me introduce myself. I am the record keeper of the library of books; that is all you need to know for now," he replied, clicking his fingers, startling me.

"Then you will know what this key is for?" I asked nervously, holding it carefully.

Looking somewhat bemused at me, he chuckled. "But madam, you have already turned the key. It belongs to you, please keep it safe."

"But I don't understand," I muttered, safely securing the key with a ribbon from my hair, attaching it tightly to the inside of my bodice.

"One day, you may understand and then again, you may not. Remember, nothing is as it seems," he said, walking swiftly away.

Baffled by his words, and placing the book back upon the shelf, I gasp at the enormity of this place; what is it? Puzzled and deep in thought, I grew aware of the ticking clock. Tick-tock, louder and louder it was, spinning me into a whirlwind of frenzied energy. Closing my eyes to avert the giddiness, I clung to the walls for support and waited for the sensations to pass.

Courageously opening my eyes, I found myself outside the Princess's private rooms. The vast library was nowhere to be seen; rubbing my eyes in disbelief, I was thrown off balance. Teetering on the edge of madness, my mind could not digest what was happening. Gingerly, I opened the door to Gabriella's bedchamber; thankfully, it was as I remembered.

Crystal chandeliers brightly lit the room, creating the illusion of diamond rays from the afternoon sun. It filtered through the heavy draped curtains against a tall window overlooking her private gardens. Peering out of the window, I scanned the landscape, perturbed, not recalling any of it. Gabriella's four-poster bed looked inviting with soft, smooth bed linen. It was dressed in seductive shades of red velvet drapes. Smelling her sweet scent, I sighed heavily. Above her bed was her signature of wealth and power which was now visible.

It was the mural of the Occult. Arousing my curiosity, my heartbeat quickened; hearing footsteps, the door started to open. Quickly I took refuge under the bed. Holding my breath, seeing glimpses of a loose buckle on a shoe as they made their way to the bed, an overriding scent of musk engulfed the room. Instantly, I knew it was the Lord, feeling the heaviness of his body as he slumped upon the bed. Hearing him groaning, I knew he was up to something, I dared not move. Moments later, in walked Gabriella, recognising her distinctive perfume, she pounced eagerly upon the waiting Lord. Moving her body, she rode his hard phallus, their noise was unbearable as they fornicated in dark rituals of promiscuous wild sex. The bed rocked ferociously, pushing the mattress further onto my squashed body; at last they stopped.

"We don't have long, my Lord. Sophia thinks she has drugged me," said Gabriella, gleefully.

"She's a fool," snapped the Lord. "No one can get the upper hand of us," he said, thumping the bed hard.

"We know you are there, Sophia, please show yourself," he ordered.

Sheepishly, I emerged from under the bed. Staring at the Lord's naked body, his face was stern and his eyes were cold as ice.

"I'm sorry, my Lord, I was to believe that you had returned to Amsterdam," I replied nervously.

"Well, that doesn't explain why you are here in the Princess's private room," he snarled menacingly at me.

"I was looking for the library, and somehow I found myself in here," I muttered quietly.

"Speak up, child and come closer," demanded the Lord.

"Yes, my Lord."

"Sophia, you can never outwit us. You are under oath and must obey my orders to help bring our plan of world domination into place," he shouted savagely.

His eyes now glowed fiercely, burning into mine. Feeling his anger, I had no choice but to agree.

"What about Lucien, is he part of the plan too?"

"He's not important! Surely you don't believe him; he is a fraudster," said the Lord, sitting on the edge of the bed, playing with his phallus.

Gabriella's golden hair seductively covered her breasts, revealing her left nipple. I easily felt aroused by her powerfully hypnotic sexuality.

"Sophia, you are here because we have enticed you into our world, and I am the Lord's wife," said Gabriella, stroking her naked body.

"But you are to marry Prince Lavin soon," I gasped, astonished.

"Yes, the wedding will still go ahead. You must not breathe a word of this; after all, you are my lover and with that comes a responsibility to keep our secret safe."

"I promise," I replied, smiling inwardly, knowing I was one step ahead of Lucien.

"Now come and join us," said Gabriella, patting the bed seductively. "You are now one of us, so you may bear witness to our seal of sovereignty to each other," she purred, erotically.

Lying next to them, strangely my fears dissipated. The Lord's testosterone was on fire; his heat was palpable and intense as he gorged upon Gabriella; they were unstoppable. I eagerly waited for my turn, engrossed in my own sexual pleasure. Magnetic energy intensified the moment, as I tightly clung to the sheets. Gabriella gazed lovingly upon me through her deep hazel eyes. Between them both, I was engulfed in their dark sexual fantasies.

"Sophia," whispered Gabriella. "We need you to recruit more women to fund our baby marketing. Boys make more money."

"Yes," I murmured as the Lord pummelled me forcefully from behind until he reached his crescendo, ejaculating deep into my womanhood. Exhausted, I quickly fell into a deep sleep in Gabriella's arms.

I awoke alone in a cold and empty bed, the smell of musk from the Lord mixed with the scent of Gabriella lingered on the damp sheets, stained with semen. Heartbroken, I remembered the Lord's spirit had seeped into mine. Mortified, I staggered from the bed, fumbling in the twilight, finding my clothes. Thankfully, my watch and key were still safe. Clasping it tightly, I felt the hands of time spinning faster. A faint smell of patchouli wafted in the air; immediately, my anxiety eased.

"Don't be fooled Sophia," said the voice in the shadows. "It's time."

"Time for what?" I replied, scanning the room, blocking the sound of the constant ticking with my hands.

Bewildered, I left the Princess's bedchamber and hurriedly made my way back towards the library, but was stopped abruptly by a sharp tap on my shoulder.

"Madam, do not make the same mistake."

"Who are you?" I enquired, turning hesitantly, expecting to come face to face with the commanding voice. But there was no one there.

"I am your rite of passage. You have the key now, so use it wisely, Sophia," said the voice.

Overcome with emotions, my vision blurred as the room started to spin. Seeing the library opening up to the sky, a familiar scent brought me back from the realms of delusion. Finding myself back in the palatial corridors of the palace, I took a seat on a cream velvet chair, and waited for my hysteria to leave.

"Madam, there you are," said Martha, looking concerned. "I have been looking for you for several hours. Come quickly. The Princess has suddenly taken ill in the morning room; she has been asking for you."

Aghast, composing myself and holding the guilt within, I ran to her aid.

Gabriella lay all in white upon a regal chaise longue looking pale and wan, her golden hair looked limp, her life force was slowly slipping away.

"Sophia, you've come," she murmured softly.

"I'm here, my dear Princess."

Holding her cold and clammy hand, she raged with a high fever; her pulse was weak. Time was not on her side. My heart was tainted with sadness.

"Sophia," she whispered. "Whatever happens to me, you must find my son, Philip. The Lord has taken him but he is not the Lord's son!" she gasped, in between breaths.

"I will," I promised. Stunned by Gabriella's news, I gently kissed her soft lips.

A cold presence filled the morning room as the wind from the north blasted in from the open windows. I shivered, sensing the Lord's darkness in the room. Cradling Gabriella in my arms, she murmured.

"Please don't leave me."

"You have my word, my dear Princess." Stroking her hair from her face, I waited by her side as time ticked slowly, minute by minute.

Chapter 17

For several months I tended to Gabriella as I watched her fragile life hang in the balance like the scales of justice weighing heavily upon me. Torn between love and guilt, I was propelled into a world I hardly recognised as the wheels of time kept ticking. She looked serene; even in illness, her beauty enchanted me with her regal presence. My infatuation with her intensified daily; she had stolen my heart with every breath she took.

The first signs of spring were bursting into life, with the freshness of the morning dawn. I embraced the light, walking among the vast gardens of the palace; it had been a long time coming. Life in the palace began to breathe new energies, as Gabriella's zest for life had now returned. The House of De Vries was calling me back; with the help of Martha, Rosa and Scarlet, my empire had grown. Sitting in the centre of the maze, I listened intently to the nature's call, only to be interrupted by Scarlet.

"Madam, it's time," said Scarlet approaching me through the endless rows of yew and boxwood bushes. Her fiery hair bounced in rhythm with the dawn chorus; she spoke with authority.

"Princess Gabriella knows you have to leave soon; she has also heard where the Lord may be hiding. Rosa and I will escort the new ladies back to the House of De Vries if that is your wish. Martha will journey with you."

"Thank you, Scarlet," I replied, scanning her face as my distrust grew, questioning her loyalty.

"I must inspect the new ladies before I make my decision," I replied sharply.

"Very well, madam. I will gather them in the lobby and await your approval."

Sighing heavily, I looked back towards the palace. I had succumbed to the richness of this world, and I was not ready to give it up. Apprehension overshadowed my thoughts, knowing I would have to face the Lord yet again.

Nine new virgin ladies stood patiently awaiting my inspection; young and delectable, they were eager to learn the ways of the night, and to earn their keep within the house.

"Welcome ladies, if you abide by my rules, you will all be showered with much wealth of golden coins. Keep your eyes on your job. Men love a virgin. There are ways to fool them; this will enhance your position in the House of De Vries. Julian, my brother, will expect the best, so please don't let me down," I said, authoritatively.

"Scarlet, you are in charge of these new recruits until I return. Please show them what needs to be done. Rosa will accompany you."

"Yes, madam," she replied gleefully, mocking the ladies with her vulgarity as she led them towards the waiting carriage.

Gabriella stood at the palace gate, waiting for Prince Lavin to arrive. She looked raw and untamed. Her golden hair billowed in the gusty wind. Gabriella's white gown loosely clung around her tiny body, giving an appearance of innocence, magnifying her beauty. I was saddened to leave her, but I knew time was ticking away. Smitten by her radiance, our eyes connected with warmth, embracing each other as our lips met with tenderness, intoxicating me under her spell.

"Dear Sophia, please find my son, Philip. He has become of age; I fear the Lord will entice him with a powerful ceremony, initiating him to the Occult. You must stop him, Sophia. The Lord has no mercy. Please be careful."

"Yes, your grace, I will endeavour to find Philip and bring him home to you," I replied, daunted by her request.

Hearing the sound of horses, the royal carriage was fast approaching. My last few moments with Gabriella were all I had. Holding her hand, I gracefully let it go. Prince Lavin was here to claim his bride. Shiny buckles on his tiny feet, he stood upright, exaggerating his diminutive height. His hair was neatly groomed, tied carefully into a ponytail. A blue crushed velvet jacket and breeches framed his small stature. Proprietorially, he gave his hand to Gabriella; she eagerly accepted as a wave of jealously caught me off guard.

"I will look after her now," he declared in his Prussian accent.

"Madam Sophia, thank you for your help. Your next stage is in front of you. Your duty now lies with us. Take my carriage; my horsemen will look after you and Martha."

"Very well, your Majesty and my dear Gabriella. I bid you both farewell until we meet again," I replied, taking my seat upon his carriage with Martha by my side.

As we passed the Chapel de Royal, the big clock chimed repeatedly. Glancing at my pocket watch, it was twelve noon. Galloping further away from the palace, my anxiety grew as we headed towards our fate. Clasping my watch tightly, a fine mist blurred my vision, reminding me of the path I must take and the power that I held within my hands. Our journey was long and arduous, covering many miles through the pathways that became visible. We sat in silence, fearing the danger we had to endure as time engulfed us.

"Madam, did you see that," yelled Martha, clinging to my arm.

"See what?"

"Look in the mist. There's a dark shadow ahead of us," replied Martha, agitated.

I stared blankly, not wanting to see, but my inner voice alerted me to the many pitfalls that lay ahead. The veil of time shrouded us in a world of vulnerability.

"Martha, we need to get out of this carriage now," I yelled.

"But madam, how will we get back to Amsterdam?" she asked fearfully.

"Just do as I say," I demanded.

"Stop!" I screeched at the royal footman.

The carriage came to an abrupt halt. Flinging us both to the floor, encouraging Martha to jump with me, we alighted onto a dusty path surrounded by many trees.

"But where do we go now?" asked Martha, brushing the dirt from her pale blue gown; looking fraught and shaken, she stared at the vastness of the deep dark glen.

"Just follow me, come quickly."

Watching the carriage speedily disappear as it turned the corner, I breathed a sigh of relief. We were now several miles away from the palace, surrounded by a blanket of mist. The trees eerily stood out silhouetted in the skyline. Cold and hungry, we carefully walked to a nearby tree for some shelter. Old oak blended with the sky, giving an appearance of mottled light; dusk was fast approaching. Resting by its vast trunk, we waited until the mist eventually lifted.

"Which way?" asked Martha, looking tired, cold and rather pale, matching the colour of her blue gown.

"It's this way." I pointed to a nearby path which had now become visible. "I have been here before."

"Are you sure?"

"Well, I think so, but there's only one way to find out," I muttered.

Hurriedly, we made haste upon the path as night quickly fell. A passing crow swooped menacingly overhead, stopping to perch on a branch that was directly in front of us. In the twilight, his eyes were silvery black, mirroring the darkness within. I flinched away, tugging onto Martha, as many crows were now following our every move. Their squawking was deafening, raising the alarm of impending danger. We ran deep into the woods, stumbling upon a small derelict dwelling. Exhausted, we took shelter and shut the door on outside life. The small hut was damp and cold, but we were out of sight from the prying eyes of the crows. Huddling together to keep warm, I drifted between two realities. The light of the moon aroused me from my sleep; it shone brightly, giving me some comfort on this cold, dark night.

"The moon will keep us safe," I said sleepily, "but we must wait until dawn before we leave. The crows will lead us to the Lord. Rest, Martha, for tomorrow we journey onwards."

The night was cold and endlessly exacerbated by pangs of hunger. We were both longing for dawn. Fatigue seeped into my aching body, wreaking havoc with my mind, seeing visions of Gabriella in my dreams.

At last daylight filtered through the murky stained window. Thirsty and extremely hungry, searching the hut for food, we found nothing. Fearing the path that we were both about to embark upon, I crouched into a ball, hiding from a bright light, which oozed through the walls. Clasping my watch, I felt time slipping away as the energy changed within the dwelling. As the light grew sharper, I started to recognise the hut, as a wave of anxiety swept through me.

"Martha, wake up. We must leave now."

"But which path do we take?" asked Martha wearily.

"The one that leads us to the Lord," I replied, looking out of the dirty window. Beady crow eyes stared blatantly through the window, intimidating me with his threatening energy. I froze, seeing the Lord's reflection in its eyes.

"We can't go out there!" shouted Martha.

"I know, shh, let me think, there has to be another way out of here."

With my hand still firmly holding the watch, my mind began to unravel.

"Yes, Martha, there is another way, I remember, there is a trap door that will lead us to Philip and to the Lord. We just need to find it."

Scrabbling on all fours, we searched the dirty rotten wooden floor, revealing a heavy slab. Heaving it away, we eventually found our way out towards our destiny. Eagerly we embarked down the rickety steps, into a dark, putrid tunnel; it was grim and endless.

"Listen, Martha, can you hear that faint whisper?"

"Yes."

"The Lord may be fearless, but he is no fool. I fear he is waiting for us to walk this path."

"What do you mean?" quizzed Martha.

"You will find out soon enough. Come, now hurry, hold on to my cape and follow me."

Daylight was in sight. Taking a gasp of fresh air, we left the tunnel, finding ourselves in a thicket, surrounded by an expanse of fresh fertile grass. Pure white snowdrops gently swayed in the soft breeze, giving me hope. Exhausted, we carried on regardless. We were not on our own for long; the menacing crows were back. They circled noisily above, tormenting us with their high pitch squawk, before descending to the bushes.

"Martha, we can do this, come on," I pleaded. Her sullen face hid the pain that she was carrying.

Warming my cold hands in my deep pockets, I gravitated to my watch. It felt warm to the touch as I rubbed my fingers over the intricate carving, feeling time ticking within my hands. The sky turned dark with angry clouds, causing the crows to disperse noisily. A storm was brewing with supernatural energy, causing electric currents that lit the sky.

Despairingly I shouted, "Watch! Please lead us to the right path."

"Your wish is my command," replied a voice in the air.

"Who are you?"

"I am the keeper of time. You have the key, so use it wisely."

"Martha, did you hear that voice?"

"No, madam, it's just your imagination," she replied, looking tired and frustrated with me.

Intrigued, I touched the tiny key which was now safely attached to a ribbon around my neck. It felt strange but also familiar, but still I was not grasping its true meaning.

"Martha, we have to go into the woods to find our path."

"OK," she replied, reluctantly and feebly.

Gingerly, we walked together as the bracing wind blew from the east, touching each tree as we passed. Overcome with weariness, we were lost in the woods, trying to find a path that would lead us to the Lord. Heavy-hearted, I glanced at my watch; uncannily, it was 2.12 pm. Shuddering fearfully as my heart raced rapidly, a path revealed itself to us.

"Sophia, you have earned the right to enter the next stage," said the voice in the ether.

"This way, Martha, there is no turning back. We must find Philip; I fear for his life."

"Yes," she replied, lagging behind me, as we walked tiredly towards our destination. It was in sight!

Chapter 18

A tall tower loomed ahead as the crows circled our every move. Sinisterly, a lone crow perched upon the vaulted roof swooping low over our heads; its menacing presence brought an unease within my soul. My attention turned towards Martha, anxiously sensing danger ahead; she looked weak and extremely pale. Still, she insisted that I should continue without her. Pangs of guilt pricked my conscience as I left Martha on the grass verge. Remembering Catalina, I called out to her.

"I'm so sorry. I will find Philip and come back for you."

"It's OK, just go," she replied wearily.

The rays of the afternoon sun warmed my cold body. Standing under the canopy of a giant birch tree, I stared at the tower, not wanting to enter. It was covered in a thick layer of ivy, which clung to every brick. Dare I proceed onwards? I had no choice. Apprehensively making my way towards the entrance, I entered a dark tunnel that would lead me into the tower. A vile, rancid smell burned the inside of my nostrils. Fearfully, an overwhelming feeling of suffocation gripped my body. Instantly, I was pushed backwards by the strong force of a powerful energy, propelling me to flee the tunnel, hastily.

Out of breath, gasping for air, I was surprised to see Martha waiting under the tree.

"I knew you would come back for me," she smiled reassuringly, "we have to do this together, don't we?"

"Yes," I replied. "But the time is not right; For now I have to do this alone, Martha. Come lean on me."

Sheltering under the safety of the tree, we rested and waited, watching the sun fade behind the clouds whilst the crows dispersed as dusk grew. Intensifying the moment as the sky turned vivid red, it was now time for me to walk this path alone. Running my fingers over my watch, I prayed silently.

"I will be back, Martha. I promise."

Reluctantly leaving Martha behind, I walked back towards the tower which loomed ahead, dark energy seeped from the building. Hesitating, glancing backwards for reassurance, I saw a hazy glow around the tree, but no Martha! Gathering my strength, I forged my way forward, knowing it was time to face the Lord yet again. Heavy-heartedly, I approached the threatening fortification, fearing every brick held a grizzly secret. Night had fallen, and the moon was just rising; sighing with relief, the light guided me through the maze of thickly overgrown ivy. Every step took me closer to the Lord. I anxiously stood at the entrance as the scent of death and decay was putrid; it clung in the air. Nervously, I walked the path into the darkness of the steeple as a cauldron of bats flew above my head. Losing my balance, I stumbled falling upon the stone floor.

"Lord, where are you?"

"I am right here. Sophia, stand up and walk straight ahead, then turn and face me," he commanded.

"But I'm in pain, my Lord."

"Sophia, get up now," he bellowed.

Slowly, I walked painfully and apprehensively towards the Lord, knowing I would be witnessing the darkness in my soul. The Lord's cold hands were soon around my mouth, holding me tightly; I gasped for air.

"Sophia, there is no turning back. You are here because you wanted to come, didn't you? Speak up, child!" he shouted, taking his hand away.

"But I don't understand. Who are you?" I yelled.

Moonlight cast ghostly shadows through the small gaps in the stone wall. The Lord's presence was deeply encased in the tower; I recoiled in disgust as his red eyes violently glowed.

"I am the Lord! Look into my eyes, what do you see?" he ordered, towering over me.

"No, I won't," I replied defiantly.

Feeling his body close to mine, and his foul breath upon my face, I reluctantly looked him in the eye, seeing his truth; I gasped, horrified!

"You will never find Philip, but seeing as you are here, I will reveal the dark side of my soul."

"I can see it in your eyes," I replied shivering, trying to wriggle from his grasp.

"Well, well, well, that is interesting. You and Gabriella have deceived me, and with that comes a price. You know what that is, don't you?" he said menacingly, as he started to grope my body.

"No!" I shouted.

Powerless, he swiftly pushed me to the floor, dragging my hair with his long slender fingers; there was no way out but to give myself to him. Feeling the weight of his body upon mine, he quickly parted my legs and crudely entered my vagina. Speaking in Latin, casting incantations, he ferociously expelled his sperm. I had reached the point of no return, as the Lord consumed me with his darkness; I was encased in his web of satanic sexual gratification.

"Eros Deo maxima ex libidine et cupidiate. Sophia, est scriptor euphoric libido crescat affectus. Expergiscimini Sophia, quod affectio corporis, quantum sufficit, ut eam sexualem attractionem. Sophia, diu et durum facere libeat. Sic fiat semper."

(Eros, the greatest God of lust and passion. Increase Sophia's feelings of euphoric desire. Awake Sophia's needs for physical affection as well as sexual attraction. Make Sophia lust long and hard. So mote it be.)

"You are mine once more. The spell has been cast," sneered the Lord venomously.

Producing a knife from within his robe, the Lord sliced his index finger, allowing dark scarlet blood to ooze upon my lips. Tasting his blood, satisfying my thirst, I was easily lured away from my path as the energy intensified the moment. Breathless, my animalistic nature made me crave more of his fetish behaviour. The Lord had seduced me yet again with his powerful, potent sorcery.

"Remember, Sophia, you are under oath. You must never reveal my true identity to anyone."

"Yes, my Lord."

Overcome with greed, I gave myself freely to the Lord of devilment. His powerful energy rapidly fed my soul, inducing me into a deep trance. Hours later I found myself lying on a field of green grass. Dazed and confused, I stared at the turquoise sky, not a cloud in sight, just the distant mellow tones of beautiful skylarks. The morning sun graced my aching body with warmth as I lay in the hazy light of a fresh new day, trying to recall my memory of the night.

"Sophia," I constantly heard in my thoughts. "Sophia, my dear Sophia."

Noticing a familiar figure standing over me, I was relieved to see Martha.

"What happened? How did I get here?" I enquired, feeling nauseated, with a metallic taste in my mouth.

Martha's kind eyes soothed my soul as she helped me to my feet. Shockingly, my gown was ripped and stained with blood. I scanned the horizon for answers, but all I could see was meadows.

"Martha," I pleaded again. "Where is the tower?"

"Look, the tower is still there," she said, comforting me in a warm embrace. "Don't you remember you went to confront the Lord?"

"Vaguely. How come you are here, Martha? I left you under the birch tree. You were weak, and now you're full of vigour."

"Don't you remember you came back for me twice? Just breathe slowly, your memory will come back in time," said Martha smiling fondly.

Concerned for my well-being, I frantically searched for my key; it had been tied securely around my neck by a length of black ribbon, but it had vanished!

"Martha, the Lord has taken it. We have to get it back," I gasped, horrified, as visual pictures flooded my mind, with the energies of rituals and sacrifices that I had witnessed with the Lord. Heart-rending words tumbled from my mouth.

"I am the mistress of the Lord, his fire burns within my soul; together, we are one."

Martha's face changed dramatically, looking shocked with a ghostly white hue. She whimpered, "If you are his mistress, then I am your sister. I was there with you both. We have both been shockingly bewitched. Yes, you must reclaim your key, we badly need it Sophia." Martha anxiously paced up and down in dismay.

"But your gown is still intact, how come?"

"I don't know, madam, all I recall is his heavy body upon mine, then I awoke here, just like you."

Rage stirred within me. The Lord had taken us both in his greed for sexual empowerment. Martha crumbled to the grass, sobbing uncontrollably. I comforted her as guilt crept in, yet again. A faint scent of patchouli drifted in on the breeze as the voice in the wind grew louder and louder.

"Sophia, wake up. Time has shifted your awareness; look up into the sky."

"But I am awake!" I whispered, perplexed. Viewing the world with fresh eyes, I looked eagerly towards the tower for answers. Through the veil of time, we had slipped into the Lord's dimension. Knowing the magnitude of the moment, standing together, we were now slaves to the Lord.

"It's time to reclaim your power, Sophia," said the voice in the wind.

Reassured with the words of reason, I turned towards Martha. Her eyes were red and swollen from many tears.

"The Lord has the key, but he has forgotten how powerful we both are."

"Yes, my dear Sophia, thank you for reminding me," said Martha, as hope grew within her face.

The call of the tower beckoned us once again. It loomed ahead, but this time, we had no fear. Hand in hand, we solemnly walked into the darkness of the building to reclaim what was rightfully ours, my key and our sovereignty. This time we were ready and prepared for the Lord.

Chapter 19

Shafts of light guided us through the dark dismal tunnel, with the sound of constant dripping water. My heart yearned for stability and love. In the depths of the rambling tower, we stared into the abyss, feeling the Lord's presence within the fabric of the building. Dark forces of nature propelled us forward, touching my heart; I prayed silently for the light to return.

"Martha, we will find them and reclaim my key."

"Yes," she replied, sighing heavily.

Entering a small dimly lit room, there was no sign of the Lord, but his musky scent lingered. The taste of his blood was still fresh upon my lips. Disgusted, I threw myself to the floor, cursing him for what he had done to us. Soft rugs cushioned me as I inwardly squirmed, knowing this was the Lord's room of dark sexual fantasies.

"Martha, we must not give up." I sensed her helplessness. "There is something we are not seeing. Let no stone be unturned, seek and we will find."

"I don't understand," muttered Martha, looking subdued, her swollen eyes reflecting her fear.

"Look, Martha, at the edges of the rugs; they are all different."

"Oh yes!" she exclaimed, taking a closer look. "The stitching is loose, and something is sticking out."

"Yes," I replied, tugging at the object and feeling a heavy weighted tube. Each corner of the rug felt similar. Carefully, we unpicked the stitching, revealing four pewter tubes. Shockingly, each one contained a miniature portrait of myself, Martha, Catalina and Gabriella. Rage engulfed me, as my hatred grew towards the Lord.

"No, no, this can't be happening, but it is. We are all the Lord's mistresses, and Catalina has paid the price with her life!" I yelled, horrified.

Holding my portrait, I stared deeply into the shadows of the painting. Seeing the darkness within my soul, I squirmed, not wanting to look again.

"Martha, what do you see in yours?"

Taking her time, she examined it closely, before angrily throwing her portrait across the room.

"I can't see anything," she sobbed, "just a heavy mist."

"Martha, it's OK, please, we have to keep going," I reassured her.

Holding Gabriella's portrait, my eyes transfixed upon hers. Immediately, I felt calm and at peace. Her beauty was captured within the painting; my heart yearned for Gabriella.

"Martha, you must look into Catalina's eyes," I insisted. "She will talk to your soul and lead us to the Lord and Philip. But first, we need to draw a pentagram on the stone floor to enhance our energy and place our names within the sacred space."

"What with?" replied Martha.

"All we need to do is visualise and draw it with our fingers. Stepping into the middle, we will cast our spell."

"Universe, overland, sea, earth, wind and fire, we seek justice. The ring of fire is burning brightly, bringing forth the vision of the Lord and Philip. Seek and behold our power, for we are sisters of the Lord. So mote it be."

Our voices echoed around the tower, amplifying our energy as a strong gust of wind whipped our legs forcefully.

"Hold on to me!" I yelled, hearing a voice within the wind.

"Sophia, dear Sophia, remember why you are here."

"Who is it?" I shouted, but no reply came, just a faint aroma of a familiar scent aroused my senses.

The energy grew within our pentagram, it was solid and extremely powerful. Remembering my task, nothing was going to stop us from knowing the truth.

"Martha, now is the time to link into Catalina through the window of her soul."

"Yes, I can do this," she replied hopefully.

Martha carefully unravelled the portrait; holding it firmly, she connected with Catalina from beyond the veil of death.

"I see a vision of a stately home in Amsterdam. There we will find the Lord. I see him counting his gold amongst the men of the

Occult. The Lord's power is tremendous; Philip is in danger, Sophia. Catalina will lead us to them," said Martha.

"Martha, we must get to Philip before the Lord initiates him into the Occult. At first light, we need to make haste."

The night was endless, cold and damp; we huddled together as the prevailing wind from the north funnelled around our feet. Hungry, I lay silently, longing for daybreak while Martha slept. I kept watch with the constant sound of tick-tock repeating in my thoughts. An owl screeched in the distance. Its piercing cry sent waves of acute anxiety through me as the pressure mounted within the tower, consuming us in its evil presence.

Daybreak finally came; I waited eagerly as the light slipped through the gaps of the small oblong leaded windows. Sighing with relief, I gently woke Martha.

"Martha, it's time to leave."

"But how will we get back?" enquired Martha, fearfully.

"There will be a way. Have faith, dear Martha."

Looking forlorn and lost, Martha's eyes were raw and puffy from crying. Her blue gown hung loosely around her petite frame, and her hair was now matted and dirty. I owed it to Martha to get us safely back to the House of De Vries.

Emerging from the darkness, the light dazzled our eyes. A crow circled overhead beckoning us to continue through the thick ivy, leading to the grass verge glistening in the morning dew. Stopping for a moment, I heard the sounds of Mother Nature comforting my soul. The deafening squawking of the crow swooped low, breaking the silence; feeling its wings touching my head, I knew it had come to show us the way. Our path soon became visible as the sun emerged into the sky, gracing the heavens with shades of pink.

"Martha, I know the way. We have to walk through the woods, following this dusty dirt track. It will lead us to a traveller's inn, nestled amongst the tall pines. We can rest and replenish ourselves before we journey onwards."

"How do you know that?" said Martha quizzing me.

"I just have a feeling; besides the crow is showing us the way. Look, it's flying right in front of us now."

"Oh yes, you are right," said Martha, smiling warmly, touching the wet grass and wiping her mouth to quench her thirst.

"Lead on," said Martha wearily.

The dense forest was full of giant pines, towering towards the sky; they gave us some comfort from the prevailing wind. We walked wearily along the path. I stopped momentarily, watching the crow above swoop low, sweeping its wings above the branches of the trees before descending into the undergrowth of wild garlic; its pungent scent whetted my appetite.

"Not long now, Martha, I promise, we will soon be at the inn."

"I do hope so," replied Martha, looking drained and exhausted.

The Crow's Nest was now in sight, nestled neatly amongst the trees. Warm and inviting, it enticed us to retreat inside. Sighing with relief, we were both eager to rest and replenish our hunger. A fire burned brightly in the corner of the inn, smelling of cedar wood, the welcome smile of the innkeeper was a pleasure to our eyes.

"Hello madams, what can I get you?" asked the tall dark-haired man.

His face was pitted with scars, his hair flopped untidily to the left, whilst his brown eyes sparkled as he spoke.

"Some food please and some drink, sir," I said eagerly.

"Yes, of course, take a seat by the fire," he replied kindly. "Two bowls of the finest broth coming your way and some of my finest liquor that will keep your belly warm." He grinned widely, revealing his stained teeth.

Moments later, our food arrived, whilst the innkeeper kept a watchful eye on us. I was not perturbed by his glare but aware that something was not quite right. Then I saw him in my peripheral vision, the Hooded Man.

"Martha, do you see him?"

"Who?" she replied, mopping up her broth with the thick crusty bread. "I can't see anyone."

"Well, I can! I must follow him. Stay here, please trust me."

"OK," she replied, hesitantly.

Watching the shadowy figure walk across the inn, I quickly followed him.

"Hey, wait!" I yelled. "I need to speak to you."

He ignored me, walking towards a bolted wooden door, then

turned around. His brown hood concealed his face, revealing only a subtle beard.

"Who are you?"

"Don't you know yet?" he chuckled lightly, handing me another key. "You haven't worked it out yet?"

"No," I replied, somewhat perplexed as he held my hand firmly.

He spoke swiftly and with authority. "Listen, Sophia. You must retrieve your key from the Lord; he is not to be trusted with it. Please take good care of this duplicate key and give it to Martha once you have retrieved yours from the Lord. The past is changing all around you. Remember Sophia, life is an illusion, and you are here for a reason. You have been told."

I wanted to ask many questions, but he turned around swiftly and was soon out of sight. Remembering his words, I scrutinised the delicate silver key, reaching inside my deep pocket for my watch. The key fitted perfectly as I eagerly turned it. Immediately, sensing a shift of energy, everything looked different; part of me was still in the tavern. I could hear the sounds of chatter, but it was all so faint, yet another part of me was in another world, seeing visions of a life I did not know; they were compelling yet oddly familiar. My heart raced as the energy intensified; two worlds collided at frightening speed. Panicking, I quickly retrieved the key from the watch, and the images disappeared into vapour. Sighing heavily, and realising the importance of the key, I tied it securely into my gown with a black ribbon from my hair before walking back to Martha.

Standing at the door of the inn, Martha looked relaxed and rosy-cheeked. Perched on her right shoulder was the crow. It cocked his head and looked directly into my eyes, connecting me with his soul.

"Martha, I do believe he's saying we must now leave."

"But there is no carriage," replied Martha. "Where have you been? You have been ages; it will be sunset soon."

"What! I haven't been anywhere," I replied, somewhat bemused by her question.

"There will be a carriage, Martha, have faith."

The crow squawked three times, then flew ahead and out into the evening light. The air was heavy as the sky turned a dramatic shade of deep fiery red.

"There's a storm brewing. We must hurry."

"But where to?"

"Just follow the crow, Martha."

The crow led us to the nearby stables as the rain pelted hard, and lightning flashed brilliantly around us. Thunderous claps echoed my anxiety; fearing the worst, I prayed for a miracle. Closing my eyes tightly, hearing a carriage hurtling towards us, my prayers were answered.

"Where to, madam?" asked the coachman.

"The Jenssen Estate," replied Martha.

"Very well, climb on board; it's hellish weather, so hold on tight."

My fingers were numb from the rawness of the rain; placing my hands deep inside my gown to thaw, I felt the key within my grasp. I held it tightly as faint pulses of energy raced through my body. Shades of light and darkness filtered my vision as we hurtled towards our destination. Feeling safe, my breathing became calmer, and eventually I drifted off to sleep, oblivious to the raging storm outside. A deafening boom echoed overhead as the carriage abruptly stopped, jerking us sharply forward. Fork lightning lit the sky in a blaze of dazzling light; as the thunder continued to rumble loudly, startling the horses, they became wild and unhinged. Stuck in the middle of nowhere, we desperately waited for the storm to ease. Time ticked slowly as the horsemen took turns to see to the horses, whilst one of them joined us in the carriage, making things more bearable. Thick mist rolled in from the valley beyond. I shivered feverishly as the cold air lingered heavily around us, knowing another long night lay ahead.

The first light of dawn emerged with the sound of a passing carriage. It stopped, and a tall, well-dressed man entered our carriage. I smiled warmly at him as he held out his hand to greet me.

"Hello, madam," he said calmly. His warm, inviting dark brown eyes caught my gaze as he carefully brushed his black flowing hair to one side.

"Let me introduce myself. I am Luka. I hear you are seeking my son, Philip."

"Yes," I replied, flabbergasted. "I'm Sophia, and this is Martha, my trusted companion."

"My carriage awaits you. We will ride together to seek my son and bring justice to the Lord."

Holding my hand tightly, he whispered softly in my ear, "Sophia, I am your destiny!"

Chapter 20

Standing proud and magnificent, the Jenssen Estate glowed in the evening sun casting its rays of light. As I approached the stately home, a strange energy rippled down my spine, sending cold shivers throughout my body.

A large golden fence encircled the whole estate, lined by fir trees; the gravel path took us towards the grand entrance, made of mottled grey marble. Gorgeous marigolds and deep russet roses evoked memories from my past. Water features of cherubic statues took centre stage in the large lily pond, showering us in a fine hazy mist. Hearing a child's laughter, I looked intently towards the trees, seeing a young girl disappear out of sight amongst the shrubbery.

"Hurry, Luka and Martha. I feel there is another way in around the back of the estate, but we need to be quick; I fear we are being watched," I said warily.

We entered through a small wooden gate that led us to the old part of the building. Dilapidated stained panelled walls darkened the passageway in a gloom of dismay. The putrid decay was unbreathable; I heaved uncontrollably.

At last, we found the door into the main building. Chequered black and white marble flooring sparkled with flecks of gold as the evening light streamed through the delicate stained-glass windows. The hallway expanded dramatically to a room of mirrors. Each was different in texture and size, decorated with intricate carvings of angels and demons, reflecting ghostly images of many faces. Worriedly, I stared into the mirrors.

"Are you OK, Sophia? You seem agitated," asked Martha.

"No, not really," I replied fearfully, tugging at my matted hair.

The evening light was fading fast. Suspiciously, I peered into the mirrors again; this time, I saw nothing. Confused, I rubbed my teary eyes as deep emotions resurfaced.

"Madam Sophia, you have to carry on," said Luka reassuringly.

"Yes, I know," I replied, fixated upon his gentle gaze. On our journey here, I became fascinated with Luka. His chiselled features were very appealing, while his hazel eyes glinted wickedly. I watched him with intrigue, listening to his deep husky tone, arousing my desire.

"You're looking very flushed," said Luka.

"Oh really? Oh dear, I must be having one of my moments," I said, feeling somewhat flustered.

"Hurry, both of you, we must disperse; I can hear footsteps approaching," said Martha, urgently.

We hid from view, as the Lord marched through the expansive hallway in the full costume of his deity, looking fierce yet dangerously attractive. Dressed in a black robe, wearing a crown made of antlers, he glowed with power and malice. I froze, gulping air between breaths. Many men walked eerily behind him wearing the same attire but with purple horns upon their headdresses. My pulse quickened as they formed a circle around the Lord.

"Dear brothers, we have gathered here today to witness Philip's initiation into the brotherhood," commanded the Lord.

Smirking sinisterly, he produced an identical small watch from his deep pocket. I gasped silently, clasping my hands around mine.

"Time is irrelevant, today we are going to bend time for our advantage," spoke the Lord.

"Step forward, Philip and make yourself seen."

Within the circle, a man stepped forward, walking barefoot upon the marble flooring, towards the Lord.

"Philip, reveal yourself to your brothers," ordered the Lord.

Carefully undressing, he revealed his nakedness, while the men eagerly watched and the tension mounted. Agitated, I feared the worst, as vivid memories of my encounter with the Lord of the Occult were deeply entrenched into my soul.

"This sacred act is deeply embedded in the ways of the old. Today we are setting a precedent for the future of our brothers," bellowed the Lord. "It's time to cast the spell."

My stomach tightened as the intensity mounted within the circle.

"We have to stop this," I whispered to Luka and Martha.

"Yes, but how?" asked Luka softly.

"Please trust me, we need to find the room of many portraits."

Silently and out of sight, we retreated back the way we came. Night had fallen, and the air was cool; flickering candlelight gave me hope as I urged them to follow quickly.

"It's this way."

"How do you know that, madam?" asked Martha.

"I don't know, honestly, but I feel somehow connected to this estate. Please hurry; we need to act fast before it's too late."

Palatial doors stood before us, embossed in gold leaf. I ran my hand over the carvings; strangely, it felt familiar as I carefully opened the door, revealing a gallery of many portraits. The room was light and airy. A fire blazed warmly in the grand fireplace. The walls were decorated in a deep shade of magenta, enhancing the clarity of the many images, depicting royal men and women looking regal in their finery. Many eyes followed me as I searched the room looking for a clue. Stopping immediately at the portrait of Lady Constance Jenssen, her soft blue eyes captivated me pushing me into another dimension. My attention grew as she enticed me into her world. For a brief moment, I became Lady Constance Jenssen. Viewing her life through her eyes, I was able to see into the future, giving me the strength to confront the Lord.

"Sophia, come on, hurry, we have an intruder," said Luka fearfully.

There was no time to hide, as the door opened and in walked Lucien, elegantly dressed in a dashing red jacket and breeches, embroidered with bold flowers. His ruffled white shirt emphasised his flamboyant charisma as he swaggered towards me.

"Lucien! What are you doing here?" I asked, incredulously.

"I've come for you," he replied, gloating sublimely.

"Please, I beg of you, don't tell the Lord we are here."

"What's it worth, Sophia?" he laughed, flicking his dark hair from his brow.

Lucien's piercing crystal blue eyes stared intensely into mine, entrapping me easily into his lair.

"Your secret is safe with me, but only if you honour your oath Sophia, by keeping your loyalty to me. You know you can never refuse me," he said arrogantly. "Now, I must return to the brotherhood who are waiting for me."

"Yes, I know," I replied reluctantly, as Lucien quickly dressed in his black gown, which was neatly folded on a nearby chair, before departing the room. He was now one of them.

"Sophia, you cannot trust Lucien. Our paths have crossed many times. He is known for his sexual depravity. The last I had heard, he had squandered his wealth away gambling," said Luka assertively.

"Of course, I don't trust him. I am fully aware of his lust for women. We must stop the Lord; we have to go back now!" I insisted.

Feeling the strength of Lady Constance Jenssen within me, I was ready for battle. Tentatively we made our way back into the grand hall, towards the gathering of the Occult. Hiding behind a large, marbled pillar, we watched, horrified, witnessing the Lord performing his dark satanic rituals.

"Luka, where's Martha? She's vanished!" I whispered anxiously to Luka. "She was standing next to me, just a moment ago." Anxiety rifled through my body, knowing Lucien had betrayed us.

"So you do have a conscience then?" said Lucien standing behind me.

"Lucien! You promised," I replied, turning to face him.

"I lied," he said arrogantly, pursing his lips at me.

"Stop, Lord. We have guests," he shouted.

"Oh do we!" roared the Lord sinisterly. His crown of antlers glowed fiercely, mirroring the fire within the circle of dark magic.

Apprehensively, I stood close to Luka. Please don't hurt Martha, I mumbled silently. A tremendous surge of energy erupted as the Lord's voice echoed in the hall of demonic shadows, diminishing my power. There was nothing I could do but to obey his orders.

"Step forward," commanded the Lord. "Enter the ring of fire, Sophia, it's time to face your demons!"

The Lord had spoken; yet again, I was at his mercy. Fearfully, I entered the ring of fire, taking my place next to the Lord in the centre. Engulfed in his mastery of dark rituals, the heat intensified as the Lord salivated over me. Knowing I was his prey, I quivered uncontrollably.

Chapter 21

Electric magnetic energy pulsated around the grand hall, intensifying the silence. I breathed anxiously as the circle of fire raged its war upon me. The brotherhood gathered closer as the pace quickened. Light and dark flickered ferociously as the gateway opened between two worlds of reality. The Lord's presence hung heavy in the hall; there was no way out but to obey his orders, as he offered me some magic snuff infused with opium. I sniffed it eagerly, breathing in the vapours as he laughed venomously.

"Oh Sophia, what have you done? Your fate is in my hands," he sneered defiantly, teasing me with my key. "The key is mine now. There is nothing you can do to stop the hands of time," roared the Lord menacingly.

Looking fierce, his eyes of steel pulled me into his lewd sexual rituals. Giddy with fear, seeing the chequered marble flooring swirling around me, I reached inside my deep pocket, clasping my watch tightly.

"Sophia, it's time," he bellowed.

His face was stern as he stood before me. Adrenalin fuelled my curiosity; watching him turn the key three times, I waited fearfully for the big reveal. Immediately a funnel of toxic energy swirled around us, taking me on a lucid journey in my mind. Watching the sky part between heaven and earth, witnessing many timelines merging into one, time momentarily stood still. We were caught in the flux of neither here nor there.

"What's happening?" I inquired warily.

"Through the veil, we can change our reality," said the Lord, gloating.

"Where's Martha and Philip?"

"You will find out soon," said the Lord. "Come, Philip and Martha, step into the fire," he roared.

"No! Not Martha," I begged.

I gasped, horrified, hearing Martha scream as she was pushed into the middle of the circle then ordered to strip. Fearfully she undressed; her vulnerability showed as she cowered away from the Lord, hiding her modesty with her hands. Philip was quick to join her. He stood naked by her side, eager for the commands of the Lord.

"Philip, take your place."

"No!" I shouted.

"It's too late, Sophia, you must watch, then it will be your turn," he sneered lecherously.

"Now strip," he ordered me.

My hand firmly upon my watch, pushing it deeper into my pocket, I prayed the Lord would not find it. My dishevelled gown fell to the floor in a heap as I hurriedly undressed, shivering fearfully. Cringing, I dared not look, holding my breath, I was desperate for this to end. Nothing could stop the Lord; he was relentless, compelling me to witness his beastly acts of animalistic sexual acts.

"Dear brothers, we have welcomed Philip into our brotherhood, he has taken his oath, and now he must show us he is a man and take these two women, Martha and Sophia," said the Lord masterfully.

Speaking in Latin, he recited, "*Fratris tempus est potestatem nostram recuperare per flammas vitae, iterum resurgimus. Et nos unum sumus. Velum temporis est nostrum, sic epulatur sororibus misericordiae.*"

"Brothers, it's time to regain our power through the flames of life we rise once more. We are one. The veil of time is ours; let the feast begin upon our sisters of mercy," he ordered.

Philips's body was battered with many bruises, but he was eager to serve his master. Pushing Martha to the floor, he held his penis firmly, encouraging it to grow, causing a stir within the gathering. Frenzied activity grew amongst the men as one by one they stripped, eager to watch and pursue their secrets of sadomasochism. Encouraged by the brotherhood, Philip's penis was ready for penetration, prising Martha's legs wide open. She screamed, terrified as he entered her crudely. Feeling light-headed, I closed my eyes as a faint waft of patchouli drifted in the air, giving me hope. I prayed silently, hearing the groans of Philip as he climaxed. A boiling pot of crude erotic energy rippled around the room; strangely it aroused my sexuality. I was bewitched as the heat intensified within the circle.

The brotherhood revelled with Philip's triumph as they welcomed him into the Occult, chanting ecstatically. The fumes of magic powders were dangerous and potent, intoxicating me into their world of perverse sexual rituals.

"Welcome, Philip, you are now one of us," exclaimed the Lord.

"Now, I give you Sophia. She is ripe and ready. Sophia, you thought you could outwit me, think again, madam, I know everything," he bellowed. "Now lie down and prepare for Philip!"

Flames of desire engulfed my soul as Philip straddled me. He was young and rock hard. Deep penetration took me to another dimension of unadulterated wild sex; I didn't want it to stop. I shuddered with pleasure as orgasmic waves rippled throughout my body.

Lying naked in the circle, oblivious to the sexual acts being performed by the Occult, dark and devious energy had consumed me, yet again.

Philip's body sprawled heavily upon me. Exhausted and elated, he gloated, "Sophia, it's not me that needs rescuing; it's you!"

"No, surely not! Get off me, you are hurting my arms, Philip," I yelled as he pinned me to the floor.

"That's enough, Philip," the Lord ordered. "Now dress brothers, watch and learn from your Lord."

"Sophia, now walk with me into the world of illusions."

The brotherhood stood holding hands around the perimeter of the circle. Their headdresses of purple horns glowed eerily in the shadows of the flickering flames. Reluctantly, I took my place by the Lord, whilst Luka tended to Martha.

"Well, are you ready?" said the Lord.

"Yes, my Lord," I whispered tentatively.

His dark fiery eyes glowed sinisterly; holding me firmly, he rubbed his manhood forcefully between my legs. Overcome with a desire to please the Lord, I gladly walked through the veil of time. Pulsating energy swept through my whole being, engulfing us in a hazy mist of seclusion.

"Where is everyone?" I enquired tentatively.

"Sophia, but there has only ever been you and me."

"What? But I don't understand."

"You will one day, or maybe not," he said masterfully. Pushing me to the floor, opening my legs wide, his tongue feasted hungrily upon my quim. Shuddering with pleasure, I gave into my sexual appetite.

The searing heat burst our bubble, bringing us back to the present moment. The brotherhood had formed a tight circle around us; they watched intently as the Lord devoured his prey. The flames of magic grew stronger and stronger, revealing his true nature. Shocked and disgusted, my whole body repelled violently, seeing his truth.

"Sophia, oh Sophia, wake up and listen. The tide is turning; many paths are now visible to you. The choice is yours, which one do you dare to walk? You decide," said a voice in the air.

"So you don't like what you see?" sneered the Lord. "I've had my pleasure. Now stand and get dressed. You will wait for another day," he snapped, clicking his finger.

Clutching my stomach, I quickly ran out of the circle towards Luka through the flames of dark forces, gasping for air; I was desperate for water.

"Luka," I said breathlessly. "This cannot be happening. We must stop him now."

"It's OK," said Luka reassuringly. "I have every faith in you. You can do it, Sophia."

His gentle and calming energy brought little comfort to my tangled thoughts.

"But how, Luka?"

"Just breathe; remember, you have the power within your grasp."

Slipping my hands deep into the hidden pocket of my gown, retrieving my watch, I placed the delicate key into the tiny groove. Carefully out of sight from the Lord, I turned the key slowly, but nothing happened. Anxiety grew as the flames drew nearer whilst the Lord danced between two realities.

"Sophia, please try again," said Martha tearfully, clinging to Luka in fear.

Sweating profusely, I turned the key again. Instantly the flames diminished, irrupting the Lord's anger. He flew venomously towards me, his eyes full of hatred; terrified, I cowardly bowed my head.

"Sophia! The path you have taken is one of betrayal. You have denounced your loyalty to the Occult. With that comes a price with your life!" he shouted furiously.

"My Lord, please no!" I pleaded nervously.

"Just give me your key," he demanded forcefully.

"Never!"

"Very well, Sophia. You have chosen your fate; there is no escape!"

Gripping my watch tightly, hearing the faint sound of time ticking slowly, I held my breath, whilst Luka and Martha looked on, powerless to help. Was this the end?

"Sophia, do not be fooled by the Lord," said a voice in the air. I caught a waft of patchouli.

Courageously, finding my voice I spoke my truth.

"How have I deceived you, my Lord?"

"Don't you know? You are the light, and I am the dark."

"But I have done everything you have asked."

"It's not enough, now hand me your key!' he ordered, raising his voice intensely. I trembled fearfully.

"No," I replied defiantly, "unless you tell me where the missing children are."

"What! You think I have to answer to you?" he roared sinisterly. "You leave me no choice." He pushed me to the floor violently. Feeling his breath upon mine, miraculously, I was able to turn the key before the darkness engulfed me.

"Sophia, it's OK; the Lord has gone. He was forcibly pushed back from you," said Martha, holding my hand tightly. "It was your watch that saved us. I saw him leave with Philip and Lucien."

"We must follow them," said Luka. "I have to return with good news for Gabriella."

"I feel it may be too late to save him, Luka. The Lord has control of him now, but we can still try," I replied, seeing the sadness within his eyes. Feeling his sincerity, my heart opened.

We were now alone in the grand hall of marbled flooring; the brotherhood had dispersed, and the fire was out. Charred ashes were all that was left of the circle. I shivered anxiously, recalling the satanic rituals of the Lord of darkness. My path was now entrenched in a web of deceit and deception. I could only move forward by following the Lord's path, leading me back to the House of De Vries, where I may find my salvation.

Chapter 22

Dawn was just breaking as we approached the canal, leaving a thin veil of mist hanging over the murky water. I sighed heavily as Martha clasped my hand tightly. Neither of us wanted to step back into the house of illusions. The imposing black front door was now in front of us; surprisingly, it opened easily, flooding my senses with its toxic fumes. Hesitating, I paused fearfully.

"What is it?" asked Martha.

"I'm not sure," I replied.

Luka stared at me intensely, revealing his sharp brown eyes; momentarily, my anxiety eased.

"It's about time you are here," said Julian appearing at the door.

His arrogance personified him, standing tall and well-groomed in a cavalier manner, not the usual attire I was accustomed to.

"You are needed; come quickly, there is much to do," he said brusquely.

The House of De Vries looked barely recognisable. Gone was the seedy décor. Now hanging from the ceiling were exquisite crystal chandeliers. The furnishings were lavishly dressed in rich deep purple, and golden drapes.

"Don't look so surprised, Sophia. While you have been away, I have made many changes."

"Yes, I can see that, but how?" I asked, scanning the room.

"I acquired a very lucrative deal," he gloated.

"We will talk later, we have guests this evening, and you need to be seen, so dress appropriately. Scarlet and Lucien are both waiting for you in the lobby. Luka, you come with me!" he said assertively.

"We meet again, Sophia," said Lucien smiling confidently.

Dressed immaculately in a black corded jacket and breeches showing his fine physique, Lucien's broody presence of sexuality caught me off guard.

"I wasn't sure you would be here."

"I have business here this evening, and if I play my good hand at cards, I will be the sole owner of the House of De Vries."

Mesmerised by his dashing looks, I was easily distracted by his news. Instead, I focused on his sapphire ring, knowing it would be mine one day! Lucian's gaze was hard to resist; his eyes were as sharp as the liquid sea, pulling me further into his dark web of desire.

"Sophia, this could be your lucky night, as I know you will carry out your task. You will be rewarded with many pleasures of the night and much more," he replied. Teasing me as his fingers gently lingered over my lips, gripping me firmly, his body pressed against mine, Lucien mockingly whispered, "Two can play at that game. Sophia, the clock is ticking. You must do what I say, now go pretty yourself, you are looking very unkept. We are entertaining very distinguished guests, men that require the touch of a virgin. Now hurry along, Sophia."

Dashing to my room in the attic, I was relieved nothing had changed. Shutting the door behind me, in need of some air, I opened the small window overlooking the canal, noticing a woman on the towpath. She was staring intently at me. Who was she? Muddled thoughts flooded my mind as I rubbed my pocket watch for some clarity. Looking again, she had vanished in the hazy glow. Hearing the grand clock in the hall chime eight times, exhausted, I crumbled to my bed and slept fitfully. Waking to a darkened room, night had fallen. I shivered profusely, sensing a sinister energy seeping into my room. Dressing hurriedly, as my stomach churned, a nagging feeling of unease grew within.

"Sophia, Sophia, it's time to be seen," said Julian, knocking on my door.

"Very well, I will be down shortly," I replied warily.

Hearing his footsteps fade, I clutched my pocket watch tightly and opened the door gingerly. The corridor was lit by many candles, reflecting ghostly shadows upon the walls. A faint whimper of a crying baby altered my awareness. I stood still, listening intently.

"Sophia, I was just coming to wake you," said Martha, approaching me in the hall.

Martha looked radiant in a lavish exquisite gown. Around her neck hung a delicate necklace encrusted with sparkling diamonds.

They shimmered brightly in the candlelight.

"Where did you get that gown from? You look beautiful."

"Julian gave it to me. Your gown is in the private lobby. It's a gift from him."

"Oh, is it!" I replied apprehensively.

"Where's Luka?" I enquired, agitated.

"He's been with Julian for most of the day. They are waiting for us. Come, hurry and change, madam."

Entering the intimate lobby, an exquisite gown was neatly laid out for me. The fabric, made of crushed cream velvet, was soft and sensuous to the touch. I smiled warmly. Delicate ivory flowers encrusted in diamonds were embroidered on the snug-fitting bodice. I eagerly dressed with a sense of grandeur, becoming entranced with its beauty. Lying on a small chest was a tiny box containing teardrop diamond earrings and a matching necklace; I gasped as it sparkled joyously at me.

Seeing my reflection, I sniggered to Martha, "Julian has indeed made a profit whilst I have been away."

Hearing a baby's faint cries, my heart sank, remembering the documents that Julian insisted I should see.

"Shh, listen, Martha, do you hear that? It's coming from the other side of the lobby."

"No, madam, there can't be, as it's an outside wall. Hurry, please, Julian is waiting for us," replied Martha assertively.

Entering the main reception room, we were greeted by bellows of smoke-infused powders; the scent was intoxicating as the fumes hung heavy in the air. The shabby interior was replaced with many luxurious velvet chaise longues and chairs. Gold-plated tables with crisp white cloths were elegantly displaying liquor decanters with matching glassware. Fine art adorned the walls, bringing the room alive with rich colours of portraits and landscapes. The windows were perfectly framed with purple velvet and golden drapes. I gasped in awe; it looked palatial and regal.

"I hope you approve, dear sister," said Julian.

"Yes," I replied, smiling approvingly.

The room was now full of men looking for a woman to seduce; their pockets were lined with wealth. The ladies greeted them eagerly by parading in front of them, touting their bodies seductively. A small fire was lit, casting golden rays of light within the room, luring me into the web of dishonour and desire. I winced painfully, seeing the Lord dance menacingly between the flames of life and death. Gasping for air, I took a seat by the window and watched the night unfold. Julian was quick to join me; he sat smugly, counting his coins.

"Hello, madam, we meet again," said Scarlet, walking towards me. Her vivid red hair stood out in the crowd as she walked confidently to us. Scarlet was eager to introduce the new recruits, looking sultry in a tight-waisted vibrant red velvet gown. Rosa slowly walked behind Scarlet; she looked subdued and lost. Guilt returned in a vengeance, seeing the pain in her eyes. I quickly downed a glass of strong liquor to block out the memory of Catalina as the new ladies gathered for our inspection.

"You have done well, Scarlet. They are virgins, I presume?" said Julian.

"Yes, I play my part well, Julian," she smirked gleefully.

"Good to hear; you will be rewarded," he replied, pulling her tightly into his grasp and placing her hand on his aroused penis. Scarlet immediately slapped Julian hard upon his face.

"Oh, I do like a feisty woman; you will wait until later," he replied, discarding her crudely.

"It's time to entertain our guests."

"Very well," replied Scarlet, seething.

As the new recruits took to their roles, Scarlet led the way whilst Rosa followed sheepishly. Depravity consumed the room in a heady mix of eroticism and lewd behaviour. I was eager to see Luka amid the mayhem, but he was nowhere to be seen. The flickering light of the fire caught my attention; this time, seeing a baby screaming in the twisting, spiralling flames, full of remorse and anguish, I shamefully looked away.

"Are you alright, madam?" spoke a tall, silver-haired, impeccably dressed man.

"Yes, of course, I am," I replied sharply, admiring his kindly disposition and eloquent voice.

"We haven't been introduced. I'm Klaus Richter, and I'm here to help you."

"I don't need your help," I replied, agitated.

"But you do, Sophia, the Hooded Man has sent me. Clearly, you have not listened to him. You are treading on dangerous ground. What you do now will affect your future. Do you understand?"

"I think so, but how can I trust you?"

"You have no option, now please come with me now," he insisted, holding his hand out to me, whilst his soft blue eyes eased my anxiety.

"Time is of the essence; now follow me."

"OK, where are we going?" I replied hesitatingly.

"To see your truth. A carriage is waiting for us, do not worry, you will be back in time for the wedding of Princess Gabriella."

"But I'm needed here. What about Martha? Can she come too?"

"No, only you can see your truth. You cannot run away from it anymore," replied Klaus sincerely.

"Martha will be here on your return. Please hurry now. My carriage awaits us."

Nothing seemed real anymore as I walked through the drunken haze of men and women fornicating amongst the realms of dishonour. Feeling safe with Klaus, I was ready to see my truth.

Chapter 23

"Where are we going, Klaus?"

"Good question Sophia. I have no idea," he replied, ruffling his greying hair from his forehead, revealing a distinctive mole which caught my attention.

"The coachman knows our destination. Besides, I have your company for the evening, so let's enjoy the ride!" he said cheekily, patting my bottom.

Smiling warmly, I gladly took my seat next to him in his comfortable carriage. His gentle disposition charmed my inquisitive nature. Admiring his elegant attire, he was dressed in a beige embroidered tailored jacket and breeches made of linen and silk, with ruffled lace cuffs and a matching collar.

"My dear Sophia, your eyes are the window of your soul. You have to decide which path to take," he said softly, peering deep into my eyes, bringing warmth to my heart.

"I need to show you something, Sophia," he said, quickly producing a rolled scroll with an embossed royal seal from his deep pocket.

"Look! your signature is here."

"No way, I haven't signed anything." I was flabbergasted, seeing my name in ink on the accounts of the missing babies. "But how, Klaus?" I replied disconcertingly.

"I'm here to inform you, Scarlet and Lucien, are behind this."

"Oh, it all makes sense now, I was aware of their involvement, but I had no idea I was implicated."

Rage engulfed me; as my anger grew, I became hotter and hotter. Unable to breathe, I screamed, "No, this cannot be right."

"It's OK, Sophia, I know," said Klaus softly, running his fingers through my hair.

"Lead on," he yelled to the coachman.

Our journey had begun as the carriage wheels moved swiftly

in time with the rhythmic sound of the galloping horses. I sighed heavily; fearing my truth, I clung to my pocket watch for comfort.

"Sophia! I need to ask you a question, so please be truthful. Are you sure you are not involved?" His soft blue eyes penetrated my soul, and I lost myself in his kindness.

"I honestly don't know; I'm rather confused. My past is somewhat blurred."

"Yes, Sophia, it is," he replied knowingly. "Now, hold on tight; it will be a bumpy ride."

Our carriage raced speedily, with the silvery moon guiding us over the many cobbled streets and into the valleys beyond. Huddling together to keep warm, a familiar feeling of love swept through my body, opening up old wounds.

"I have met you before, haven't I?" I enquired tentatively, staring at the black mole on his forehead.

"Yes, you have, my dear Sophia, a long time ago," he replied, smiling fondly.

Exchanging a gentle kiss, our eyes connected, rekindling lost love; it stirred a deep passion within me, as I encouraged his hand between my thighs. Reaching the deepest point of my moist vagina with his fingers, I moaned contentedly, enjoying his gentle but firm touch, giving me waves of euphoric pleasure.

"Please don't stop," I purred, holding his hand over my pulsating womanhood, taking me to a place of blissful nirvana of deep sexual gratification.

"You've done this to me before, haven't you?" I whispered seductively.

"Yes, many times, Sophia," he chuckled.

"Now, please rest, Sophia; we have a long journey ahead, trust me."

Feeling safe and protected, I heard the gentle sound of tick-tock reverberating in my pocket. Reaching inside, I clasped it softly, drifting in and out of sleep.

"Sophia, you don't need that anymore," said Klaus, awakening me gently.

"What," I replied, bleary-eyed.

"Your watch."

Instantly I clenched my hand around it. "How do you know about that?"

"The Hooded Man," he replied.

"Oh, really!"

"Yes, Sophia, I am the guardian of time and justice. You may keep the watch for now. Tomorrow you will see your truth."

Clinging to Klaus, I hid my face in shame. "But what if I don't want to see my truth?" I replied hesitantly.

But you must," he insisted. "Stop!" yelled Klaus to the horsemen. Our carriage stopped abruptly, causing me to jolt forward.

"Why here, Klaus?" I peered out of the carriage window. "It's a cemetery!"

"You will see, my dear; the moon's light will guide us."

The night sky was alive with abundant stars; they dazzled brightly as the full moon glowed sinisterly. Seven sisters spoke to me as I stared intently at the constellation, knowing it was my home, feeling the stars within my heart. A passing crow flew over my head, sending a wave of anxiety throughout my body. The graveyard was vast with many tombstones; I clung to Klaus, shivering.

"To the left, please, Sophia, tread carefully, the ground is boggy." Again I asked, "Why here?"

He didn't answer. We walked silently as the moon beamed across the eerie graveyard, highlighting the many shrines. Each building was different in size and lovingly kept.

"I can't go on," I said fearfully.

"Yes, you must, Sophia; you need to see your truth."

Quaking, heavy-hearted, I stood at an unkempt shrine. Its gothic features spookily stood out under the moonlight, whilst a statue of a cross glowed menacingly, depicting a clock face with the hands of time. I froze, not wanting to enter.

"No! No no, Klaus, please don't let me see this," I replied, pulling my hair anxiously with my clammy hands.

Panic-stricken, with the world's weight in my hands, I looked up towards the moon, praying for guidance as my whole body trembled fearfully.

"But what if I don't want to see it?" I said reluctantly.

Intense pressure mounted within as each step took me closer to the gate. Breathing heavily, I gasped nervously as crippling pain from my neck ravaged through my body, crushing me in a wave of despair; clinging to a branch of a nearby tree, I wept silently, knowing this was yet to come.

Klaus spoke softly as he fumbled in his deep pocket, producing a large rusty key.

"Sophia, please unlock the door."

Gingerly, I pushed the old decaying iron gate open with my fingers quivering with the coldness. It squeaked noisily as a passing bat flew overhead; its high pitch shrill altered my senses. With the key in hand, I froze at the brown rotting door of the shrine. A heavy bolt with a padlock was waiting for me; I stood on the steps with long grass around my legs, cold, damp and petrified.

"No, Klaus, I can't go in," I pleaded.

"Yes, you can; there is nothing to fear, just your shadow, trust me."

Dead leaves crunched underneath my feet as I carefully headed towards the iron door. Hesitant, I felt the ground open up before me, as the key turned slowly in the lock. Tentatively I pushed the creaky door open. Immediately, I was confronted by six coffins, three on each side, stacked upon each other. A large wooden cross was nailed high up on the back wall; a bold giant pentagram stood beneath.

"Klaus, why have you brought me here?" I inquired, unhinged.

"Look at the top coffin on the left side."

Brushing the cobwebs away, I shivered uncontrollably, seeing my name etched on the lid. It read, "Here lies the headless body of Madam Sophia De Jung."

Quivering, trying to find my voice, I wailed, "What happened to me?"

"Nothing," replied Klaus.

Darkness came with a thunderous roar, and I became one with the night sky as the velvet stars pulsated throughout me. Seeing myself rise above my body with silvery light emanating from my hands.

"Come back," urged Klaus, holding me tightly. "You have entered another realm."

Heaviness in my numbed feet brought me sharply back into my body.

"Now look at the coffin again, Sophia."

As I touched it apprehensively, I saw my name disappear between my stinging fingers. "What has just happened, Klaus?"

"You saw into your future."

Holding my stiff neck, trying to ease the pain, I stared with intrigue at Klaus as erratic sensations riffled throughout my body. Cold, then hot flushes of subtle energy warmed my soul, bringing clarity to my scattered thoughts.

"Klaus, can I change my future?"

"Yes, but I cannot guarantee it."

Placing his hand on my heart, I immediately became calmer as the light of the moon shone brightly upon us against the backdrop of millions of stars, dancing in the night sky.

"Sophia, it's time to go."

"Go where?" I asked tentatively.

"To where it all began, but first, it's time to hand me your pocket watch."

"But why?" I replied curiously.

"Sophia, the past always catches up with us; now pace yourself, we must unravel your timeline. The watch has magical powers, but you have all you need inside your heart from this moment onwards. I will keep it safe and return it to you sometime in the future."

The complexity of emotions arose from nowhere; reluctantly, I gave the watch and key to Klaus.

"Sophia, it's for your own good; please believe me."

Nodding begrudgingly, I walked silently by his side as we weaved our way through the cemetery towards the warmth of our carriage. "Lead on," yelled Klaus to the horseman.

Overwhelmed and holding back the tears, I whispered to Klaus, "Do we have to go on?"

"Yes, Sophia, there is more to see. Are you ready?" said Klaus.

"No," I replied warily as the carriage sped away in the dead of night.

"There's no time like the present," he replied, glancing at the small pocket watch. "Tick-tock," he chuckled.

Chapter 24

Night became dawn as the sky turned cerise pink. I was becoming increasingly alarmed, knowing instinctively where I was. The morning sun rose over the valley, bringing rays of light that glistened upon the meadow, invoking childhood memories of a distant past.

"We've arrived," said Klaus. "Look!"

My heart pumped ferociously and feeling sick, I dared not look.

"Do not fear, my dear Sophia, this is a past you need to see. Now open your eyes."

In front of us stood a grand cathedral of gothic designs. The tall building towered over us; its intricate carvings stood out against the facade of the building. Searing pain in my eyes brought many tears as I witnessed my younger self.

Morning prayer had just begun, seeing myself amongst the chorus of many nuns gathering in the vestry.

"Remember, Sophia, this is your past."

"I looked so young, full of life and eager to learn. Where's my mother, Klaus?"

"Don't you remember? Reluctantly, she had no choice but to send you away to this convent run by the order of the Occult. The nuns cared for you until you were enticed by the lure of money, selling your soul as a lady of desire. At night you became a creature of the darkness within your soul. By day, you became the light which healed your heart."

"Please, Klaus, no more," I pleaded. "It's too painful."

"Sophia, our past is why we are here. Don't you remember that?"

"No," I replied quietly, feeling bewildered, running my hands anxiously through my matted hair as my agitation grew.

"But you do remember me! I came to you in your dreams of lightness. I held your hand through the darkness and taught you how to be a lady. I am just as guilty as you are, Sophia; it's time we readdressed the balance. Remember Sophia. I am the keeper of time, tick-tock," he laughed, grinning profusely, revealing his gleaming white teeth, which complemented his distinguished features.

"Show me our past, please, Klaus," I pleaded, holding his hand for comfort.

"Very well, I will take you there. Close your eyes, take three long deep breaths, then open them quickly."

A delicate hazy purple light funnelled around us, consuming us in a safe haven, transporting us back in time. Breathing in the vapour, I could sense and smell the memories we shared. Mesmerised, I held my hand out to Klaus. "I'm ready," I replied softly.

"Now focus your attention within the aura of the light; see how it changes and grows minute by minute," urged Klaus.

Weirdly, I was instantly transported back into his carriage.

"How did that happen?" I inquired, flummoxed.

"Remember, I am the keeper of time; look at us now!" he replied, smiling broadly.

Sunlight poured through the carriage's windows, basking us with golden solar rays. Klaus shimmered as I touched his face; his youthful energy intoxicated my young body. Images flashed before my eyes of our past. Smiling contently, I whispered, "You taught me well, Klaus."

"So you do remember, Sophia, all those nights we spent together."

"Yes, vaguely, but you just vanished. Where did you go?"

"I didn't go anywhere, Sophia. Let me show you," he replied warmly. "Ride on," he commanded the horseman.

"Sophia, our flame has been lit many lifetimes; now we are together again," he said softly, kissing my neck.

"Klaus," I whispered gently, revealing my love for him.

"I know Sophia, I've always known. We have a long ride ahead of us, tick-tock," he smirked.

As the light diminished, holding hands, the veil of time closed, bringing us back to the present moment. I turned to Klaus. "Please help me find my mother."

"All in good time, Sophia; our journey together will be fruitful for both of us. The seed has been sown. Only you can decide what happens next," he said, teasing me with his tongue and seducing me to submission.

Sensuous sensations filled my desire as our bodies again entwined breathlessly; we rocked back and forth in tune with the galloping horses.

"You haven't lost your touch, Sophia," he chuckled seductively.

"No, most definitely not Klaus," I replied coyly. "Where are you taking me now?"

"Just enjoy the ride, Sophia! Look at the sun, and see how it dances between light and dark, so we must do the same. Our lives are like intricate pieces of a clock. Each mechanism turns the wheel; which way it turns is up to us," he chortled.

Liberated, I was running wild with the horses, forgetting my oath. I remembered the night Klaus entered my dreams as a familiar scent caught my attention, hearing a voice clearly in my mind.

"Remember why you are here, Sophia!"

"Klaus, did you hear that?" I asked anxiously as my past caught up with me.

"No, my dear, it's just your imagination. Come, rest your head, my dear, on my lap," he replied with warmth and sincerity.

"You know I will do anything to oblige our fantasies," I whispered.

Our journey of self-discovery was very pleasing, but alas, our time together was nearly over. Darkness flowed like a chasm of iron; trying to forge my way through it, Klaus shouted to me, "Light is always with you; it's everywhere. One more destination Sophia, before I return you safely back to Martha. Now that we have reconnected, you need to know the bigger plan. Let me show you what is going on. Place your hand over the watch Sophia, close your eyes and connect with Lucien, be an observer and reveal what you are seeing."

"Lucien is with Scarlet," I said shockingly.

"Go on, Sophia, please keep going. I'm watching with you."

As the clock ticked rhythmically, we witnessed words that danced before my eyes, conquering vivid scenes of Lucien's demise within my mind.

Dark satanic vibes filled the air like a vacuum of desire, greed and lust. Lucien was a victim of his success, caught in the grip of the Occult. He stood looking out of the window, daring not to see his truth. His blank expression told many stories that were hidden deep within his soul. Nightfall crept up on him, and he knew he had nowhere to hide. He paused, flicking his black hair between his ears.

"Lucien, where are you? I'm waiting for you," shouted Scarlet.

She walked towards him. Her pursed red lips were full of passion and desire.

"Scarlet, there is much that I cannot share with you," replied Lucien.

"And there is much you don't know about me," replied Scarlet sharply.

Her flaming red hair flowed around her ample bosom as she strutted towards Lucien.

"Lucien, I know you are a fraud," she said arrogantly.

Lucien dropped his head in shame, grinning, then laughing hysterically.

"Well, two can play at that game," he replied menacingly.

Quickly grabbing Scarlet's neck without hesitation, he pushed her towards the window.

"You like to play dirty then," said Scarlet, reaching inside his trousers and groping Lucien's penis with her hands. "Let me go; you know we are good for each other," she squirmed.

"Yes," he replied, pulling her closer as their lips touched briefly before swiftly pushing Scarlet to her death through the open window.

I gasped, horrified. "No, Klaus, we have to stop this from happening."

"It may be too late, Sophia. Only time will tell. Lucien's fate is now in your hands!"

Chapter 25

"Please, Klaus, take me there," I pleaded.

"Very well, Sophia, but you may not like what you see."

"I know, but I have to take that risk," I replied, sighing heavily.

The change in direction was quick as we sped through the dense wood. The glare of the midday sun was upon us as it beamed through the carriage. Feeling safe in his arms, Klaus smiled warmly at me as we watched the countryside race by until we stopped at our destination.

"We have arrived," said Klaus.

Eagerly I clambered down from the carriage.

"You have to do this on your own, Sophia. I will be back, I promise," said Klaus.

"But where am I?" I replied anxiously.

"You will know," he called out. "You have twenty-four hours Sophia."

"But I don't!" I yelled as his carriage swiftly departed.

I stood still and alone in a small village, not wanting to move. The sound of silence intensified the moment. Squinting, I glared at the sun; there was no cloud in sight, just a shimmering haze that blurred my vision.

Startled, hearing a familiar cough, I turned swiftly around, becoming face to face with the Lord.

"Well, Sophia, what did you expect?"

"I don't know," I mumbled, staring at his steely eyes as he stood towering over me in his black gown and robe, looking fierce.

"Speak up," he commanded.

"Why am I here?"

"Because you asked."

Thrown by his remark, I swayed back and forth as the blazing sun warmed my back.

"Sophia! Remember your oath," he shouted.

Gasping for air, falling upon the gravel path, I hit my head hard and entered oblivion.

Shades of dark and light flashed before my eyes; momentarily, I stared the darkness straight in the eye, dissipating the fear.

"I'm not afraid of you anymore," I screamed.

"Good, you have passed the test Sophia," replied the Lord.

Rubbing my eyes in disbelief, I lay still, mesmerised by the sharpness of the blue sky. A passing swift flew past me. Sitting upright, expecting to see the Lord, he was nowhere to be seen. I stood, eager to find some shade from the searing heat. Steadying myself, I walked down the cobbled streets with tiny premises lining my view, giving the illusion of endlessness.

Hearing voices, I quickly ran for cover, hiding behind a nearby tree and witnessing Lucien and Scarlet in deep conversation.

Intrigued, I watched them from afar. A slight breeze ruffled my hair, bringing relief from the fiery sun. Sniffing the air, a familiar scent of patchouli alerted my senses.

"Sophia, follow them," I heard in the wind.

Watching them enter the nearby tavern apprehensively, I peered through the small murky window. It was empty inside, with a door swaying to and fro at the back. Silently, I followed their path, wondering why no one else was around. A gentle tap on my shoulder unnerved me.

"It's OK, Sophia," spoke the voice. "Remember, nothing is what it seems; life is like a game of chess. You have to play the right move."

Bewildered, becoming increasingly hot, I made my way to the bar, and guzzled a large tankard of ale to quench my thirst.

"Take your time; there is no need to rush, Sophia," said the voice in the wind.

My mind drifted to my first encounter with Lucien. I was gullible and weak, but his touch pleased me in every way. I quickly jumped behind the bar as they entered the room. Scarlet's flowing red hair now looked unkempt. Her face was wild with anger as she stormed out, her gown tattered and torn. Lucien casually brushed his hair with his right hand; smirking, he laughed.

"When will they ever learn?"

"Sophia, I know you're there," said Lucien.

Containing my fear, I stood my ground, ignoring his words.

Approaching the bar, he tapped his fingers impatiently just above my head.

"I'm always one step ahead of you; you can't hide forever."

Catching sight of his reflection, he brushed himself down, fixed his trousers and, with poise, strutted out of the inn. Grabbing Scarlet by her arm, he spoke authoritatively.

"We have business to deal with now; you were not enough for me! Find me a virgin and meet me in the old warehouse. I will be waiting for you, Scarlet, and I need that list you promised. The Lord is running out of patience, and I am too!"

Pushing her to the ground like a rag doll, he left her wilting under the sun's glare. Running to her aid, I was stopped abruptly as the tavern door swung tightly shut in front of me. Through the murky windows, I was relieved to see Scarlet walking away. Pushing the door open finally, I was determined to find the warehouse.

Heat haze bubbled from the ground, exposing me to the toxic energy that clung to every dwelling. Then stillness came, pausing by a tree, unsure which path to take. Clasping my heart, I instantly knew which direction to take.

Scarlet stood at the entrance, looking vague and forlorn. A young woman appeared from the dwelling crying hysterically, propelling me to come out of hiding.

"Rosa, is that you?"

"Yes, madam," she said, sobbing uncontrollably.

"Sophia, I am so pleased to see you," said Scarlet.

"Can I trust you?" I replied, hesitating.

"Madam, my name is what I am, mistress," said Scarlet tossing her red hair over her shoulders.

"I will deal with you later; let me attend to Rosa."

Rosa stepped forward, her face hardly recognisable through her tears of torment. Her scrawny figure was a shadow of her former self. Her long blonde hair was her pride; now it looked unkempt and matted as she nervously played with it.

"Whatever has happened to you?"

"I'm forbidden to say," she said, whimpering.

"Was it Lucien? Rosa?"

"No, madam," she insisted, avoiding eye contact.

"We are still waiting for him to arrive," said Scarlet, biting her bottom lip.

"You know who it is, Scarlet, don't you?"

"I may do, but it will cost you," she replied brashly.

"Enough! This has to stop now!" I demanded.

"Who is it?" I shouted as my annoyance grew.

"It's you!" she gloated.

"What? How absurd."

Flummoxed, my mind became foggy as sweat trickled down the nape of my neck from the searing heat. Through the sun's hazy glare, Lucien swaggered towards me from behind the warehouse, his fists raised in anger.

"Yes, Sophia, you betrayed us all; you let me take the blame for Catalina's death. If it weren't for Scarlet, I would be dead now!"

"But I didn't kill her," I protested.

"Are you sure?"

"Yes," I insisted.

"The truth hurts, doesn't it, Sophia?" smirked Lucien.

"But I don't remember anything of that night; all I recall was the intoxicating fumes that swept through me. Remember Lucien? And why would I kill Catalina?"

Bursts of energy pulsated through my body as strong images of that fateful night flashed before me, seeing my blood-stained hands. I shook my head in disgust.

"No! It wasn't me," I protested. "It was Julian, that vile brother of mine; he made me do it with him. I had no choice but to frame you, Lucien."

"Rosa, I'm so sorry. You do believe me."

She looked intensely at me through her tears; bedraggled, she fell to the ground, mumbling.

"I don't know whom to believe anymore," whimpered Rosa.

"But I'm telling the truth!" I yelled defiantly.

Truth, lies and deception, I was now a pawn in Lucien's games. Where do I go from here? Maybe I am guilty. In a sea of torment, my body grieved whilst Lucien and Scarlet relished the moment.

Chapter 26

Not wanting to hear the truth, tormented tears streamed down my face as the realisation hit me hard. Engulfed with the guilt, I turned and ran.

"So you think you can outrun us?" shouted Lucien.

"Stop!" he commanded.

"Never," I cried out in vain.

"You can't get very far; look around you, Sophia."

A slight breeze ruffled my matted hair, taking in my surroundings as the moving wallpaper of the skyline changed dramatically. A dusky glow descended around me, covering the sun as it disappeared behind a dark cloud. A cold shiver swept through me as the temperature suddenly dropped.

"Sophia!" called out Lucien.

His voice changed with softness, stopping me in my tracks. Lucien was now behind me, catching my arm; his radiant eyes stared deep into my soul.

Flustered, I whispered, "What do you want with me, Lucien?"

"We can help each other, I have a plan, and you are a key part of this," replied Lucien.

"Why me?" I asked, wiping my tears away.

"Because your brother has deceived us both."

Pausing briefly, my mind raced with frightening thoughts of Julian, knowing I could not trust either of them. Lucien's charming hypnotic manner enticed me back into his web of sexual power and deception.

"OK," I stuttered. "What will I get in return?"

"My ring, the one you most desire, will be yours if you accept my proposal and become Madam De Vries."

His golden ring with an alluring sapphire radiated riches of wealth. Deep, intense velvet blue, it mesmerised me. Caught in the moment, I knew this would never work, but the ring was so exquisite;

how fine it would look on my wedding finger.

Smirking, I replied, "Are you asking for my hand in marriage?"

"Yes, Sophia." His voice deepened, causing my heart to flutter. Feeling flushed as a surge of warmth entangled my whole being and quivering with excitement, I somehow spoke calmly.

"How can I trust you?"

"You can't," he replied, laughing, making big gestures with his hands.

"Together, we can bring down your brother and claim back the House of De Vries."

My stomach churned and tightened. Julian's face was etched in my mind. Filled with hatred, I was desperate to have my revenge on him.

Hesitant, I replied, "Yes."

"You just can't resist me, can you?" said Lucien, preening himself.

"No, it seems not."

Our lips met hungrily as we feasted upon each other.

Scarlet and Rosa were watching nearby. Scarlet's flaming hair was tossed around her angry face as her eyes bulged with jealousy.

"Lucien will break every rule, Sophia," she cackled with malice.

"Yes, but I am willing to take that risk."

"Well, you must prepare yourself, as there are three of us in this marriage. I am Lucien's mistress," raged Scarlet.

"Very well, I will do whatever it takes to bring my brother down," I replied calmly, knowing Scarlet was dispensable.

The air pressure felt heavy and thick as the energy grew between us; electric storms flashed vividly before our eyes. Rain was on its way. Feeling cooler, I was eager for Lucien's touch, but his gaze was now towards Scarlet. His face glowed radiantly, knowing he would bed us both.

"Three lovely ladies, I'm going to enjoy myself tonight," said Lucien smirking whilst placing his hands on his pelvis.

"That's what you think, Lucien, but Rosa is not part of the deal," I said firmly.

"Yes, she is; she has already agreed."

"Rosa, is that true?"

"Yes, madam," she said sheepishly, grasping her gown tightly.

A torrent of rage erupted within me. "No! I won't let this happen," I shouted angrily, grabbing his testes hard.

"You bitch!" he squirmed. "So you like to play dirty, just like me; well, now you've got my attention. Come with me to our world of sexual fantasy," replied Lucien lustfully.

Lost in lewd thoughts, I was easy prey.

"Scarlet and Rosa, meet us back in the warehouse; I have unfinished business with Lucien."

"We will be waiting for our master and mistress," replied Scarlet.

Her anger was now defused as they walked hand in hand towards the warehouse.

Alone, I finally whispered, "We don't have much time."

"Oh yes, we do. Time is irrelevant," he replied nonchalantly.

He pushed me to the ground in a frenzy under a canopy of birch trees whilst the storm erupted around us. Oblivious to it all, Lucien ripped my gown and pulled my legs wide apart. His fingers quickly parted the way, opening me like a flower, moist with dew; his intoxicating power consumed all of me.

"Sophia, you will always remember me," he said.

"Yes," I moaned with pleasure, riding the waves of sexual desire.

Like a tigress, we mated until nightfall. Exhausted, I stared at the blank canvas, seeing nothing but the darkness in the sky. I turned towards Lucien.

"Your ring please," I demanded.

"No, not yet; we will wed after Princess Gabriella's marriage to Prince Lavin, and then you can have my ring. This has to stay our secret."

"But Scarlet and Rosa know."

"Yes, but they are in this together with us. Come, Sophia, it's getting late; we must return to the warehouse now. There's a coldness in the air."

Damp grass muddled my view. Lucien's face became distorted as a sharp pain stabbed my heart.

"What am I doing?" I yelled, clutching my chest.

"You are mine, Sophia," he declared.

Startled by his disguise, as the light projected ghostly images, he added, "Sophia, there is nothing to fear."

My confusion rose to the surface as Lucien's eyes penetrated my soul. Hearing the rhythmic sound of tick-tock within my mind, I became aware of a faint voice in the wind calling my name.

"Sophia, you are seeing what you wish to see," said a voice in the wind. "Remember why you are here."

"Yes," I mumbled under my breath, "to seek the truth."

Lucien's gaze was still upon me; his eyes glowed like pools of liquid crystalline ice. I was entranced. The sound of my heart sharpened my awareness; remembering his deception, I spoke firmly, looking deep into his soul.

"Lucien, you are lying. I know who you are."

"Really," replied Lucien sarcastically. "I have no time for this now; my needs must be met," he shouted. Grabbing me firmly, Lucien marched me into the cold and bleak warehouse.

"Sit," he demanded as he pushed me towards a darkened corner, where Scarlet and Rosa waited patiently for our return. They had lit a small fire; the warmth felt comforting on a chilly evening.

"Sophia, I'm ready for anything," said Scarlet pursing her lips. Her long legs were wide open as she fondled herself, then licked her fingers as her eyes were on her catch. Her red mane of hair cascaded seductively around her neck.

Rosa stood silently, naked, watching every move. Her tender lips quivered as Lucien walked towards her. He was soon upon her, thrusting himself deeply; she lay motionless, eager to please the man she adored. Intently, Scarlet strutted towards me, removing her clothes; she stood before me. I was in too deep to care, trying hard not to be aroused by her sexuality, but her touch I couldn't resist. Succumbed, I admitted defeat as she persisted with her sexual games. One by one, Lucien took us all whilst we watched, indulging and purging our desires for a woman's touch. Crackling fire rose as the heat between us grew wild and frantic. Bound by the oath, we were trapped in the lair of Lucien. The scent of opium overcame me as the evening came to a close; darkness came quickly.

Through bleary eyes, I faintly saw Klaus. His distinguished stature was more prominent as he stood towering over me; his gentle energy warmed my soul.

"Sophia, Sophia, wake up!" he whispered.

"Well, Sophia, I hope you have learnt your truth," he said kindly. "I gave you twenty-four hours. Now it's time to depart."

"Yes, Klaus, I am ready to return; please take me with you now."

"Very well, now hurry before they awake."

Chapter 27

The persistent sound of a ticking clock increased my awareness. Intrigued by the constant noise, I enquired, "What is it, Klaus," looking up at the celestial sky.

"My dear, that is the sound of the universe."

Perplexed, I scratched my forehead. "What? But where is it coming from?"

"You will find out soon; come now, my carriage awaits you."

Looking up at the night sky, it was filled with many stars that seemed to dance as they shone brightly. I breathed a sigh of relief.

"It's good to see you again, Klaus."

"The pleasure is all mine," he replied with warmth and sincerity.

Feeling safe in his warm embrace, I held his hand tightly, not wanting to let go.

"Where are you taking me now?"

"Back to the House of De Vries, my dear Sophia. I must leave you there; your journey continues alone for now."

Deflated, my heart sank, with a heavy feeling clouding my judgement.

"But Klaus, I need you! Will I see you again?" I enquired nervously.

"Yes, of course, my dear," he replied softly.

His kindness melted my heart, and his wispy grey hair caught the light from the stars, radiating him in a golden glow of magnificence. He didn't seem real, just a figure of a man whose company I enjoyed. His calming voice soothed the darkness of my soul, whilst his carriage was lavishly furnished with gold and soft red cushions that were warm and comforting to the touch.

"Klaus," I said, turning towards him. "We have met several times before, haven't we?"

"Yes, of course," he said hastily. "You may hold the pocket watch one last time until we reach your destination."

Clasping the watch, I held it firmly with both hands. Holding it over my heart, I closed my eyes as the sound vibrated through me and into the cosmos. Strange visions of a world that was alien overwhelmed me. Tall buildings engulfed the skyline, and many people entered them wearing peculiar clothing. Then I saw a woman similar to me jumping from one reality to another. My whole being became one with this vision.

"Sophia," spoke Klaus as he gently stroked my hair from my eyes. "Did you see yourself?"

"Really!" I was repelling the thought. "Was that me?"

"Yes, Sophia, but you will forget this until it's time to remember again."

Between the veils of time, I slipped in and out of consciousness. With Klaus by my side, I felt content and at peace.

Morning light parted the dark sky as the dawn chorus aroused me from my visions of the night. Turning the corner towards the canal, there stood the house. I shivered as my stomach tightened.

"No! Klaus, do I have to take the next step alone?" I whimpered.

"Yes, Sophia, it's time to say goodbye. Now hand me the watch, please."

Reluctantly I let it go. Our eyes locked instantly, knowing our separation wouldn't be forever.

The House of De Vries stood out amongst the facade, glowing crudely; I knew there was more to come. Hesitantly, I knocked on the imposing door as I watched Klaus swiftly depart in his carriage.

"Good morning, madam," said Martha. Her warm smile eased my tension as she ushered me in through the door and into the grisly shadows of the house.

"So glad you are back, madam. Julian is asking for you," said Martha.

I inwardly squirmed.

"How long have I been away?"

"Just the night, madam, the party is over. Thankfully, Julian has only just stirred."

Confused thoughts raced in my mind about my time with Klaus.

"I feel like I have been away for ages," I replied, bemused.

Martha looked puzzled. "Are you OK? Please hurry, madam and

prepare yourself. Julian will be waiting for you; he has a surprise for you."

Frozen rigid to the spot, I asked nervously, "What?"

"Sophia, there is nothing to fear," she replied confidently.

"Very well, Martha, if you say so."

Walking into the house this time, I felt restored and in charge for once. The remnants of the night before were evident, men and women in a drunken stupor sprawled naked upon the rugs that covered the stone slab floor. Poker cards spread randomly on the sparse oak tables. Discarded bottles of wine decanted into goblets were left unattended.

Sniffing at one, choking as the fumes hit me, I realised it was laced with opium. Hurriedly, I made my way to the attic room, changing my gown, before entering the study to meet Julian with an air of anticipation.

He stood pensively by the grated fireplace, which spat out sharp rays of golden light. His tall thin figure looked rigid. His long, grubby fingers appeared emaciated, and his face tired, etched with lines upon his forehead; he frowned at me. Resentment rose within; as my anger grew, my desire for revenge mounted.

Suppressing it, I composed myself. "Julian, what is it you want with me now?"

"Nothing," he replied briskly, rubbing his hands towards the fire.

"I thought you were asking for me, Martha told me."

"Oh, did she now?" He looked straight through me.

A chill in the air and the warmth of the hearth beckoned me towards him. Standing tall, I swallowed my pride and reached out to Julian, holding his hand firmly.

"Julian, my dear brother, we must work together; Lucien seeks to bring you down."

His body straightened as he sniffed hard. Grunting, he replied crudely, "I don't need your help, only for sex!" His hand then gravitated towards his penis.

Wincing, I stepped backwards, avoiding his glare.

"You will wait for another day. I am aware of Lucien's plans. I am always one step ahead, Sophia! Don't ever cross me, as you will feel the full harsh hand of myself and the Lord if you do."

Rage engulfed me like a volcano that I could not suppress

anymore. Grabbing Julian around the neck and throttling him, I squeezed the air out as his eyes soon glazed over, but his strength outwitted me.

"Sophia," he said, choking and spitting vengeance at me. "That is a very silly move to make." Pushing me to the floor like a rag doll, mortified, I knew I would have to pay the price.

"Now, I will have you, Sophia," he raged angrily.

My body shook in terror as I awaited my fate. Fixating on the ceiling, blanking my mind, taking solace as I sniffed the air, catching a fragrant waft of patchouli, I submitted to Julian.

His dirty hands were soon under my gown, pushing my legs wide apart; he crudely forced his way inside my vagina. I lay there rigid until he had done his deed.

"Now stand up," he demanded. "Sister, we have a visitor. Luka is here."

The grand clock in the hallway chimed loudly; its presence was deafening, bringing me back to the moment. I screamed at Julian, "You can do what you like. One day I will have my revenge on you."

The study grew colder as a blast of chilly air flew in from an open window. Resting on a chair, processing what had just happened and studying my hands, I exhaled, knowing soon I would be rid of Julian.

"Sophia, this a game; I will be waiting for your next move," he laughed benevolently at me as he marched out of the study.

Alone in my thoughts, the room was empty, with no desk, cabinets, or books. What had Julian done? I grew increasingly aware of a crying baby. Jumping to my feet, my heart filled with guilt as I shamefully remembered Catalina's baby. Surely not? Inquisitively, I followed the sound from room to room, but nothing. Exhausted, I retreated to the attic room. Delirium fuelled my thoughts; nothing seemed to make any sense anymore, just the sound of the grand clock ticking, giving me hope that this nightmare would soon be over. To my surprise, my door was wide open, and Luka was waiting for me, sitting on my bed.

"Good morning, madam," he said, bemused by my attire. My gown revealed my overflowing breasts, making Luka smile warmly. His olive skin shone brightly as the light streamed through the small porthole attic window.

"Where did you go?" I inquired.

"On a lead, madam. I feel there is a baby here, where I do not know, but we must find it before the Lord does. I feel it's Catalina's baby."

My face paled. Sickened with remorse, I hid behind my hands.

Quietly I spoke. "Yes, I have also heard a faint cry, but like you, I don't know where to look."

"The Lord has already corrupted Philip; it's too late to save him. We mustn't let him do this again."

His voice, rich with deep velvet undertones, vibrated throughout my being.

"Yes," I replied, "we must find the baby."

"Come lay with me for a while." He patted my bed comfortably.

Enticed by his intense masculine energy, I eagerly responded to his friendly charm and wit. His strong arms engulfed me, comforting me in my hour of need.

He whispered calmly. "Soon, Sophia, Julian's ending is nigh."

Sighing heavily, no words were needed. Luka's gentle energy warmed my body, bringing me lightness and much-needed love as he held me still wrapped in his arms. I was captivated. Would he help me? I prayed he would, but for now, he was my only salvation.

Chapter 28

A fine hazy mist swept through the attic window, engulfing us in a shroud of light. Glancing towards it, I noticed a dark, sinister shadow growing more significant and prominent in the corner of the room. Feeling overwhelmed, realising how fragile life is and gripping Luka's arm for support, I enquired nervously, "Luka, can you see that eerie shadow?"

"Sophia, there is nothing there."

"But there is!" I shouted. "If you don't believe me, I will prove it."

Pulling myself away from Luka, I was eager to investigate. The nearer I got to the shadow, the intensity grew within me. Light and darkness swirled around me like a cocoon pulling me into obscurity; the more I tried to fight it, the bigger it got. I was exposed to an endless sea of helplessness.

"Sophia, come closer," said a voice in the mist.

"Who's there?" I mumbled anxiously.

"Luka, please help me," I asked fearfully, finding my voice.

Standing in the murkiness, I placed my hand upon my heart and crumbled to the floor. It was cold; the hardness and density of the floorboards creaked and groaned as I waited for the light to return.

"Sophia, it's OK. I'm here by your side," replied Luka.

Relieved, I held onto his hand. "Now do you believe me?"

"Yes, I do, listen," said Luka.

The sound of a baby crying propelled us deeper into the shady depths of the underworld that lurked in the room's dimness. We walked together hand in hand, unaware of what we might find. Through the veil of time, we found ourselves in a bleak corridor. Light from a small crack in the wall encouraged us towards a door that became visible, transporting us into a world of ambiguity. Hearing the crying louder heightened our anxiety.

"Look!" I whispered, peering through the door, recognising what I was seeing.

"What is it, Sophia?"

My body stiffened as disbelief mounted within.

"How can this be happening?"

"I can't help you until you tell me, Sophia," replied Luka.

"I don't know, but something is not right. We are standing behind the grand portrait in the hallway; I remember those eyes; they seem to follow my every move as if it was me!"

I was flummoxed and dumbfounded, seeing myself in those eyes.

"What the hell is going on, Luka?"

He looked bemused, smiling warmly at me whilst shaking his head.

"Oh, Sophia, it's your mind playing tricks again."

"No!" I replied harshly. "I wish everyone would believe me."

"But I do, Sophia."

"But you just said it's all in my mind."

"Yes, I did; maybe this is all an illusion, Sophia."

Distracted and thrown off balance by his cutting remark, I wavered, holding myself up by the wall. I was in a turmoil, torn between what was real and what wasn't.

Baffled, I said softly, "But you are here right by me, and the sound of that baby is real."

"Yes," he replied, "now follow me quickly."

My chest pounded against my skin, feeling overcome with emotions, sensing the eyes of the Lord feasting upon me.

"I can't, it's a trap," I replied fearfully.

"It's OK, Sophia, the Lord has lured my Philip to the darkness, but we can save Catalina's baby."

"Can we?" I said pitifully. "But all I can see is the Lord. He is everywhere." I cupped my ears as the Lord's voice bellowed, "I am here, Sophia."

"No," I yelled angrily.

"Sophia, it's me, Luka."

Touching his face, I ran my hands up and down his chiselled chin, stroking his stubble. I was relieved but somewhat confused.

"We must get out of here, Luka."

"We have to find the baby first," he replied, looking for an escape route.

Reluctantly I nodded.

"Now hurry, Sophia, come back from your thoughts and stay focused; we owe this to Catalina."

"Yes," I replied, bowing my head in shame.

Silently we walked together, holding my breath for fear of being caught by the Lord. Carefully guiding our way through the darkness and into the light, neither of us knew where this would lead us.

"Listen," said Luka, "can you hear the crying?"

"Yes, we are getting closer," I replied eagerly.

Placing my ears upon the corridor wall, which now seemed much more expansive, I heard a woman's voice singing a lullaby. Tears started to swell in my eyes, remembering my mother's voice; my heart ached for her love and her tenderness.

"How do we get inside, Luka?" I tentatively asked, wiping the tears from my face.

"I'm not sure, but there has to be a way in."

"Look! There's a light ahead," I replied quickly.

I stood still, listening intently, sniffing the air, catching a familiar scent wafting past me. I breathed deeply.

"Listen, Sophia, to the sounds and sights you see, for they reveal your deepest fears as you unlock your past; many secrets will be found. Listen, Sophia, push the wall," said the voice that breezed through the air on a vapour of perfume.

"There is a way in Luka, look." I pushed my hands on the cold wall, sending cold shivers up my arms. "Look! It's sliding across."

Prying it open as much as possible, we squeezed through the gap, finding ourselves in a nursery. The room was sterile and cold; a small fire was lit, giving off fumes from the smoke. I stood back in angst, seeing many cribs. Trying not to cough, I turned to Luka, my face etched with sadness.

"How did we not know of this nursery?" Mystified and angry, I voiced my concern. "Where are the babies?" I said alarmingly.

All the cribs were empty, but one was still warm to the touch. Noticing a piece of cloth, I became cold, as I knew this was from Catalina's gown. Holding it close to my heart as old feelings resurfaced to the fore, I knew I had to make amends.

"Luka, we must find her baby!" Holding back my tears, urgency mounted as I feared for the infant.

Scanning the room, I noticed another door in the far corner of the nursery; pulling me closer to investigate, I called out to Luka.

"This house has many dark secrets; I am starting to unravel them only now."

"Yes, I know, and I'm sure there are more to come," replied Luka as he gazed towards the door in trepidation.

Gingerly, turning the small brass doorknob, I felt a pulse of energy run up my arm, tingling. I started to sweat with anticipation.

"It's OK, Sophia. I'm right behind you."

The door led us into another passageway; with barely any light, we forged on blindly, but something was holding me back and I came to a halt.

"Stop, Luka," my voice wavering as I spoke, "we cannot go any further."

"Why not?" he replied sternly.

"Because I need to tell you something. It was me; I killed Catalina with my own bare hands." I stared angrily at them.

Luka shook his head in disbelief; his face turned red as his annoyance grew within him. His hazel eyes bored into my soul; I looked the other way, not wanting to hear his words.

"Sophia, we have all done bad things; I do not believe it was all down to you. Julian was behind it."

"Yes, I feel that too," I muttered, sighing with relief.

"You can't help Catalina now, but you can save her baby from the grips of the Lord. Time is running out, so we need to keep going."

"Yes," I replied, exhausted, trying to find the strength to carry on, knowing there was more to discover.

"Where is this leading us?" I feared the worse. A faint light ahead gave us hope of reaching the end. My tired feet ached with soreness; heavy-footed, I marched on solemnly. At last, we came to a grated barred exit. I froze, seeing the Lord staring at me through the iron gate.

"Sophia, how naive of you to think you can outwit me; I have the power. You, my dear Sophia, are my property, and I will tell you what you can and cannot do," said the Lord forcefully.

"Luka, do something!" I shouted, pulling my hair in desperation.

He didn't respond; I was trapped, once again, under the evil eye of the Lord. Anger and resentment rose within me.

I glared back at him, eyeing the hard phallus covering his genitals.

"My dear Lord, I am here to serve you, and I will gladly let you taste my nectar. In return, please open the gate so I can attend to your mistress, Princess Gabriella. If I do not attend her wedding, you may never know the true meaning of her fate."

"Sophia, only you can pass this gate. You know that, don't you, Sophia?"

"Yes," I replied reluctantly.

"Luka, you have to go back."

"But," he said, stuttering, "I can't; I am your future; you have to let us both through my Lord." He bowed to his knees.

"And what will I get in return?" he snarled menacingly at Luka.

"Freedom to be your true self, without your mask, your Majesty."

"Your Majesty!" I replied shockingly.

The Lord's dark fiery eyes glowed intently; we were at his mercy. My fate hung on the whims of the Lord. I knew I had to pay the ultimate price for Catalina's baby.

The deafening sound of darkness erupted around us. Still, I was not afraid, remembering my mother's last words before she gave me away as a child. "You are the light; always remember that, Sophia."

The Lord's voice deepened as he spoke. "I have decided; you can both enter but on my terms. Sophia, you need to satisfy my burning desire whilst Luka takes me from behind. It's time for men to be men and women are just mere sex objects. The gate is now open; come and join me in my reality," he growled mischievously.

Inwardly, I groaned; this time, I was ready. Sensing lightness within me, I knew I could tame the Lord to my wants and desires. If I could serve him well by letting go of my fear, he would now be my fantasy of erotica, as I had nothing to lose, only my dignity.

Chapter 29

Erotic energy erupted between us as dark carnal behaviours of the Lord whetted my appetite. The three of us become one, sharing our elicit cravings for lurid sex. The doorway had opened, and we were in the midst of his power. He devoured us, bound and gagged against the gate, ripping my gown apart; he gorged at my flesh as I begged him for more, whilst Luka penetrated the Lord hard and fast. Powerful energy intensified. It was palpable; tasting his seed, my inhibitions had vanished. Surely I had succeeded in pleasing the Lord.

"Enough!" shouted the Lord. "I have done with you both; you have served my needs. Now go, but remember, Sophia, you are under oath and will always obey me."

"Yes, my Lord," I replied, cringing at his words.

Time evaporated fast as the energy changed dramatically around us. Passion whittled like a dying rose. The moment had passed as we surveyed the landscape. Hazy grey clouds formed in the sky, big and bold; they were overbearing us in a heavy vacuum of nothingness. I shivered uncontrollably as the rain pelted hard.

"Where do we go, my Lord?" I enquired nervously.

His scar deeply bedded into his right cheek, his face stern, showing no emotions. The Lord's eyes glared menacingly at me, piercing my heart. Lightheaded, I knelt before him.

"My Lord, please reveal your true identity."

"Never," he growled angrily. Turning swiftly, he simply disappeared into the darkness.

"Where did he go, Luka?"

"I'm not sure, but we must take cover; a storm is brewing."

Finding some shelter under a canopy of a birch tree, we waited, drenched and cold, not knowing which path to take. Menacing crows circled high above us; they flew so low that I could see their fiery eyes.

"We need to go, Luka, now before it's too late."

"What do you mean?"

"I feel it won't end well for Catalina's baby."

Through the misty skyline, a path soon became visible to us. There was no turning back; we could only move forward, a step closer to our freedom. Thunderous clouds raged their war upon us as lightning lit our path. There was no time to rest, just the truth we sought.

Muddy waters, thick with grime, we forged our way through the storm. Eventually, we came to a crossroads as the sky became clearer, bringing us some comfort.

"Two paths. How do we know which is the right one?" said Luka.

Pausing, I sighed heavily as a slight breeze ruffled my hair; a familiar scent reminded me which one to take.

"We have to take the left path," I urged Luka.

"Are you sure?" he replied.

"Yes, now hurry, please."

Grabbing his hand, I stumbled over the stony track, lined by tall hedges which overhang our path, cocooning us from the bracing wind. Hearing the distant sounds of a nearby village, I prayed we still had time to find the truth. The pathway became treacherous as we battled onward. Catalina's baby kept us moving forward, urgency mounted as the desire to take revenge on the Lord grew with each step I took.

"Listen, did you hear that, Sophia?"

"Yes," I replied.

A loud boom ricocheted over our heads; it was deafening.

"It's a cannon," said Luka.

"What! Where are we?" I asked nervously, hearing the sound of the ocean.

The path widened, and to our amazement stood a grand galleon of the seas. The ship was ready to leave the harbour, looking proud and firm with her sails hung high. We watched from afar as many men alighted the boat. Their black hooded robes concealed their faces. I instantly knew they were the brotherhood; my whole body started to quiver internally.

"We have to follow them." My voice trembled as I spoke. "They will lead us to the truth."

"It's OK, Sophia, we can do this," replied Luka reassuringly.

"Yes, you're right." A wave of calmness swept through me. Letting go of what I witnessed, I became lighter and rose to the challenge.

"Hurry, we need to get on board without being seen," said Luka calmly, "I have a plan, Sophia; follow my lead. Over to your right, see the tall gentleman walking towards us? He is the captain of the *Gallant*."

"Yes," I replied, "how do you know him?"

"I've seen him in a tavern, bragging about his wealth. Seduce him, Sophia, with your charm. We need him on our side."

"Really, do I have to, Luka?" I looked dismayed as the elderly gentleman approached us. His strong presence filled me with horror. Overweight and full of facial hair growth, he repelled me. Luka nudged me forward.

"Good day, sir. I believe you are the captain."

"Yes," he snarled at us both. His foul breath stunk of ale, he snorted, wiping his dirty fingers up and down his greying beard.

"Well, what do you want? I set sail on the evening tide," he said hurriedly.

His gaze now upon me, he smiled warmly at my ample breasts.

"Sir, I would like an hour of your time to tend to your manly needs. In return, we ask for a safe passage on your ship."

He looked bemused at my request, ignoring my words.

"Nah, I don't have time for that, but later, I will be waiting for you in my cabin," he sneered.

"I am Captain Diederik Van Baas, and only I can give permission to set sail on my *Gallant*; she's a grand fine ship. Stowaways never succeed and pay the price with their life."

"Please, captain," we both pleaded.

"Meet me here at high tide; I will give my answer then," he snarled through his cracked teeth, then quickly brushed me aside as his portly stature swaggered towards the nearby tavern.

Crashing waves ripped upon the harbour walls as the storm raged its war. The sea frothed and foamed, covering us with its spray.

"Will you be setting sail in this storm?" Luka shouted.

"Nothing stops the *Gallant*, so you'd both best have the stomach to ride the waves with me," he chortled.

"How can we trust you?" I enquired tentatively.

"You can't," he replied curtly, then swiftly marched through the inn's door.

Bewildered, we stared at the bleak horizon as the sea purged towards us, praying the storm would soon pass. We waited anxiously by the ship, watching the hive of activity in the harbour, catching sight of a buxom woman cradling a baby boarding the *Gallant*.

"We have to get on board, Luka."

"Patience, Sophia, it may not be Catalina's baby. Only time will; the captain will be here soon."

The captain gave us his word. The storm, at last, had eased as we set sail to London on the evening tide. The crimson sky became the new light; with a freshness in the air, we were eager to seek the truth. With Luka by my side, we blended with the masses that alighted the galleon.

Chapter 30

Leaving the harbour's safety behind, the *Gallant*, with its three masts, hung high, bellowing as the gusty wind propelled us forward. Tide and time were not waiting for us; another storm was fast approaching, and we had to trust Captain Van Baas to sail his ship through the crashing waves.

"Choppy seas, all men to the deck," the captain ordered as he steered with a steady hand.

The *Gallant* was vast; the smelt of the sea spray spat on the deck, and frothy white foam, showered upon us. Soaked to the skin, we hurriedly made our way below deck. The ship creaked and groaned. I held on tightly to the rope as I clambered down the rickety step ladder, becoming more nauseated with each step.

"Luka, what cabin is ours?" I inquired, agitated.

He didn't reply, he looked withdrawn and very pale in colour.

"Luka, are you alright?"

"No, excuse me, madam, I have no sea legs."

"Come, please lean on me, Luka." I held my cold hand out to him.

"Can I help you, madam?" spoke a tall, gangly man; his voice penetrated my soul as my left leg shivered, noticing he walked with a limp.

"Please, we are looking for our cabin, sir," I inquired, staring at his left leg.

"Right you are, madam, the captain, is expecting you both in his private quarters."

My stomach tightened as images of the foul-breath-bearded captain draping himself around me came to my mind.

"This way," he ordered. "Weather is turning again, but the *Gallant* is a fine ship and has seen many a storm. I'm the quartermaster; now please hurry, the captain does not like to be kept waiting."

Dutifully we followed him down two flights of wooden ladders, turning left when we reached the last rung.

"I must warn you both, don't go right; you will be eaten alive," he laughed, shaking his head from side to side, "by the vampires."

"Whatever do you mean?" asked Luka.

"I'm just pulling your legs, and I've only got one," he chuckled, "but I would stay well clear of them, all dressed in black robes and chanting nonsense, led by the man they call the Lord."

My whole body shook with a deathly sickness that overcame me. I was eager to follow the quartermaster to the captain's quarters upon hearing the Lord's name.

"What you need is rest, madam. The captain has his eye on you, and so do I," he gloated with delight, ogling at my cleavage. "It's straight ahead; now both get some rest and don't turn right; I must get back to my duties."

Entering the captain's quarters, a strange sensation of familiarity swept through me. Bewildered, I scanned his cabin; it was sparse and tidy. Hazy light from the candles flickered, causing a veil of thin mist and revealing distant memories of my past. The windows were small and frosted from the battling storms of the elements. Lanterns swayed as the ship rocked from side to side. Upon a desk stood a golden sextant with an unfinished chart, beginning to map a route. Inquisitively I scrutinised it and was surprised that I knew instantly how to finish it. Adrenalin pumped through me as a strong feeling of coming home filled me with hope.

Upon the window seat was a chest, secured with padlocks, hiding secrets from my view, until I could find the key. The captain's log was there to be seen on his desk next to a silver tankard. Eager to read his entry, I took a seat in his chair; I read in awe, spellbound by his writing abilities.

"Sophia, we must rest," pleaded Luka.

"Yes," I replied reluctantly. "The captain certainly knows how to write; his language is rich, with a passion for his *Gallant*."

"He won't take it kindly, you reading that," snapped Luka. "Now come and rest, please."

Muted blue light trickled through the panelled windows as I lay precariously upon the hammock. Ghostly images haunted my dreams of days of old when pirates ruled the oceans. The sea swelled high, rocking me from side to side, stirring me from my slumber. The outlook was bleak, but this was the only passage to London. I prayed we would have a safe journey. Fearing the captain would be ordering me to his private quarters soon, I lay there apprehensively. My body was just an object of desire to him, but it was to my advantage, giving me time to find the truth, whatever that is. I was playing a dangerous game, fuelled on by a ticking clock, knowing deep inside what needed to be done. Eventually, my mind eased and sleep came.

"Sophia, wake up."

"What is it, Luka?"

"Listen, can you hear it?"

As I listened intently, I heard a muffled whimpering of a crying baby. My heart ached with sadness. Guilt-ridden, I pleaded to Luka.

"We have to find that baby."

"Yes," he agreed, "but how? The Lord will be watching our every move."

"We need a plan; I may have one," I replied.

Luka stared at me. "Really, Sophia, can you outsmart the Lord?"

"I hope so, Luka."

Still feeling nauseated, somehow, I found the strength to carry on. With a sense of trepidation sweeping through me, knowing I must face the darkness of the Lord again, this time, I would be prepared.

The cabin door creaked wide open as the captain swaggered towards us. His high-waisted breeches concealed his distended belly, whilst his flimsy dirty grey shirt clung tightly around him. A broad black jacket with wide shoulders and his tricorne hat complemented his look.

Flummoxed by his appearance, I realised we were on board a pirate ship.

"I see you both made yourself at home," grinned the captain. "My bed will be waiting for you, Sophia." He was teasing his tongue at me. "Now fetch me some ale," he commanded.

"I'm not your lackey," I replied angrily.

"Well, well, we have a feisty one here; I like that in a woman," he snarled. "Let me remind you of who I am, this is my ship, and I'm in charge!" he roared.

"Very well, I will fetch you some ale; please tell me where to go, captain."

"Don't you know anything? It's in the galley."

"It seems I do not," I replied curtly.

"Luka, you best go with her; we don't want her to get lost and be enticed into the brotherhood, do we?" he smirked candidly.

The *Gallant* propelled us forward upon the open sea. We weathered the storm with the wind behind us, riding the waves towards our destination. We weaved our way to the galley, holding on tightly to the rope as the ship swayed from side to side. Many barrels of ale were stacked up high in the stern, each one sliding forward with the force of the powerful waves.

"This one is open," said Luka, handing me a cask.

Precariously we staggered back towards the captain's quarters, reminding ourselves not to turn right.

"Luka, we must confront the Lord again to find Catalina's baby."

"Yes, I agree, but now is not the right time. You must fulfil the captain's orders to gain his trust, Sophia."

"Yes," I nodded, torn between head and heart, as we approached his private quarters.

"You took your time," snapped the captain. "I run a tight ship, now come both of you and sit with me," he said, offering us some ale. "Drink up," he chuckled.

The ale was strong and bitter, with a heavy aroma of hops. I soon became inebriated as my stomach gurgled for food, and my vision distorted. Laughing hysterically as the captain fed me with his outrageous stories, whilst Luka slept slumped over the table.

"Now I have you all to myself," grinned the captain.

Feeling very giddy, I tried to stand, but my legs turned to jelly.

"Well, madam, you had best bunk down with me for the night. I can make good use of you," he smirked.

"I'm sure you can. Lead the way, captain," I replied, sobering up quickly and remembering my task.

His bed smelt of him, musky and sweaty, but to be able to outwit the captain, I had to play at his game. His scruffy beard pushed into my face as he kissed me roughly, tasting the ale upon his breath. I quickly used my womanly powers to seduce him, much to the delight of the captain. Caught in the moment of sexual persuasion, he was easy to please and satisfied my needs as he parted my legs and tasted my juices. Begging for more, I gripped his hard erection, sighing heavily as he penetrated me with much gusto. Harmoniously we rocked together with the rhythm of the *Gallant* as it swayed back and forth, then darkness came swiftly.

"Sophia, Sophia, wake up!" shouted Luka, throwing a bucket of ice-cold water over my face.

"What?" I replied, dazed and shocked.

"Don't you recall, you were with the captain last night?"

"Yes, vaguely." I smiled as I looked down at my nakedness.

"Where is he now?"

"He's gone up on deck, so this gives us time to investigate. I hope you managed to find the key to his chest whilst you engaged in your sexual appetite."

"Yes, of course, it's under my pillow." I grinned profusely.

"Good, now hurry and get dressed. We need to act now."

"Yes, of course," I replied hurriedly. "Time is of the essence."

"Exactly, Sophia," replied Luka, pulling his big black boots on.

A familiar scent wafted in the air as the ticking clock in my mind became louder and louder. Strange sensations surged through my body, alarming me that all was not what it seemed. Regaining my posture, my strength regained; with the key in my hand, we were both ready to unlock the captain's dark secrets.

Chapter 31

"What is it, Sophia? Why are you hesitating?" asked Luka.

The sturdy oak chest sat proudly upon the window seat, inviting me to turn the key in the lock. I paused as waves of anxiety swept through me.

"I'm not sure," I replied, hesitating, clasping the key as my hand trembled. "What if we see something we don't want to see, Luka?"

"I have my reservations, too, but we must find out; it's now or never."

"Yes, you are right; I owe this to Catalina."

Composing myself, the key effortlessly turned with a click. Momentarily we were both transfixed as I carefully lifted the lid. It was just full of old navigation charts. I sighed disappointedly.

"Is that it? There has to be a secret panel, surely," said Luka.

"Wait, I think I have found something." I pulled at the bottom of the chest. "There's another part, but how do we get into it?"

"Let me look," said Luka impatiently.

"No, I need to do this," I retorted.

"The clock is ticking, Sophia, now hurry. The captain will be back soon."

"It's OK, I've worked it out, look." I slid the secret compartment forward.

The captain's secrets were laid bare to us as I gasped in horror. Time shifted to another dimension. For a brief moment, I stood alone, caught in two realities; one I recognised, and the other felt hostile and alien.

"Luka, where are you?"

"I'm right here; what have you found?" he replied.

"Oh my, this is big; you had better sit down, Luka."

"What! Really?" he replied, biting his lip anxiously.

"The captain holds the key to everything. He is the instigator, the master of all masters. He decides what happens next. Look!" I replied, waving a document in front of his eyes.

There in black and white, was inscribed, "I, Captain Diederik Van Baas, am the Master of all. The Lord is my slave; he only answers to me."

Overwhelmed, I was lost for words as my head spun with violent images. I fell to the floor with a thud.

"Sophia, come on, find your strength; you have the power within you to overcome the Lord and the captain," said Luka coming to my aid, helping me gently to my feet.

"Then who is the Lord?" I asked fearfully, knowing he has many guises.

"We will find out. The truth always comes to light," declared Luka as he searched through the chest.

"I've found a list, Sophia! It's a list of names. Look, Catalina's name is here, and so is my Philip; he was taken at birth by the Lord!"

"What can we do?" I feared the worst for Catalina's baby.

"We must wait for the right time and obey the Lord for now. Hurry, we had better put these papers back and lock the chest. The captain will be back soon."

"Yes, OK." Nothing made sense anymore. Tick–tock, tick-tock grew louder in my mind. The vastness of the ocean expanded my view, knowing my internal clock was ticking fast. Still, somehow I knew without any doubt that I could outwit the Lord and the captain.

Steadying myself, I regained my posture, feeling the presence of the Hooded Man as a hint of patchouli wafted past me. I smiled, reassured, knowing I would always be protected.

"I will do what needs to be done; rest assured, I will find a way. Justice needs to be done," I snapped at Luka.

"You can trust me, Sophia."

"Can I really?" I enquired timidly.

"Yes." He embraced me with his strong masculine arms and softly whispered, "We are in this together, remember?"

Tentatively he held me close to his chest.

"It will be OK, Sophia. Look at me, please," asked Luka, lifting my chin.

His soft hazel eyes gazed lovingly at me. Comforted by his sincerity, I relaxed a little.

"We don't have much time," replied Luka impatiently.

I quickly replaced the documents, locking the chest, then replacing the key under the captain's bed linen, where I found it just before he returned.

"Please take your leave, both of you now; I have urgent business to attend to," commanded the captain as he marched hurriedly into his cabin.

"Very well, captain," we both replied.

The sea swelled high as the ship rocked back and forth. Holding onto Luka, we made our way up on deck. Physically exhausted, both nauseated with seasickness, the waves leapt in front of our eyes.

"Where is the crew?"

"I don't know," replied Luka.

A deluge of waves hit us hard, throwing us to the deck. I held on tightly, shivering fearfully, not wanting to look as the Lord called me in my thoughts.

"Get up, you two, the sea is swelling high; take cover below," ordered the quartermaster; his black boots were awash with frothy sea foam.

Confused, I lost sight of Luka as the sea roared violently upon the *Gallant*. Dark clouds raced in the sky; we were now plunged into the murky depths of a violent storm. Delirious with cold, somehow I managed to clamber below deck as the ship rolled from side to side. An eerie glow descended upon the boat; clinging on with all my might, I called out for help.

"Sophia!" The Lord's voice violated my entire being. His evil presence hung over me as his menacing eyes bored into my soul; I was yet again at his mercy.

"I knew you wouldn't disappoint me," said the Lord.

"What do you mean?" I was feeling perplexed as my anxiety grew.

"Follow me; the brotherhood is waiting," commanded the Lord.

"No! I'm not playing your games anymore."

"Sophia! Where can you run to?" he laughed menacingly.

My heartbeat grew rapidly as my mind cleared. Watching a movie screen playing out in my thoughts, taking me back to the ceremony that brought me face to face with the Lord. I shivered with anger, defying the Lord.

"No!" I screamed at him.

"You leave me no choice," he bellowed, dragging me by my hair. "Your services are needed now. You are coming with me!"

Silenced by his anger, my heart numb with pain, I knew I had to retrieve Catalina's baby from the evil clasp of the Lord.

Down we went to the depths of the ship, gasping for air as the Lord's hands were now firmly around my neck.

"Now, you will obey me."

"Yes," I replied breathlessly.

Nine of the brotherhood were gathered around a pentagram, their black hooded robes hiding their identity. In the centre was a cradle. I shrieked with horror seeing a tiny baby wrapped in a loincloth.

"No, please, Lord, I beg of you, please, release the child to me. Give it to me," I pleaded.

Pushing me aside and ignoring my words, he proceeded with the ceremony.

"Dear brothers, we meet again with Sophia as our host."

My eyes shifted from left to right, looking for a way out. My stomach churned rapidly.

"It's time," he ordered.

He lifted the cradle high in the air, chanting incantations in Latin as the baby screamed, jolted by the sudden movement. My heart lurched.

"*Hic puer est nostra et sacrificium salutaris noster. Et non frustra moriar, ut eam famem nostris in sanguine pascat te. Pueri in tenebris non receperint vos in ordinem.*"

(This child is our sacrifice and our saviour. She will not die in vain, for her blood will feed our hunger. Child of darkness, we welcome you into the order.)

"We take this child with her life, for she is not worthy of her light, born to a whore of the night; she must pay the price," the Lord declared.

My whole body quaked with terror, seeing the Lord produce his dagger from within his robe.

"No!" I shouted. A torrent of rage ripped through me, as I threw myself towards him.

"Take me, please, and let the child live," I pleaded.

"There is a time and place for you to die, but that is not now," he roared violently.

With a jerk of his hand, he drew his dagger. I closed my eyes tight, not wanting to see. A gush of wind spun around me as the ship rocked back and forth in slow motion.

I screamed in anger, "Stop right now. You are not in charge, Lord; the captain is the master of everything."

"Yes, I am," replied the captain, revealing his identity as he threw off his robe.

"No!" I cried, "this cannot be happening."

"But it is Sophia. Now, take your place with us and witness her death."

A loud bang from up on the deck halted the ceremony.

"All hands on deck," shouted the quartermaster. "The *Gallant* has taken a blow. All hands on deck now!"

My time had come. Swiftly, I grasped the infant, clutching it protectively in my bosom. I took flight and ran up on deck with her, trying to find Luka. The Lord was soon upon me, pinning me against the ship's edge. Sea and sky were all I could see. Saturated and cold, the baby slipped from my grasp as the boat turned sharply, spinning me around and around. I watched helplessly as the beautiful wailing child fell into the boiling sea. My heart sank as she disappeared amongst the deluge of purging waves, plunging her to her watery death and swallowing her into the vastness of its depths.

Staring out to sea, I waited but dared not look, fearing the Lord and the Master were behind me.

"Take her down below now," ordered the captain.

My head low, I bowed to them, yet again, taking my place at the pentagram. I satisfied their lust as they purged themselves upon me, one by one. They devoured my body with their masterful, powerful sexual energy. Oblivious to the mayhem that had erupted around me, I lost consciousness, overcome by the scent of opium.

"Sophia, Sophia, wake up; we have arrived in London."

Finding myself in the captain's bed, Luka looked lovingly at me.

"Luka, is that really you?"

"Yes," he replied fondly.

Then I remembered the fateful events, crying hysterically as tears streamed down my face.

"The baby, I tried to save her, Luka. I really did."

"I know you did; it's not your fault."

"What about the Lord and the captain?"

"They jumped ship, taking a raft with the rest of the brotherhood. The quartermaster took the helm and brought us safely through the storm."

I sighed with relief but was deeply saddened, as I couldn't save Catalina's baby.

"She was so fragile, like a delicate rose, and that is what I will call her. She will have not died in vain. Together we must overrule the Lord and the Master."

"Yes, Sophia, there is always a way," replied Luka.

"Come now. It's time to embark on your next journey. In the streets of London, you must seek Madam Genevieve. I hear she has magical powers of the light that can help you."

Hearing her name, a wave of sadness swept through me as my childhood memories flooded back.

"Luka, how do you know of my mother?"

"I don't, but I have heard from other sources that speak highly of her. Really, she is your mother? How interesting," he replied, adjusting his neckerchief.

"Yes, she gave me away when I was seven. I'm not sure why, but she told me to remember the light is always within me."

"Then we must find her, Sophia. Let us now embark on the sights and smells of London town. Are you ready, Sophia?"

"Yes, I feel safe with you by my side. Lead the way Luka," I replied tenderly.

Chapter 32

Leaving the docklands behind, we headed towards the city. Dusk was fast approaching; we waded through the murky shades of decay with little light. A thick fog hung in the air; the foul stench was overbearing; I heaved as my stomach churned. Who could we trust? Men with black faces covered in soot, women begging with their bodies, and children running barefoot in the filthy streets. London looked grim, a far cry from the lavish palace in Paris. My thoughts then turned to Gabriella, remembering her soft touch and voluptuous body. I smiled inwardly.

"Luka, you do know I must get back for Princess Gabriella's wedding?"

"Yes, I know that, but she won't like the news regarding Philip," sighed Luka.

"But there is still time," I insisted.

"Yes, but how much time do we really have?" asked Luka.

"I have no idea, but we mustn't give up."

Nightfall came in a vengeance, making it impossible to see at all. Only noise was our guidance.

"This fog will last all night; you had best make your way to the tavern up the hill," shouted a young man who came into our vision.

"Where is that?" replied Luka. "We have just arrived from Holland."

"If you give me some silver, I will take you," he replied, coughing as he spoke.

His fair hair was long and unkempt, his clothes torn and tattered hung from his wasting body. Taking pity on him, I wanted to help him. I reached into my pocket and was surprised to find the brooch I had given back to the Hooded Man.

"How did that get there?" Confused, I held it in my hand and offered it to the young man.

"No, Sophia, you need to keep that; it's important. Here lad, take these coins and lead us to the inn."

The young man grinned, seeing five shiny coins in his hand.

"It's a deal!" he shouted. "This way, please."

"How do you know of the brooch, Luka?" I asked with curiosity.

"Now's not the time; just be thankful you've got it back."

His slender body silhouetted in the hazy fog, catching a glimpse of his bright eyes gave me some hope and reassurance. I nodded thankfully towards him.

"Come on, the fog is coming denser; you don't want to lose sight of me," shouted the young man.

"OK," we both replied as I clung tightly to Luka. Holding hands, our cold fingers touched raw skin; we both longed for some warmth. Keeping a close eye on the lad, we followed him in earnest. Neither of us had been to London before, but somehow, it seemed strangely familiar, causing a ripple of uncertainty within me. I shivered uncontrollably. Thick fog now consumed us all, and the taste of soot lingered in my mouth.

"How much further?" I replied wearily, my feet throbbing with every step. I winced painfully.

"Just up this hill, Mrs; hold on to my arm."

Out of breath, we finally made it to the tavern. The Ship's Compass invited us in. Eagerly we stepped inside and into the warmth. The inn engulfed us in a blaze of fire as we sat huddled around the hearth, warming our bodies from the cold. The innkeeper looked sharply at as.

"A fine pair you make," he smirked, looking at me.

The intensity of his stare caught my attention.

"Who are you?" I inquired.

"The owner, Mrs, now don't ask anymore. Food will be served shortly, but have these drinks on me for now."

His hands shook as he passed the ale to us. A man of age, he was clearly not that well. His face was pitted with scars, and his greying hairline was visible under his black-rimmed hat.

"Drink up." His voice was hard to hear over the raucous that was going on in the next room.

"Troy!" he yelled to the young man. "Once they have eaten, please show them to their room."

"Yes, sir."

Both tired and hungry, we were glad to be in the tavern. Bathing in the golden rays of the fire, it blazed powerfully. Mesmerised, I watched the flames dance before my eyes. I screamed, in shock, seeing baby Rose's cherubic face entwined in the flickering sparks.

"Luka, look! I can see Rose."

"Sophia, it's OK, you're seeing things again," he replied softly. "Now eat up; our food is here."

The bowl of thick broth was rich and tasty, nourishing us as it fed our souls. I breathed a sigh of relief; our stomachs full, we were both ready to retire.

"Come this way," spoke Troy as he led us to our room.

"What's going on in the room next door?" I asked nervously.

"Just fishermen playing their games, nothing for you to concern yourself with," he replied.

Too tired to answer, I solemnly followed him with Luka by my side. Three flights of stairs later, he finally opened the door to our room for the night.

"I will wake you at dawn. Now rest."

The room was sparse but adequate. A bed was all we needed. Exhausted, I lay down staring at the ceiling, noticing similarities to the House of De Vries. Eerily all was quiet as I watched the night tick by until I eventually gave into sleep, drifting between the veils of time. Tossing and turning, I finally awoke to the sound of life coming from the street. Peering through a small window, I squinted to see what was happening. The brotherhood had gathered in a circle; they seemed agitated as they waved their fists in anger. My hands clamped to the window as my anxiety rose, feeling hot and giddy with fear. I quickly woke Luka.

"Luka, we have to go now."

"What!" he replied bleary-eyed. "What's the rush, Sophia? Come back into bed; I have something for you," he grinned seductively.

"Stop it. Look out the window; the brotherhood is waiting for us. Is there any escape from them?" I cried out in vain.

"OK, I hear you," said Luka, quickly jumping to his feet. "It's OK, Sophia, let's go now."

Making a dash from the room, we headed quietly down the three flights of wooden stairs.

"Where do you think you're going?" shouted the innkeeper, stopping us in our tracks, his eyes questioning our every move.

"We have to go; you can't stop us," said Luka.

"No, you're right there, but you aren't going anywhere until you tell me what those men want with you."

"We can't tell you, sir, but you must let us go," I pleaded.

"What's it worth?" he replied.

"Our freedom, sir; I'm here to find my mother, Madam Genevieve."

"So you are her daughter?" he said, bemused.

"Yes," I replied, surprised and concerned he knew of her.

"She said you would come, but I didn't believe her; she's crazy and dabbles in magic, but she sure knows how to please a man. You have a look of her; I can see it in your eyes, " he said, smiling broadly at me.

"Those men outside are not trustworthy. They are using dark magic to get what they desire; it's not good. My mother can help us. Where can we find her?" I asked hurriedly, hearing them beat the door loudly.

"Last I heard, she had gone underground. You had best go out the back door, now hurry. I will get word to your mother, just head east from the city and take refuge in the church spire."

"Thank you," we both replied.

The mist had finally lifted. Through the hazy light of dawn, we could see the spire in the distance.

"We can hide there until the coast is clear," said Luka.

My feet ached raw as we ran, daring not to look back and knowing I had to reach the church before the brotherhood would be upon us. Breathless, the stone tower was now in front of us. Stopping at the entrance, a bright luminous light beckoned us in. From the depths of the building, the light grew significantly, glowing vividly as we walked up the spiral staircase leading to the belfry. Instinctively, I knew my mother would be there. She stood patiently waiting for us in the golden light, a vision of splendour, giving me much comfort as she held me close in her arms.

"Hello, Sophia, I always knew you would find me one day when you most needed me!" she said affectionately.

"Hello, mother, I need your help."

"I know you have strayed from your path, my child of the light, but you can redeem yourself."

The bright light intensified as it spun into a vortex around me. I quickly became lightheaded as my mother stared lovingly at me. Her serene face was now rounded with age, and her greying hair was tied neatly into a bun. My heart melted as her soft blue eyes connected with mine. As we held each other in a warm embrace, her familiar scent of sweet jasmine brought powerful memories. Feeling safe, I sobbed with relief.

"Dear Sophia, there is more to come, but in the end, you will do the right thing," she whispered gently.

"Yes, mother, I will," I replied, daunted by what may lie ahead of me.

"Remember, you are the light!" she said softly.

"Who is my father?" I inquired nervously.

"You have already met him. It's the Lord!"

"No!" I screamed in disgust, feeling the heaviness in my heart. Mortified, throwing myself at her feet, as anger rose within, I yelled, "But why mother, why him?"

Chapter 33

Finding the strength to stand, I stood motionless, leaning against the cold stone wall, staring at my mother in disbelief. Without warning, a raven appeared and flew above me, feeling the full force of its wingspan overhead. Its giant claws landed with ease upon my mother's left shoulder, as she shamefully bowed her head, whilst Luka walked impatiently towards her. My stomach sank as my whole being quaked, reeling from the news. A sharp pain pierced my heart as I screamed, trying to block the images of the Lord cruelly pillaging my naked body.

"Mother, how could you!" I yelled.

"It's time to tell her, Madam Genevieve," said Luka.

"Tell me what? You said you didn't know my mother, Luka."

"I lied, but it was for your own good."

"Really!"

"So, mother, tell me now!" I replied angrily.

"Very well, it's time for you to know," she replied, hesitating as her eyes glazed with sadness. "Sophia, there was a reason I gave you away; I had no choice. I was only fourteen when I encountered the Lord. He was just a prince then; he lured me from the light and into his darkness. Seduced by his distinguished black hair and his eyes of steel, he converted me to his ways. Realising I was with child, I managed to break free from him. You were born into the light of our coven, and then the Lord came and took you away to the House of De Vries. I'm so sorry, Sophia. I tried to bargain with him, but it was no use; I had to let you go. Now, my dear child, it's time for you to cut earthly ties from the occult and rekindle your past, bringing forth the light once more."

As she spoke, golden rays emanated from the lantern she carried, casting us in her mystical powers of wonderment. Spellbound, she held my hand tightly as the raven perched silently upon my mother's shoulder, his beady gaze now firmly transfixed upon me.

"How can I, Mother! I'm under his oath! And who is Julian's father?" I said harshly.

"It's OK to be angry at me, Sophia, but you owe it to yourself to break free. Julian is not your blood brother; he is your stepbrother. His mother was my sister, Chantel; she died during childbirth. The brotherhood came and took him away; that was the last I saw of him."

"Stop it!" I yelled, overwhelmed with emotions as the tears started to flow. Falling into my mother's arms, I pleaded with her to tell me who the Lord really was.

"Sophia, my dear child, you must seek your own truth; only you can find out the real identity of the Lord. You have the power within you to break free from his chains; just believe it. Now, look into the lantern's light. Tell me, what do you see?" She placed her warm hands upon my heart.

Time evaporated before me, spinning fast in a vortex, whispering fleeting memories in shockingly vivid detail. It revealed a clear vision of myself, old and haggard, running from a crime I had just committed. A lifeless body was on the ground, covered in blood. It was Princess Gabriella!

"No! Surely this cannot be the truth?" I yelled, "I love her so deeply. Why would I do this, Mother?"

"Only you can answer that, but you can change your path, my dear child. The light is always with you and always will be."

"But how?" I replied, feeling bereft.

"Sisters of the light, step forward," she commanded.

Within the shadows, seven ladies of the light appeared mysteriously. Dressed in white hooded gowns, they paraded in front of me, chanting incantations as they sprayed me with a potent potion of neroli orange blossom mixed with the sweet scent of white oleander and herbaceous. It was powerful and hypnotic, leaving a trail of strong vapours.

"Welcome to the Sisters of the Light, dear Sophia," said Madam Genevieve.

Her voice changed tone as she spoke in Latin. No! Not more, I prayed, surely not my mother! I held my breath, fearing the Lord would appear.

"Cum omni studio tenebrasque accipimus. Et nos per te iter quod

sit amet ante. Nos ex antiquis et illud est. Et educ nos ibamus iter "

(Shadows of the night, we welcome you with all our might. Let you lead us through this maze and into the majestic light. We are of the old witchcraft, so mote it be. Bring forth our path and guide us on our way.)

With her words, a luminous golden-white winged being of light engulfed the whole tower. Dazzled by its beauty, I stared in disbelief whilst the sisters gathered around me, forming a circle and placing their hands on the crown of my head. Their virginal silk gowns shimmered as they walked slowly around me, casting and weaving the enchantment. It was magnetic and pure, engulfing me back into their coven.

"Sophia, step forward into the middle; please let me have the brooch; it needs recharging, then you and Luka must find the missing children. Only then can you redeem yourself."

My face etched with sadness, crumbling to the floor, I sobbed, reliving the moment the sea engulfed Rose's tiny body. "I tried to save Catalina's baby from the Lord, mother, I did."

"I believe you, my child."

"Sisters, please step aside," she ordered.

My mother's warm hands were now hovering over my head, omitting energy currents that pulsated through my whole body. Startled, I stood up, hearing the voice of the Lord in my mind.

"Stop!" I shouted. "The Lord is here."

"Yes, I know, he's here all of the time Sophia, he is the dark, and I am the light. It's his energy that you are feeling."

"But I don't understand?"

"You will one day, Sophia," she replied, smiling warmly.

"Now keep this safe, take it and use it wisely; remember you are as powerful as the Lord," she said lovingly, handing me the brooch.

Holding it firmly, the golden jewelled cluster glistened radiantly. Shutting my eyes tightly gave me a clearer vision. My heartbeat became rapid as the Lord's menacing presence came closer. Taking a deep intake of breath, I opened my eyes, finding my mother and the sisters had vanished within the vapours of time. The tower was now in darkness, with just the sound of water trickling inside from a borehole in the stony ground.

"Where did they go, Luka?"

"I don't know; I was under their spell too; we must continue our search."

"Yes," I nodded, deep in thought.

Morning light faded under the greying clouds; no one was to be seen. Agitation grew within me as my insight became heightened. Rain fell heavily from the sky; I shivered, watching the crows fly high above. Indistinctly I knew the Lord was close.

"Where do we go now?" asked Luka.

"To the monastery, It's near a river. I'm sensing a strong current that flows continually. We must return to the dockyard to find the right path."

Luka didn't question me; he just stood in front of me. His masculinity magnified his aura, causing me to falter.

"Come on, Luka, I haven't got time for your silly games."

"Oh, but you have," he laughed, firmly grasping my hand.

"You know I excite you, Sophia." His brooding presence towered in front of me, activating my sexual glands. Avoiding eye contact, I stared at the ground.

"We have all the time in the world, tick-tock," he smirked.

"Stop it!" I yelled.

"We are too exposed here, and I must redeem myself. We need to find Philip."

"The day will come, Sophia, when you cannot resist me, come what may!" he smirked candidly.

The rain eased as a shaft of sunlight reflected upon Luka. His pale skin brought a softness to his eyes, revealing his fragility. Instantly, I felt his sadness.

"Yes, one day, but we have to stop the Lord; then I'm all yours, I promise."

"That's good to hear," he replied, wiping droplets of tears from his cheeks.

"Lead on, Sophia."

Chapter 34

Transcendent light filtered through the grey clouds, hugging the air; it consumed us. Wearily we walked the path back towards the docks. Evergreen trees became our new friends; as we passed each one, they seemed to be saluting us on our way.

"Luka, I don't recall seeing this before, do you?"

"No, we must have taken a different path," replied Luka.

Clasping my brooch for comfort, I held it tightly. A familiar scent aroused my senses as a voice from within spoke. "Sophia, keep going; time is ticking."

"Luka, it's OK; we just have to keep moving forward. Look! The trees are guiding us."

"If you say so," said Luka flippantly, snapping a branch from a nearby tree, causing the many crows to squawk. Their shrills echoed eerily, mirroring my insecurity.

The afternoon sun peered through the gaps in the sky, casting shadows of our innermost fears. Everything seemed surreal as if I wasn't there, but I was. Feeling my feet and toes throbbing with the coldness brought me back to the present moment.

"Luka, what day is it?"

"Friday, why are you asking?"

"Because the next ship leaves on Monday, we must be on it," I urged Luka. "I have to put a stop to the wedding."

"I know," he replied.

"How do you know?"

"Because it's all part of the plan."

"What plan? You know where we are going, Luka?"

"Questions, questions," he replied, "all in good time, but I can tell you we are going back to the beginning."

My face tightened as he spoke, and my lips quivered as I silently bit my lip. As I knelt before him, I stared intensely at Luka, quizzing his face for answers.

"What are you not telling me?" I whispered nervously, watching his every move as he played nervously with his fingers.

"Sophia get up," he demanded. "All will be revealed, but not yet. You have a task to do; that's all you need to know for now."

A fine layer of mist descended from the clouds; it lingered heavily upon us, bringing dampness into the air. I shivered uncontrollably. The trees were no more; they were gone, shrouded in a veil of uncertainty.

"Hold on to my hand, Sophia."

"Yes," I replied, hearing my heart pound against my chest.

"We must be nearly at the docks," said Luka reassuringly.

Solemnly we walked together through the density of the fog, unsure of our path, knowing I had no choice but to keep going. The thick, rancid smog was now becoming unbreathable.

"I can't get my breath, Luka," I panted.

"Here, put this scarf around your mouth," replied Luka as he produced a pink silk scarf from his pocket.

"That's Gabriella's! I recognise her scent; how come you've got it?" I stared at Luka defiantly.

"She gave it to me to give to you, dear Sophia."

"Oh, I see, thank you," I said, feeling somewhat perplexed and baffled.

As I gently stroked the scarf, a warm glow filled my heart; sniffing her sweet fragrance reminded me of Gabriella's beauty. I smiled reassuringly, knowing her love for me was deeply enriched within her soul.

"We can do this, Luka."

With each footstep we took, the light diminished under the thick blanket of London fog. We walked blindly together. Holding hands solemnly, we guided each other as our thoughts turned inwards. A chilly breeze kept us moving forward. At last it lifted, revealing the monastery in the distance. Its shadow stood tall against the backdrop of the hills beyond.

"Do we really have to enter?" I enquired nervously as a cold shiver ran through my body.

"Yes."

I winced in pain. "But Luka, the Lord, is there. I feel his energy; it's big and menacing."

I stood still, unable to move any further. Light and dark energy consumed us; it changed moment by moment as the gusty wind blew hard upon us. Clutching my jewelled cluster for comfort, I waited for the wind to pass.

"I can't do this, Luka."

"Yes, you can. Remember your mother's words," he replied calmly.

"OK," I replied, hesitating, as my heart pumped fast. I took another deep breath.

"It's time, Luka, to unmask the Lord."

The monastery loomed upon us. A gothic building with stained arched windows brought me closer to the Lord. I looked up towards the bell tower. Hearing the Lord's voice in my mind, I reminded myself why I was there. The darkness of the monastery chilled my bones; it felt cold and uninviting.

"I have to do this alone, Luka."

"Sophia," he called out, stopping directly before me. "Very well, but I won't be far behind you."

The door was heavy and solid, made from oak. Cast iron hinges secured it to the blackened, reddish bricks. Pushing the door hard, it silently opened, like a whisper in the wind; it chilled my bones.

"Stay here, please, Luka," I begged him.

"Very well," he replied begrudgingly.

The heavy door slammed behind me, bringing me face to face with the Lord. Standing in the centre of the many arches of the cloisters, his threatening shadow flickered all around the hall. I stood pensive, eager to have my revenge on him.

His now greying black hair was swept to one side, concealing his scar. His cold eyes glared like ice, piercing my soul. Placing my hand on my heart, I took another deep breath and prayed for the truth.

"Hello Sophia, I knew you were coming. Welcome, dear daughter, child of the light!" he laughed, enticing me into his arms.

"How could you?" I screamed, pushing him away.

"Because we are the same, Sophia."

"What do you mean?" I pleaded with him. "Who are you?"

"The Lord, of course," he said furiously. "Now follow me; the brotherhood is waiting."

"No! Bring the brotherhood to me so I can see them in the light," I demanded, finding my voice.

"All is not what it seems, Sophia; the brotherhood is already here."

Stunned and confused, stumbling for answers, I began to question everything.

The vestry opened up before my eyes, revealing the grandeur of the building. Oddly it felt familiar as I walked the aisle following the Lord and the brotherhood, touching each pew for reassurance. Incense with a scent of cedar wood bellowed from the altar, reminding me of my childhood. I squirmed anxiously, tugging my tousled dark-brown hair from my eyes. Tears started to swell, holding my tongue, trying to advert my anger.

"My Lord," I pleaded again. "Why! You are my father!"

"Indeed I am, now sit child," he ordered.

"Dear brotherhood, the Master has decreed that I must reveal myself today."

There was a rush of noise as faint whispers between the brotherhood stirred the quietness of the moment.

I took a seat at the front, with the brotherhood behind me, and waited for the big reveal. My hand was firmly clasped around my brooch as I silently called my mother for help.

The bells chimed nine times, and with that came a deathly silence. A faint light of a glowing candle lit the Lord's face as he stood, commanding his audience. His manly figure tugged at my heart, catching me unaware, forgetting he was my father. Who was he? I stared hard at him, trying to see through his darkness, and then suddenly the energy shifted, revealing his truth. I gawped, astonished, seeing the true identity of the Lord.

Reeling from the revelation, I hung my head in shame. How could this be so?

"Sophia, you look shocked," said the Lord, as his facade slipped away.

"Yes, I am, your Majesty," I said, seeing images of myself projected upon the Lord.

"Then you have nothing to fear."

I nodded silently and took my place by his side. The spell had been cast between us, light and dark; we merged as one. As the brotherhood faded into obscurity, I had regained my power. Light filled the vestry momentarily; smiling inwardly, I knew the day of reckoning was soon.

Chapter 35

Intoxicated and delirious, I laughed hysterically as I knelt before the altar. Crimson light from the stained-glass windows flooded the vestry, illuminating the grand oak pillars that supported the building. My gaze was now firmly fixed upon a hard block. It stood prominently, waiting for its next victim. Its carved, worn edge was stained with blood spilt by the executor's axe. I shook violently, paralysed by a spine-chilling energy rising up from the ground.

Immediately my hands flew to my heart, expecting every part of me would pause. Yet, still, rapid thoughts raced in my mind trying to find the light through the murkiness of darkness.

"Sophia, you know your truth," said a voice in the air as a familiar odour of patchouli awakened my soul.

"My Lord, where are you? I want answers," I expounded, raging with anger.

But he didn't answer; the Lord and the brotherhood had simply vanished. Just their shadows were left, like a memory that lingered, trapping us between two worlds. Hesitantly, I placed my fingers on the block, praying for the light to return. Images of my future self constantly penetrated my mind. I looked different in a city of tall buildings, strange feelings resurfaced, viewing my life through different eyes. I questioned myself, calling my name.

"Hello, Sophia, is that me?"

"Yes," she replied, "I am your past, present and future self."

I swayed back and forth, unsure of what was real; I wept profusely at my immortality.

"Sophia, you know we are the same."

"Yes," I silently whispered.

Regaining my posture, I slowly walked to the front of the monastery, where the Lord had returned; he stood beckoning me. There was nowhere to hide; I had to take my place by his side. Steadfast and strong, his energy seeped into mine as I entered his world. His steely eyes looked into mine; I bowed before him knowing judgement day was fast approaching.

Our energies fused together as our bodies locked with the sacred union of light and dark. Weak for his needs, I was lured from my path as we rode the waves of euphoria, encapsulating the moment of frenzied sexual indulgence.

"Sophia, Sophia. Come back," said the voice in the air.

"Where are you?"

"In between the emptiness," I replied casually.

"Come back," urged the voice again.

"Yes," I replied. "Anna?"

The coldness of the vestry woke me from my inertia. Finding myself alone, sprawled out amongst the pews, my gown pulled up to my neck, exposing my bare flesh. Alarmed, I looked down at the rawness of my vagina, swollen and covered in semen; I felt disgusted, used and abused by myself and the Lord. I stared at the wooden cross nailed high above the altar, begging for salvation; I gagged profusely as I tasted his sweat upon my lips.

"I will get the better of you, Lord!" I screamed. "I know where to find you!"

"I will be ready and prepared," he shrieked menacingly as he calmly walked towards me.

His immaculate, preened body stood over me; I scanned his eyes for compassion, but they were cold and calculating. I had yet again been hooked into submission by his dark satanic ways. Speechless, I watched him disappear through the haze that blurred my vision.

"Sophia, there you are," said Luka coming to my aid. "Let me help you."

"No, it's all my fault, Luka."

Seeing the torture in my eyes, he held me close, comforting me with his love.

"Where did the Lord go?" asked Luka.

"I don't know, but I have an idea. Hold onto my brooch and view what I see."

"Sophia," he said flippantly, "this isn't a mind game."

"I know," I replied indignantly. "Trust me, Luka, please."

Holding the jewelled cluster firmly, we held hands and closed our eyes, seeing images of the Lord's demise.

"The tide is turning, Luka. Are you with me? I have a wedding to attend, and we must find Philip before it's too late."

"Yes," he replied. "Now, I can take you back to the beginning."

"What do you mean, beginning? I don't understand."

"Sophia, it's time to finish what you started and discover why you are here."

Confused and overcome with emotions, I surrendered to his words as they sunk deep into my soul. The time had come to finally let go of the Lord; I now had the power to diminish him forever.

"I'm not sure I can do this," I said wearily. "The Lord is my father, Luka!"

"Light will always find a way to help you; trust me and have mercy for your father. You know deep down in your heart you have to forgive yourself, and you will."

"Yes, you're right, Luka. I can do this."

A sharp breeze rustled around my legs, reminding me we needed to take our leave. Hearing a heavy thud vibrate around the chamber, I stood at the altar, praying for guidance.

"Luka, please sit with me."

"We haven't got time; our ship sails at noon tomorrow, and we still need to find Philip and the missing infants."

"I know; I just need a moment."

Reluctantly he bowed to my wishes. We sat in silence, waiting for divine intervention. A sense of calm swept through me as the light started to fill the vestry, illuminating all the dark places.

"For the grace of God, thy will be done; please forgive me," I whispered.

"It's time, Sophia," said Luka, as he clasped my hand tightly whilst he carefully handed me his razor-sharp dagger from within his tunic.

"Yes," I agreed shockingly, staring at the gleaming blade. I gulped nervously at my task before composing myself.

"I believe we need to exit through the side door; I feel the Lord hasn't gone far. He is still here."

Dusky pink sky greeted us as we emerged from the monastery, with the sound of the evensong. Momentarily, I breathed a sigh of relief, and then, through the shadows of the trees, a figure loomed ahead of us. It was the Lord. Instantly I repelled his advances.

"Hello, Sophia. We meet again."

"Yes," I mumbled through gritted teeth.

His grotesque shadow grew nearer towards me. His energy engulfed me, encapsulating me in the moment. Feeling insignificant, I clung to Luka for support. I watched, mortified, as twelve hooded men wearing purple gowns appeared through the realms of darkness. They encircled us in their cloaks of dishonour as the full moon emerged from behind the trees, revealing the truth, yet I found the courage to move forward. Stepping into the middle of the circle, my energy grew as the intensity mounted and my power returned.

"My Lord," I declared. "You have served me well," I mocked, "but your downfall is you let me into your world. Now I can see clearly who you are; I will never fear you again!"

The Lord, cold and calculating, stood his ground, twitching; I had caught him at his own game. Quickly he snapped his fingers as he spoke.

"Brotherhood, disperse you to Luka. This is just between Sophia and me."

"It's OK, Luka, I've got this," I called out to him as he left the circle with the brotherhood.

Then there were just two of us. The Lord's eyes glazed over as they bored into mine, his face now tormented in pain as his scar was visible beneath his facade.

"Sophia, I am your father and taught you well; remember your childhood."

"Yes," I said quietly, regrettably, as vivid memories of his doctrine came flooding back, consuming me with powerful images of dark witches and druids.

Anger rose within me like a phoenix rising from the ashes. I yelled at him.

"I was only seven when you took me from my mother, and I became your object of loath!"

"Yes, Sophia, but I waited for your return. Don't you remember you disappeared? Where did you go?"

"I can't remember," I murmured quietly.

The full moon beamed upon us as whispering shadows danced in the wind. Glaring at each other, I knew it was time to release him once and for all.

"I do not fear you anymore, you can do what you wish, but I have won, my Lord. Goodbye, it's time to meet your maker."

Swiftly I pulled the dagger from my gown. Charging forward, I stopped abruptly, for a brief moment seeing compassion in his eyes.

"Just go," I yelled at him, taking pity, as I withdrew the dagger inches away from his heart. He turned and withered, fading into the void. I could hear his words, "Sophia, I will be back."

"No, never!" I yelled. "You are dead to me!"

The Lord had vanished before my eyes; where did he go? I stood mesmerised, staring at the untainted dagger, relieved not a drop of blood was to be seen.

"What's happening?" I shrieked as his vile silhouette hovered over me, causing electric currents that ricocheted throughout my whole being.

I leapt upwards, awakening myself from the years of torment; the Lord's reign was finally over. Looking over my right shoulder, his shadow eventually diminished. My heart returned to a steady pace as I sat, waiting for Luka to return. The moon's silvery light was now gracefully hugging the sky. I sighed heavily with anticipation, knowing I will back at the House of De Vries soon.

"I knew you could do it," said Luka, smiling lovingly at me as he joined me by my side, retrieving his dagger.

His deep rich voice soothed my soul, and our eyes met passionately as we held each other close.

"Take me now, Luka," I whispered seductively, hearing the repetitive tick-tock rhythm in my mind.

"Not now, Sophia; time is fading quickly. We have to find Philip."

"I fear it's too late, Luka, but we can still try to find the missing children."

Luka's eyes grew heavy with sadness. "Sadly, we may never find them, well, not in this lifetime," he replied.

Despair turned into desperation as we continued along the path towards the docklands. My thoughts drifted towards Gabriella, knowing I would soon be reunited with my beloved, if only for a short while.

Chapter 36

Our journey back to Holland was long and arduous. Sleep didn't come; with that came an uncertainty of what may happen next. I stood on the deck gazing out to sea and beyond. The night sky was lit with millions of stars, giving me hope. Fractions of light entwined with the fabric of time, starring at the vastness of the universe, I pinched myself hard, trying to recall why I was here. My mind raced forward to a time of nothingness. Eagerly, I wanted to reach out and touch that space; instead, I placed my hands upon my beating heart.

Tick-tock, tick-tock got louder and louder in my thoughts; it grew stronger minute by minute, magnifying the enormity of life. I cupped my ears hard, blocking out the noise.

"No more!" I screamed at the voice in my head.

"You're safe," said a faint voice in the air.

"Anna, is that you?"

Inner calmness returned, and the sound of the sea soothed my thoughts. Waiting for the sunrise, I sat comfortably upon the deck, catching a glimmer of first light; sleep came at last, with strange erotic dreams enticing me with the spirit of an asp.

"Sophia! Wake up," said Luka. "Look," he demanded.

"Where am I?" I replied.

"Oh, Sophia, you know exactly where we are."

"Do I?" I said sleepily; my thoughts were still in the dream.

"Look," he persisted, handing me a spyglass.

Peering through the lenses, I could easily see the docklands at last. Rubbing my tired eyes and taking another look, I was pleasantly surprised to see Martha waiting at the quayside with Lucien.

Our ship docked, at last, now standing on firm ground. I was relieved to be back in Holland. Martha looked tired; her complexion was sullen, and her tiny frame was now lost in her oversize gown, as she held on to Lucien for support. I was shocked to see her fragility.

"Martha, I'm so pleased to see you see. What has happened to you whilst I have been away?" I inquired, concerned for her well-being.

"My dear madam, I am so pleased to see you again. I have been waiting for your return. You must hurry back to the House of De Vries; it's a matter of much urgency."

As she spoke, beads of sweat nestled upon her forehead, highlighting her anxiousness and the severity of the crisis.

Becoming rigid with fear, not wanting to hear her words, hesitating, I replied quietly, "But I have to attend the wedding; it's next week."

"I know," she replied reassuringly. "You will get to the wedding, but you are needed at home first."

Reluctantly, I nodded. "OK."

"Lucien, what is going on? Please tell me, is it, Julian?" My stomach churned violently, speaking his name.

"Yes," he said hoarsely.

Lucien looked thinner; his demur had diminished, and his blue eyes now told a story of pain and illness.

"You must return, Sophia," he insisted, coughing profusely.

Martha's blue gown bellowed in the prevailing wind, nearly knocking her off her feet. Lucien gently held her hand; they both looked weak and frail. Have I been away that long? Time seemed irrelevant to me as timelines merged into one another. Confused, I searched for answers in Martha's eyes, but all I could see was her pitiful distressed state.

"Lucien," I said sharply. "What has happened!"

"You will see when you return. Our carriage is waiting; hurry now."

Luka looked apprehensively at me, his voice not heard through the gush of wind.

"Sophia, you must return with them alone. I will meet you in Paris for the wedding. I have to find Philip."

"Yes, I understand," I said regretfully, sighing heavily as his kindness had opened my heart.

"Promise me, Luka, a dance we will have at the wedding ball."

"Of course," he replied, kissing my hand with softness.

The sound of galloping horses grew nearer. I flinched, not wanting to return to the House of De Vries. The golden royal seal of Prince Lavin stood out amongst the black glossy shine of the carriage; it gleamed in the early morning sun as it made its way to us.

"Lucien, why the royal carriage?" I inquired timidly.

"It's by the orders of Prince Lavin for your return to Paris," said Lucien candidly.

Apprehensively, I climbed on board. "I hope I won't be blindfolded this time, Lucien," I said anxiously.

"That was then, Sophia. This is now," he said feebly.

As the horses picked up speed, the rhythmic sound of tick-tock became louder and louder. A sense of unease grew steadily within me, dreading what I may find on my return.

"Martha, can you hear that loud tick-tock?"

"No, madam, all I can hear is the thunder in my heart," she replied tearfully.

Her face was wet with tears, tormented in anguish; she looked right through me as if I wasn't there.

"Martha, you must tell me what has happened."

"I can't, madam, you must see for yourself," said Martha, whimpering.

Holding her hand, I nodded. "OK."

Lucien's facade had now vanished, revealing his true nature. He looked different even though he was in pain. He seemed smaller, and his arrogant behaviour had now disappeared. His dazzling sapphire ring still allured me to its beauty, knowing one day, it will be mine.

The House of De Vries was now visible; I squirmed further back into my seat, not wanting to venture inside. The formidable red house reeked of danger. Giddy with apprehension, the big black imposing door was now in front of me; an icy chill ran down my back as the door creaked open by itself.

"Sophia, there is no turning back," said Lucien urging me forward.

Gingerly we entered into the world of the House De Vries and all of its vices. The grand clock in the hall chimed four times. The sound was deafening; each chime sank deeper into my soul. The house felt cold and strangely different.

"Where's Julian, and where is all the furniture?" I insisted.

"Upstairs in his room, Sophia," said Lucien coughing badly. "He will tell you."

Julian sat slumped over his chair; his emaciated body looked decrepit, and his face pale and grey. I began questioning my motives as to why I was here at this moment.

"Julian, I'm here. It's me, Sophia. What has happened?"

"The truth – that's what," he whispered, gasping for air.

"I don't understand."

His room was cold and sparse, with no bed, no furniture, just the chair he was sprawled over. The room looked smaller and dark; just a single candle was lit on a shelf, lighting the only portrait on the wall. The grand fireplace was no more, just empty spaces. I surveyed the room, becoming increasingly disillusioned. Despairingly, I shouted, "I need to know the truth, Julian."

The door flung wide open, and in walked Scarlet brazenly, with Lucien by her side.

"Hello, Sophia, I'm in charge now; this is my house now," she said triumphantly.

Scarlet's flaming red hair bounced with ease, defining her features. Her lips pursed as she spoke, revelling in her own success.

"Can someone please tell me what the hell is going on?" I said impatiently.

"She's blackmailing us," muttered Julian.

"Why?" I demanded.

"You haven't worked it out yet, Sophia," smirked Scarlet.

I stared vacantly at her, then towards the portrait; seeing Scarlet's fierce eyes penetrate my soul within the painting, I froze momentarily.

"Scarlet," I demanded, "how did you become the owner?"

She stood defiantly admiring her portrait, flicking her luxurious long red hair behind her back, revealing her delicate bare shoulders.

"Don't you think it has captured every essence of me?" she smirked gleefully.

"Sophia, can you not see?" said Julian, his voice now weak and his breathing laboured.

"See what? All I can see is your pathetic body riddled with guilt and shame, and as for you, Scarlet, I knew I couldn't trust you."

"You are absolutely right," said Scarlet laughing menacingly, as she walked towards me. Her presence dominated the whole room, alluding to the Lord. I shrank fearfully under her spell.

"Oh, I see. You are an offspring of the Lord," I said, repelling her words.

"Yes," she replied, gloating. "It's so good to have my brother and sister held to ransom," cackled Scarlet.

"What!" I yelled, flummoxed, turning to Lucien for answers. Shamefully, he looked the other way.

"Are you in on it as well, Lucien?"

"Yes," he muttered under his breath.

Pushing Lucien aside, Scarlet raged her resentment towards me.

"I've had to work hard to earn my keep. The Lord chose you and not me. Now you and Julian must pay the price," she shrieked, cursing me.

"Why is Lucien involved?"

"There's bigger fish to fry; he just got caught up in my trap. He is damn good in bed, but not for anything else. I've done with him now. Luka will soon fall under my spell," she yelled violently.

Julian's voice was weak and feeble. Hurriedly, I held his hand as he whispered, "Please forgive me, Sophia."

He looked small and insignificant, crumbled up in his chair. I felt nothing for him.

"What have you done to him, Scarlet?" I demanded sharply.

"I poisoned him; it was all too easy," she smirked gleefully, staring intensely at me, "but he will live. I didn't have time to finish him off completely. One more dose, that's all he needed, then you showed up," she said venomously, waving her fists at me.

"You don't scare me, and Luka will never stoop to your level."

"That's what you think; it was his doing," she replied, infuriated.

"No, I don't believe that," I retorted. "Lucien, do something, please," I begged him.

"Scarlet, enough is enough. I have done exactly what you wanted; you have the house now. Let us both go," he pleaded.

Charged energy filled the room as my heart pounded against my chest; who could I trust? I snapped angrily.

"What do you want with me, Scarlet?"

She stood by the window, drawing breath, as she opened the window and shutters, allowing daylight to flood the room. Seeing the cold light of the day, I remembered my brooch. I clasped it tightly in my clammy hands.

"Sophia, hand it over to me now!" she demanded. "It's mine."

"No!" I replied defiantly.

As the light rays caught her face, it became distorted with rage revealing the darkness within her.

"Give it to me," she roared venomously.

My power had diminished, and my grasp weakened as my jewelled cluster fell to the floor.

Instantly, Lucien raced towards Scarlet and was the first to retrieve it. Holding it firmly in his palms, light emanated from the five-pointed crystal brooch. A multitude of colours depicting red, purple, yellow, green and blue vapour trails engulfed him in the energy of white magic, giving him his power back.

"Scarlet, your reign is over; that brooch is not yours or Sophia's. It belongs to Princess Gabriella. I am under instructions that Sophia must give it back to her the night before her wedding," said Lucien assertively.

"No! It's mine," she yelled angrily.

"But, Lucien," I replied hastily. "My mother gave it to me."

Lucien stood in front of me. His charismatic charm had returned as he looked deep into my soul through his hypnotic blue eyes, beckoning me into his world. I was quickly charmed yet again by his alluring sexuality.

"But it was never hers," he replied indignantly, pushing me aside as he swaggered towards Scarlet.

"Well, it's time to say goodbye, Scarlet," said Lucien, pinning her against the open window.

My thoughts quickly returned to the vision I witnessed with Klaus.

"No, Lucien, don't do it," I pleaded, trying to stop him. "Remember your promise to me?"

"I don't make promises, Sophia, you should know that. I won't stop at anything to regain the House of De Vries, now out of my way," he replied furiously.

Swiftly, with one push, Scarlet screamed profusely as she fell through the open window, plummeting to her death with a mighty thud as she hit the cobbled street.

Chapter 37

Eerily, the grand clock chimed six times, breaking the sound of silence. Its high-pitched tone vibrated in my ears. Becoming fixated, I counted the chimes one by one, knowing time had no meaning; I was living moment by moment. Fragmented visions of images and voices played out in my mind, causing me to doubt what I had just witnessed. Hurriedly, I went downstairs and out the front door, seeing Scarlet's lifeless body splattered grotesquely on the ground as blood oozed from her head. Shockingly, I felt no sadness, just pity for her soul.

"It's OK, Sophia, you are safe; it's nearly time to come back," said the voice in the wind.

"Come back from where?" I muttered under my breath.

A gentle tap on my left shoulder brought my awareness back to the present. The enormity of what I had just witnessed engulfed me in a sea of tears. Shaking with shock, Martha firmly cradled me in her arms.

"Martha, I feel Lucien will frame me for this and for his other crimes. He has no morals, only greed, sex, and power are his vices; they feed him constantly. What can I do, Martha?"

"I've had my suspicions for a while, Scarlet enchanted Lucien, and now we will have to pay the price," she said, walking towards the lamp.

"Yes," I said, regrettably.

Martha's slender frame silhouetted against the gas lamp; she looked younger and brighter, and her face had come alive with an eagerness to help me. Her kindness shone through. Now Scarlet was dead; she was free from her spells.

"Madam, you must rest now. Lucien has to attend the wedding with you, so we have a few days to plan our escape."

Feeling drained and exhausted, I agreed gracefully.

"We have to dispose of her body; we can't just leave her there."

I was questioning myself and my motives as I ran my sweaty hands through my matted hair.

Lucien was now at the scene of his crime. He glowed with contentment, showing no remorse, as he hovered over Scarlet's battered and bruised body. Flicking his hair, grinning broadly, he then turned towards me. His sharp blue eyes beckoned me into his soul. Averting his stare, I spoke calmly.

"Well, Lucien, now what? Am I to be your next victim?"

"That depends on your loyalty. Remember, we have made an oath and sealed it with a heart engraved on the old oak tree," replied Lucien assertively.

"Yes, vaguely," I whispered softly.

"Now we can wed."

"What! No, not yet; I thought we would wait until after Gabriella's wedding." My face burned as anger rose within me. "This is not what we agreed, Lucien."

"Change of plan," he replied, mocking me. "Brothers of the order, I beckon you to us now," he bellowed.

Six hooded men in black robes appeared through the rising mist that lingered over the canal. Brooding and menacing, they gathered around us. My heart skipped a beat; no more, I pleaded under my breath.

"Not the Lord, please no, Lucien!"

"The Lord has gone, and so has the Master. Brothers of the Occult, you will answer to me now, and you must follow my orders."

"Yes," they replied, bowing their heads to their new Lord.

"Gone where?" I replied curiously.

"You don't need to know Sophia," said Lucien abruptly.

"Six of the best, I have called you here to help dispose of Scarlet's body, and at 10 pm, you will witness my marriage to Madam Sophia. Martha, please attend to her and prepare Sophia for her duty."

"Yes, sir, very well," she replied.

"We will wed here, on this exact spot. Now hurry, time is money; I have the urge and desire to feed my hunger upon your delectable body," he smirked ferociously.

Fooled yet again by his dashing good looks and charisma, compelling me back into his sexual animalistic powers.

"What about your ring?" I was mesmerised by his dazzling sapphire ring. "You promised me that would be mine."

"You may or may not have my ring," he replied flippantly. "Only time will tell if you follow my orders. A dress is ready for you in your room; it was Scarlet's."

Lucien laughed wickedly as he preened himself, adjusting his breeches. Captivated by his alluring presence, I was hooked yet again.

Hurriedly Martha and I returned to the safety of my attic room.

"Martha, I can't go through with this; my heart is yearning for Gabriella's touch and to hold her in my arms one last time."

"But you have to, madam. You have to gain his trust and his love; in return, you will be set free."

"But I don't want to become Mrs De Vries," I said in anger, stomping my feet hard against the bare floorboards.

"Then keep your name; it will be better for your safety and mine, too," replied Martha sharply.

The crimson velvet dress was laid out on my bed. Heavy-hearted, I reluctantly run my fingers over it. Scarlet's gown was bold and brash, just like she was.

"Why this gown? It reeks of Scarlet." I could smell her distinctive aroma, which lingered in the fabric.

"I was just following orders, madam. Now come, let me dress you."

"Martha, promise me you will always be faithful to me."

"Yes, always," she replied, pulling my corset tighter to fit into Scarlet's gown.

Holding my breath, I felt suffocated as the dress hugged my body tightly. I caught a glimpse of my reflection in the small mirror, barely recognising myself. My hair, now in a bun, with tiny delicate red rosebuds neatly placed around my head, complemented Scarlet's dress of lavish vulgarity. Looking like a smouldering siren, I was ready for anything. Shockingly I smirked contentedly, knowing I would soon be the sole owner of the House of De Vries.

My shoulders were bare, and my ample breasts swelled over the tight bodice; Lucien was more than a match for me. A familiar scent aroused my senses. Sniffing the air, catching a waft of patchouli, I turned to Martha.

"Why? I didn't ask for this," I scratched my head.

"But you did, madam," she replied calmly.

"Really!" I replied indignantly, sensing the room becoming smaller and hearing strange noises outside.

"Can you hear that, Martha?"

"No, madam, all I can hear is the last clang of the chiming clock. It's 10 pm, now hurry. Lucien will be waiting for you."

Strange surges of energy pulsated through my body; with that came a realisation that I had to proceed with the marriage to Lucien.

"Yes, it is time," I replied, smiling. "Lucien does bring out the sexual goddess within me; perhaps Scarlet's dress has magical powers that surrender himself to all of me," I smirked candidly.

"Madam, you are now ready; that ring you so desire will be yours," said Martha assertively.

"Yes, I believe it is destined for me," I replied, unaware of the ring's real purpose and value, which had enticed me onto this path.

"Martha," I paused momentarily.

"Yes, what it is."

"I'm not sure; it's just a feeling in the pit of my stomach. Have we done this before?"

"What, of course not, don't be silly; that's the magic of powders," said Martha, smiling gleefully and composed. Her face glowed in the candlelight, revealing the true essence of her, a woman with much strength and integrity whom I could trust. She was indeed a most loyal and courageous companion to me.

The full moon was now visible, bringing clarity of much light as its shadow shone upon the canal, dispersing the fine mist. I stared lovingly at the moon, gazing up at the Milky Way, it was so far away, yet it felt so near. The North Star glowed fiercely, witnessing all that we do. I trembled with anticipation as Lucien stood before me. Neatly groomed, his ruffled white shirt was tucked into his tight black breeches, revealing his endowment of manly sexual powers. His jacket was finely embroidered with golden tweed, which complemented his shirt. As Lucien held his hand to me, my eyes now feasted upon his dazzling sapphire ring.

"Are you ready?" said Lucien, eyeing my cleavage.

"Yes, but I have one condition: I keep my surname," I said,

staring intensely into his alluring blue eyes.

"It makes no difference to me; you will still be mine, and mine to do what pleases me," he smirked benignly. Rubbing his penis against my body, feeling his hardness, I was eager to become his wife, if only for his ring; besides, he knew how to satisfy my appetite for sexual enslavement.

"Dear brothers and sisters, please gather into a circle, and the one to marry us, reveal yourself now," commanded Lucien.

Instantly the circle grew around us as more hooded men appeared in the moonlight. Now there were twelve of them. A wave of anxiety swept through me, sending me in a spin.

I whispered to Martha, "Where did they come from?"

She didn't answer as she was transfixed, just as I was.

The moon's shadow enveloped the sky as the wind changed directions, stirring the murkiness of the canal. A Hooded Man stepped forward into the silvery moonlight, revealing his face to all; I squirmed in anguish, seeing Luka standing before me.

"No, surely you're not one of them! Why you?" I pleaded.

"It's part of your plan, Sophia. You invited me into your world, and so it is; I'm here to marry you both and to witness your oath upon the vow you took from the day you were born."

My heart raced with the sense of an inner knowing that Luka was right. Speechless, I took my place next to Lucien and silently waited for the wedding ceremony to begin. I was about to become Lucien's wife; was I prepared for what may come? Only time will tell.

Chapter 38

Lucien snapped his fingers impatiently. He seemed agitated as he scanned the brotherhood, smoothing his shirt as the wind teased his ruffles.

"Luka, please proceed with the ceremony now!"

"Yes, sir," he replied, looking directly at me.

"I cast a circle of light around you both. Dark and light come together to meet as one. Two souls are divinely different but share the same path. The vows you took many years ago are here before you. Lucien, you speak first," he said, handing him a scroll neatly bound with red twine.

As I stood before Lucien, my whole body started to tremble. His captivating blue eyes caused a shiver within, then instantly it went, and all I could see was the good in Lucien.

"Sophia, I vow to desire your womanly body every day, to be with you in every sense. You are mine, and I am yours. Together we reign through the veils of light and dark," spoke Lucien attentively.

"Sophia, please say your vows," said Luka handing me my scroll bound in green twine.

"I, Sophia, will willingly be your husband, to devour you in your sexual pleasures. I honour the man in you, and I will be the light in your darkness."

The light of the moon beamed upon us, bringing a surge of sexual energy that was highly charged; it was tangible, toxic and yet very addictive. I was utterly spellbound.

"I now pronounce you both man and wife," declared Luka. "It is now time to seal your wedding with the ring of sovereignty."

I gasped in awe at its beauty; breathtaking, it was so utterly exquisite. Staring intently at the sapphire blueness of the gemstone, it was now firmly on my wedding finger, seducing me into its world of mystical powers.

"Now seal your marriage with a kiss," said Luka.

Lucien tightly held me in his arms as my heart thumped noisily against my chest. Our lips met again, sending waves of euphoric energy throughout my body. The fire was lit with a burning desire for deep penetrative sex of wild abandonment.

The brotherhood had now dispersed. Alone we stood, captivated by his charm; I was eager to please him and to satisfy myself. Grabbing Lucien's hands, placing them under my gown, and feeling his gentle touch rub up and down my thighs, I sighed heavily, wanting him right now.

"Sophia, all in good time," he replied, teasing me with his tongue whilst nibbling on my ear.

Catching a waft of patchouli oil, I instantly remembered a life that was me, but I looked so different, bringing me back from the realms of dishonour.

"Lucien, where did Luka go?"

"What? Sophia, you must have been seeing things again; he left a while ago. Don't you remember?"

"No!" I replied indignantly, "but he married us."

"Oh, Sophia, that's what you wanted to see."

My hair now free from the tight bun, I ran my fingers through my mane whilst annoyance grew within; yet again, I was fooled by the trickery of my mind.

"But I saw him, Lucien," I replied defiantly.

"I can assure you that it was the Master that married us," replied Lucien.

Flabbergasted, I hung my head in shame. "How can this be so?" I enquired nervously.

"It is irrelevant; remember, the Master has many faces. Now come Sophia, it is time to seal our marriage with your body that is now mine. I'm all yours, feel me, my dear, look how hard you make me," said Lucien charged with testosterone, placing my left hand on his erection, arousing my womanly powers. The sapphire ring had awoken the sexual goddess within me.

The road we tread is not always easy; we travel to make peace with ourselves through timelines of history. Standing by the formidable black front door, I was about to enter the House of De Vries, this time as Lucien's wife. Hand in hand, I walked eagerly into his web and into his reality.

The door closed quickly behind us as the grand clock in the hallway struck midnight. Flickering candlelit guided us to the master bedroom. The luxurious four-poster bed dominated the room. With red satin sheets and drapes to match, it beckoned us to grace our bodies under the moonlight that danced through the small, grated window. Its shadow side was visible to my eyes. Tension arose between us as frenzied sexual chemistry simmered until we could not refrain from ourselves. I was ripe for his hardness; lustfully, we sealed our marriage, riding the waves of pure unadulterated sex. We purged and rocked to the natural rhythm of our desires, bringing us to a climatic end of sexual gratification with each other. The lost spirit of the asp was alive once more. Now entwined in its grasp, it slithered slowly between us, locking us with its power and strength.

Exhausted, we slept heavily in the moonlit room until the first signs of dawn. Awaking first, I lay still, staring at the ceiling with intricate carvings emphasising the room's height. Daylight projected over my sapphire ring, dazzling with radiance; it glowed magnificently as fractions of blue light bounced around the room. Its majestic energy captivated me, awakening my magical powers; I smiled warmly as my heart fluttered, knowing this ring was my future.

"Sophia, it's nearly time to come back," said a faint whisper in the air.

"But from where?" I murmured. "I'm here."

"But you're not Sophia; the clock is ticking," said the voice.

Closing my eyes tightly, then opening them quickly. Lucien was still lying next to me, I felt the warmth of his body next to mine; I sighed heavily. Strange tingling sensations swept through my body as waves of pulsating calming energy covered me from head to toe. My gemstone of wealth and beauty gave me so much joy. I stared lovingly into its power, rubbing my hands excitingly as Lucien roused. His shoulder-length black hair, now untamed, highlighted his features, causing me to explore his body again. He looked incredibly sexy in a devilish manner that was so enticing and alluring. I was ready for his touch, pulling the red satin sheet from me, revealing my nakedness; I let my body do the talking.

"Morning, wife," he smiled, placing his hand between my thighs.

Our passion soon ignited, fuelled by the powerful energy of my sapphire ring. We indulged in our desires of eroticism; I tasted his juices. I begged him for more as our bodies entwined with the energy of the asp. Becoming as one, I was caught in the moment of light and dark; there was no going back, only moving forward in time was my salvation.

A loud knock on the door interrupted our rhythm; frustrated, we both shouted, "Go away!"

"But sir, you are both needed," shouted Martha through the door.

"By who?" replied Lucien.

"He didn't say, but he's wearing the royal seal of Prince Lavin," replied Martha.

Lucien teased my hair from my eyes, looking intently at me; his crystal blue eyes matched the intensity of my gemstone. I instantly knew there was more to come.

"It's OK; please tell him to enter our room."

"Lucien, who is it?"

He smiled charmingly. "He is your wedding gift, my dear Sophia."

A tall masculine man entered our room. His neatly tied, fair hair was immaculately groomed. His beige breeches were fitted snuggly around his manly features. His torso was loosely covered in a red, golden, tweed jacket, revealing his masculine physique.

"My dear wife, this is Carlos, Prince Lavin's private valet; he has come to assist us," he smirked cheekily.

"Carlos, please do join us," said Lucien patting the bed.

Carlos didn't hesitate. He quickly stripped before me; his rippling, toned muscles oozed his sexuality. I was eager for him to indulge in our fantasies. I drooled in anticipation.

"Madam, let me take you to a place of wildness," said Carlos, masterfully pulling my legs out wide.

His warm tongue was soon upon me, licking me ferociously, bringing me to a climatic end as I clung to the bedsheets in the ecstasy of heightened awareness whilst Lucien took him from behind. Our bodies merged with the heady scent of intoxicating powders; it was intense yet compelling. Delirious, I became increasingly aware of a woman's voice calling me.

"Sophia, not long now," she said.

Carlos interrupted my thoughts with loud shrieks as he reached his point of no return. I sighed delightedly with contentment as he climaxed deep within me. Burying his head on my chest, he whispered, "Sophia, don't let your ring out of sight. Princess Gabriella wishes it to be hers and will quickly turn on you with jealously."

"No, surely not," I whispered to him, seeing Gabriella in my mind. Her golden flaxen hair flowed gracefully around her bare shoulders. I held my ring tightly, not wanting to hear any more.

"We rest until noon, then prepare for our journey with Carlos. We leave at midnight," said Lucien. "The royal wedding is fast approaching."

A surge of bright light mysteriously appeared in the room, causing illusions within my mind, waking me from my inertia. Momentarily, I was somewhere else.

Chapter 39

As I drifted off to sleep, light and darkness constantly flickered, changing energy moment by moment, a strange presence loomed over me. Tick-tock constantly repeated in my mind, hypnotising me into an altered state, as I danced through the veils of my most intimate thoughts and into the depths of darkness. Lucien and Carlos were now deeply embedded into my dreams of erotica. I slept well, content with my acquisitions, knowing this was the beginning of the end of Lucien. The ring of wealth was now in my possession; no one could stop me, not even Princess Gabriella, whom I loved deeply.

"Sophia, hurry now," said Martha, gently waking me.

Her kind face hovered over me, bringing me back from my dreams. She looked serene, with her dark-brown hair swept from her face. Martha seemed taller, elegantly dressed in a dark-blue tight satin gown. I smiled warmly at her.

"My dear Martha, you are my constant companion. Are you coming to Paris with me?"

"I'm afraid not, madam. I have been instructed to stay here to look after Julian and to oversee the house until you return safely."

"Oh, but I need you with me," I pleaded, despising Julian, annoyed that he still lived and I must endure his loathsome pathetic hold over me.

"I know, but I must follow orders," she replied hesitantly.

"Whose orders?"

"The Lord, madam"

"But he's gone!" I replied, alarmed.

"He will only be gone when you return," she replied with authority. "Now, hurry and dress. The carriage leaves at midnight. Lucien and Carlos are downstairs in the lobby waiting for you. Remember, you can outwit Lucien."

"Yes," I replied, remembering I had many questions that needed answering, but time was not on my side. The menacing sound of tick-tock grew louder in my thoughts, and the smell of opium hung in the air. Light-headed, I stood at the full-length mirror. It was beautifully framed in golden leaf; I was seeing different reflections of myself. Confused, I took another look, rubbing my eyes to gain clarity, but still, my vision was muddled.

"Everything will become clearer, madam, I promise you. Now drink some liquor, and I will help you to dress."

"Thank you, Martha."

Now I was dressed in a fine delicate gown made of satin and lace, decorated with intricate stitching on the bodice was the royal seal of Prince Lavin. Blue ribbons were placed in my long brown hair, and a royal-blue velvet hooded cape was tied securely around my neck. I was now ready to be the lady in waiting for my beloved Gabriella. Opening the door to the outside world, leaving the House of De Vries behind, I turned to Martha taking my seat on the carriage with Lucien and Carlos.

"Martha, promise me you will be here on my return."

"Of course, madam," she replied fondly.

The royal carriage swept me further along my path. Sitting beside Lucien and Carlos, I rubbed my ring for comfort, knowing I would soon be with my dearest. My brooch was now in the possession of Lucien, and I was instructed that he must witness me returning it to Gabriella. Looking back towards the house along the canal, I felt nothing; was it just a distant memory? Then I remembered why I was here, as my sapphire ring glowed deliciously. I smiled with contentment as the horses gathered speed, galloping through the streets of Amsterdam and out to the valleys and beyond.

"Dear Sophia, you look happy. My wedding present did you a power of good," said Lucien.

"Yes, my dear husband, thank you. You will receive your wedding gift in Paris," I replied candidly.

"I shall look forward to that," he replied. "Please tell me more," he pleaded, staring intently at me. His eyes were as bright as my sapphire, captivating me into his world of dark rituals.

"You will have to wait, Lucien, but rest assured you will enjoy every moment," I replied wistfully.

"I'm sure I will," laughed Lucien, running his hands through his dark mane.

"What about me?" said Carlos mockingly.

"Well, we are journeying together, so anything can happen," I said lustfully.

Night and day merged as one; time passed slowly as we approached our destination. In between our sexual entanglement, I had time to review my life, vowing that I would do the right thing this time. Sleep became erratic with vivid dreams of the asp. It haunted me during the days we travelled. Relief came when we stopped to refresh and sleep in a nearby inn, fuelled with ale; it was a welcome reprise from the small interior of the carriage. A warm comfy bed enticed us to explore dangerous sexual acts between the three of us. This made the days more bearable, and soon we were over the borders of Belgium and into France.

My heart fluttered as we approached the Grand Palace, recalling Gabriella's shapely body as we shared our love for each other. It was the day before the royal wedding, and I hoped we could spend one last night together before she was married. Her touch was so sensual and yet so comforting that I blushed profusely.

"Are you OK, Sophia?" said Lucien seeing my redness as we turned into the vastness of the royal courtyard.

"Why, yes, of course, I am," I replied, staring out of the carriage and seeing rows upon rows of neatly flowered beds.

It was late September, and the morning sun danced through the clouds, bringing much depth to the glorious array of the many sweet-scented roses and gardenias. Their fragrant perfume instantly reminded me of Gabriella. Overcome with emotion, I yearned to see her, and there she was, sitting by the ornamental lake. She looked serene and beautiful; her golden wavy hair hung seductively around her shoulders. At last, our carriage halted, and I quickly alighted, eager to greet her.

"Not so fast," shouted Lucien. "Remember, you are my wife, so please act accordingly. You will see her this evening."

"But surely I can say hello?" I inquired, disgruntled by his command.

"Yes, but only to give her the brooch," he said, reaching into his lapel.

"Here, take it, Sophia; I have to witness this at the request of Prince Lavin."

"Very well, walk with me, husband."

A soft breeze rustled the trees, and with a chill in the air, autumn had come early. Golden red leaves scattered our path as we walked hand in hand through the courtyard towards the lake of many fountains. I smiled joyfully, seeing Gabriella's soft hazel eyes looking directly into my soul; I was utterly smitten by her beauty and allure.

"Hello Princess Gabriella, I have returned as promised with Lucien, now my husband, to give you the brooch. I believe it belongs to you," I said, holding it towards her. Magnetic energy glowed from the coloured gemstones that decorated the five-pointed star as our hands gently touched.

"Thank you, it was my mother's, stolen by Madam Genevieve, your mother!" she said assertively. "Lucien, please leave us. I wish to speak with your wife; I won't keep her for long."

"Very well, your Princess," said Lucien begrudgingly.

"Sophia, remember my wedding gift," he called out as he marched towards the palace, huffing and puffing.

Alone, we finally hugged tightly, neither wanting to let go. Gabriella's sweet scent was reminiscent of our last embrace, bewitching me with her captivating beauty. A nightingale flew around us; it perched high on a tree, perfectly timed and in tune with our love song.

"Please, Sophia, do you have any news about my Philip?" asked Gabriella, her eyes starting to swell with tears.

"We did find him, but Luka and I were too late; he had already been enticed by the Lord. Luka is still searching for him. Please don't cry, my beautiful Princess." I kissed her tears away.

"I have kept you long enough; Lucien will be waiting for you," she said, pushing me away promptly.

"Come to my private room this evening; I have a proposition for you."

"Yes," I replied eagerly.

The Grand Palace silhouetted proudly against the backdrop of extensive gardens; I walked alone, unsure if I could trust Gabriella. The warning words of Carlos ricocheted in my thoughts. I glanced at my ring, as my stomach tightened. Disturbed, I turned around to see Gabriella, but she had vanished amongst the plumage of tall purple delphiniums; she blended effortlessly amongst the flowers. Heavy-hearted, I entered the main lobby. It was just as I remembered it, light and airy. The late summer sun shone through the giant windows giving life to the marbled statues gracing the vestibule. The fine art of erotic sensual images aroused my curiosity. Was I just a bystander? Or was I really here? Pausing at a portrait of Princess Gabriella, I was stunned to see she was wearing a sapphire ring precisely like mine.

"Madam Sophia, let me escort you," said Carlos opening the door to a magnificent, lavishly furnished drawing room. The walls were whitewashed with golden panelling giving an illusion of grandeur. Soft brown rugs brought warmth to the room of many chairs. A brightly red chaise longue trimmed with golden tassels caught my attention.

"Thank you, Carlos. Where is Lucien?"

"He's out riding with the Prince, madam. Wait here, and please take a seat; I have something to show you," he said, reaching into his tunic pocket and producing a letter.

"You had better read this, madam. It's concerning the Princess."

Raged engulfed me as I read the wording stating that she and Lucien were the main instigators of selling and stealing babies to feed the Lord's wealth and theirs. Disgusted, I threw the letter back at him. Torn between her deceitful ways, my heart could not accept the truth as my body ached for her touch. Tonight, we will spend our last night together and embrace each other passionately; this time, Lucien will be joining us! Threesome for the truth or behold them both. My sapphire ring glowed benevolently; feeling its power, my strength had returned. I smiled in anticipation. A new royal seal will be set on the eve of the wedding, sealing our fate before the sun rises tomorrow!

Chapter 40

The night of festivities had begun. Concealing my news, I entered the grand ballroom with Lucien by my side. Bright golden ornaments graced themselves upon the delicately carved walnut cabinets. Their reflection in the mirrors distorted my view. Lucien quickly left my side, seeking solace in the many potent powders readily available. A faint smell of patchouli caught me by surprise as I scanned the many dignitaries that had arrived for the wedding. The Hooded Man was there amongst the crowds. Intrigued, I started to follow him. I soon lost sight of him through the midst of the masses, but his scent lingered in the air. Who was he?

"Madam, it's me, Luka. You seem lost, my dear." I felt a tap on my shoulder.

"Yes, I am, Luka, but so relieved to see you."

Luka's presence gave me strength; his sharp features and expressive eyes were always a pleasure to see. He wore red velvet breeches up to his knees with a matching waistcoat and tunic. He looked elegant and defined, his black court shoes clipped on the polished wooden floor as he walked with me to the dance floor.

"May I have the pleasure?"

"Yes," I replied.

The ballroom was now alive and vibrant as the music began to play; it lifted me to another place, taking me away from my thoughts of revenge. The headiness of wealth oozed into every corner. My sapphire ring magnified the enormity of the moment and was admired by many. Countesses dressed in their finery, revealing their shapely figures with tightly fitted ball gowns of many colours. Men of gentry connected with Prince Lavin guarded the Prince and the Princess as they took centre stage in the ballroom. The Princess's golden silk gown shimmered as she danced, catching rainbows of light from the crystal chandeliers that hung high upon the ceiling. Spellbinding, her beauty personified her. Gabriella's sensuality and charismatic personality had captured my heart; it was all too easy to forgive her deceitful ways. Our night of passion was soon approaching, and I was ready for anything.

"Luka, please excuse me; I feel a little faint."

"Yes, of course, you do look rather pale; let me fetch you some liquor," said Luka smiling fondly at me. "Then I must take my leave, to carry on with my search for Philip."

"Oh, so soon; please stay a bit longer," I pleaded, disheartened.

"I will not rest until I've found him; I have to pay for my undoing, and so do you. One day our paths will cross again, but for now, we have to go our separate ways."

Reluctantly I agreed, watching him disappear amongst the gathering of dancers, with their vibrant lavish garments, eager to flirt their wealth in gay abandonment. I had grown rather attached to Luka; his kindness softened my heart. Seeing him walk away made me question everything. My attention quickly turned to Gabriella as she danced seductively with Lucien; resentment mounted within me. Cursing them, I bit my lips hard.

My thoughts grew muddled as the music got louder. My internal clock ticked ferociously. Tick-tock, the clock is ticking, Sophia, said the voice in my head. Finding a nearby seat, I sat, deep in thought, plotting my next move.

The room was filled with many rich colours, exquisite and elaborate, rare tapestries hung on the walls, bringing much warmth to the palace's grandeur. This is where I belonged, with Gabriella by my side, not with Lucien. Sadness pained my heart. Crestfallen, I gazed at the sparkling crystal chandeliers. A moment of truth swept through me; instantly, I knew what had to be done. A brief encounter is all it is, and games we must play to remind us of who we truly are.

"Ah, there you are, Sophia," said Lucien. "Take this. It will help you." He handed me a golden snuffbox with the royal seal embossed upon the lid.

Breathing in the magical medicinal powders, normality swept through me; all thoughts of revenge had dissipated. Reasoning with myself, I asked for more powders, of which Lucien eagerly obliged. Rays of coloured lights flickered before my eyes as the room swayed back and forth.

"Come, Lucien, let's dance, dear husband!"

"Yes, my dear wife, I'm all yours," he said, pulling me closer to his chest.

His bewitching eyes caught me off guard, seducing me with his charm. Secretly, I adored his flamboyant, arrogant sexuality. He was not afraid to explore the dark side of sex, and neither was I. My master plan was coming together; I smiled inwardly as we danced intimately. As the music played, courtiers gathered around Gabriella, tending to her needs; I was desperate to be with her, but Lucien held me close.

"Sophia, it's never too late to change," said a voice in the wind.

"Who are you?" I inquired nervously.

"The Hooded Man," was his answer. "Don't turn around; just listen. Tonight you must decide which path to take; only you know the right one you must follow. Your time is nearly up."

"What do you mean by that?"

"The clock is ticking, tick-tock," he replied menacingly.

Impulsively, I turned to face him, but he was nowhere to be seen, just the grandeur and opulence of the ballroom in full swing; it was loud and raucous.

"Lucien, did you see him?" I enquired anxiously.

"See who?" he replied flippantly.

"The Hooded Man."

"Oh Sophia, those powders are giving you illusions," he laughed, teasing my hair with his left hand whilst his right hand rubbed my inner thigh. "I shall be waiting for my wedding gift later. Together, we can build our own reality," he smirked wickedly.

Flummoxed and bewildered, I stumbled across the ballroom as the music intensified with a high-pitched frequency. Wincing in pain, my vision began to blur, and the room looked smaller. With Lucien by my side, he guided me to the seating area tucked out of sight from the mayhem of the festivities.

"Sit," he demanded, "wait here. I will fetch Gabriella; she will show you what needs to be done."

I watched him fade into obscurity within the energies of the room. Tangible and fragmented layers started to form around me. One by one, they melted into another; each layer took me further away from my reality. I closed my eyes as the light was bright, seeing strange images and places of the world I had never seen before. Giant structures gravitated high in the sky; they loomed over me, engulfing me in the realms of darkness, where the Lord receded in my deepest thoughts. "Sophia, Sophia, Sophia," spoke the Lord's menacing voice, waking me from my tormented dreams.

"Sophia, wake up; it's me, Gabriella. I have been waiting for you."

Gabriella's golden hair cascaded around her soft, delicate features; she looked magnificent and radiant. Her hazel eyes were pools of liquid light, inviting me into her sanctuary of womanly love. My heart melted. Besotted by her beauty, I stared deeply into her soul, enthralled by her enticing feminine energy. Forgetting my promise to myself, I longed to be in her bed again, feeling her exquisite tender touch as she pleasured me.

"Sophia, my dear, it's time; the men are full of liquor and powders. Prince Lavin will be busy for a few hours," she said, touching my cheek with her delicate hands.

I breathed excitedly, sniffing her seductive perfume.

"What about Lucien? He is expecting to join us."

"Yes, I know, and I have agreed, only if he keeps his promise," she replied.

More questions flooded my thoughts, but I was sharply interrupted.

"Sophia, we need to go now to my private chambers whilst we can," said Gabriella softly.

"Yes," I agreed eagerly, holding her hand as she steered me towards her private room. The sultry evening was only just beginning. We walked silently through the many corridors of the palace, knowing this would be our final liaison of crime and passion.

Chapter 41

As I followed Gabriella through her sumptuous palace, I was reminded of my plight to regain my power. Her golden wavy hair swung, with the rhythmic sound of tick-tick repetitively playing out in my mind. At last, the ballroom music eased as we turned a corner and entered the grand hall that led to her private chambers. It was barely lit, cold, dark and dismal; I shivered uncontrollably. An uneasy feeling gained momentum as I quickly walked with her. My mouth became dry with each footstep; I gagged profusely with the smell of excrement mixed with the corpses of many rats.

"What is it?" asked Gabriella.

"I don't recall this."

"You won't," she snapped nastily.

Perturbed, I scanned the hall, spotting grand paintings of dark satanic rituals. I gasped, horrified, staring at the one in front of me. It mirrored my encounter with the Lord!

"I don't know why you are so shocked," said Gabriella, looking annoyed and rather bored with me. "You loved it! Didn't you, Sophia! I recall our encounter with the Lord; you embraced it all," she mocked.

Flabbergasted, I turned to run as the overriding energy of malice unnerved me.

"My dear Sophia, you want me, and I want you."

"Yes, I do!" I replied quietly.

"Then ask no more questions; just follow me, but first, let me taste your succulent lips."

Gabriella drew me in with her enticing presence; her delicate shoulders were soft to the touch. Our lips met hungrily as she bit into my insecurity; my needs were more significant than the fear.

"Come this way," she ordered. "My private suite is just around the corner through the library, remember that?"

"Yes, of course," I replied flippantly.

A light glowed in the distance, guiding us towards the library. My heart flinched painfully as I stood amongst the many rows of ancient books and artefacts. Neatly stacked ceiling to the floor, I felt small and insignificant as the room encroached around me. Strange sensations surged through my body; I was lost in the sea of endless books and an object of desire that caught my attention. A golden jewelled crystallised oval jug stood out prominently in a glass cabinet. It gleamed magnificently of wealth and power. Mesmerised by its artistry and elegance, my eyes were drawn to its delicate handle. Encrusted in diamonds depicting a naked woman, it instantly captured my imagination.

"Gabriella, where did you obtain this fine vase from?" I inquired.

"My dear Sophia, it is my wedding gift from Prince Lavin. It is so divine, don't you agree?"

"Yes," I replied, staring at the precious vase as it evoked a strong memory from a distant past, one that I could not comprehend.

Gabriella's eyes sparkled wickedly as she pulled a book from a shelf, revealing a concealed lever; she pulled it hard, opening a secret panel leading towards her private chambers.

"We don't have long, Sophia, before Lucien joins us," she said, undressing me with her eyes.

Gabriella's room was a feast for the eyes. It was rich in colour with deep velvet curtains dressing the small stained-glass windows. Candles flickered brightly, radiating a sense of warmth to the room. Gabriella's scent was intoxicating and evocative as I breathed her heavenly bouquet, beckoning me into her world. Muted red tapestries hung seductively with images of sexual fantasies, whilst the portraits of the Princess brought her powerful energy into the room.

"Come to me, Sophia," she whispered longingly, pulling me to her sumptuous four-poster bed.

We kissed deeply and passionately whilst undressing each other. Lying naked together on the bed, our feminine bodies danced together as the explosive sexual tension escalated. Gabriella's beautiful hourglass body rippled as I gently caressed her with sensuous kisses. She murmured contentedly as my moist fingers penetrated her swollen labia. In return, my appetite for her womanly touch intensified the moment. Heat rose between us as she climaxed upon my fingers;

clinging to the bed, Gabriella writhed in ecstasy.

"Now it's your turn, Sophia," said Gabriella straddling me and then tying my wrists to the bed with two delicate white silk scarves, my head propped up by pillows. Now powerless to resist, I succumbed to Gabriella's advances.

"This is your time for pleasure," she murmured softly as our tongues met, seducing me completely. I was utterly enthralled by her erotic sensuality.

I looked lovingly at her. Gabriella's long cascading blonde hair brushed my face as she licked my breasts tenderly. Euphoria swept through me in waves of endless sexual pleasure. Catching our reflection upon a mirror hanging high on the ceiling above the bed, I became sharply aware of a sinister energy that quickly engulfed us in a fog of toxicity. Distracted, I watched intently as she parted my legs and tasted my sweet juices. Engorged by fantasy, I begged her for more.

"So you want more?"

"Yes, please," I replied lustfully.

"Well, Lucien will be here shortly," she said, producing a whip from under the bed.

Toying with the tassel, she teasingly flicked it over my body, seducing me with her bewitching powers; I was eager to please her sexual fantasies.

"Harder!" I shouted as Lucien entered Gabriella's private bedchamber.

"Well, wife, I see you are ready for me. Gabriella has been busy," he laughed candidly, smoothing his dark hair from his eyes and quickly pulling his breeches off. "I have been watching you both through a peephole in the library," said Lucien triumphantly.

He stood by the edge of the bed with his hand firmly around his stiff erection. I glared jealously as Gabriella engulfed his penis in her mouth. With my hands still tied to the bed, yet stirred by passion, I was forced to watch but not be part of their climax.

"Stop!" I shouted. "You've both gone too far! Lucien, remember, I am your wife."

Lucien looked arrogantly at me. His penetrating blue eyes bored deeply into mine, revealing the dark side of his soul. He was high on powders, fuelled by adrenalin; his energy was immense and extremely powerful.

"Please untie me," I pleaded fearfully to Lucien.

"Not until I have finished with you. Gabriella, you know what you have to do."

"Yes," she replied as she struck me repeatedly with the whip before she fed me a potent cocktail of opium and powders. Blackness came swiftly as my eyes grew heavy, inducing me into a deep sleep.

Hours later, I awoke alone, desperately trying to sit up but still tied to the bed. Frustrated, praying for the morning, I lay motionless, listening for sounds, but all was quiet and dark.

"Sophia, come back from where you are," said a female voice in the wind.

"Who are you?" I asked nervously.

"You will remember soon, but you are in charge of your destiny," replied the calming voice.

I sank deeper into the bed, not knowing where I was and who I was. As the night faded into daylight, I found the strength to wriggle free from the scarves. Rubbing my sore wrists, I crunched my fingers, noticing my ring was gone. I sat on the edge of the bed, distraught, trying to remember how I got here.

"Sophia, where are Lucien and Gabriella? You must retrieve the ring," said the voice in the air.

"Gone," I murmured as vivid memories flooded my vision, and my anger festered violently. Quickly dressing, I searched the room for a weapon. Finding a small, loaded pistol tucked inside a drawer, I left the room, determined to take my revenge.

The palace felt different; the facade of wealth was still visible to the naked eye, but the beauty had vanished. Tainted with noxious energy, it was deathly quiet and cold. Dark, satanic energy had engulfed the once-grand palace. Apprehensively, I entered the courtyard towards the stables, finding Lucien and Gabriella in deep conversation. Keeping well hidden, I listened intently as they gloated about their wealth and conquests. Rage quickly engulfed me; reaching for the pistol, I stumbled on uneven ground and was seen.

"So you think you can escape us?" said Gabriella sternly. She stood glaring at me; her soft hazel eyes were now venomous with hatred, and her beauty dispersed under the disguise of greed.

"Lucien, take the ring and keep it safe. I will follow you after I have put an end to Sophia," she demanded as she reluctantly handed him my sapphire ring.

"Very well, my love, I will meet you back in Amsterdam, and leave a message on the old oak tree near the House of De Vries," he replied swiftly as he departed on his horse.

Gabriella then furiously flew at me, pushing me to the ground as she placed another silk scarf tightly around my neck. Breathless, I was in peril; my life swung in the balance. Fuelled by panic, I was not yet ready to die. Somehow, I reached the pistol. Pulling the trigger, it fired a bullet directly into Gabriella's chest. I watched the Princess crumble and die before my eyes as dark crimson blood gushed from her heart, leaving a pool of gore seeping through her gown. A cold icy wind ruffled my bedraggled hair as I stood over her lifeless body. The Princess had met her maker. I turned to run, leaving no sign that I was the killer of Princess Gabriella.

"Not so fast!" shouted Lucien, hiding out of view. "You are not going anywhere. I witnessed it all, Sophia."

"But you had gone; I saw you ride away."

"That's what you thought; I could never leave Gabriella. I loved her, and you killed her. Now I must do the same to you," he roared violently.

Trembling, I tried to run, but I slipped and fell upon the slime of the cobbled courtyard. I waited fearfully for my end.

"You will wait," he sneered, gloating at my downfall. "Never fear, I will have my revenge on you," shouted Lucien. "But I have the ring; that's all I need now."

I sighed with relief, pulling the tight scarf from my neck, revealing deep scars of pink from the silk material. Devoid of all emotion, I had taken the oath. The Lord's words were deeply etched into my mind. Feeling cold, I shivered uncontrollably as the early morning sun shone, witnessing my crime. I limped painfully to a place to rest, my ankle, now sore and swollen after my fall.

"Oh Sophia, oh Sophia, I'm still here," taunted Lucien marching through the courtyard towards me.

Rage engulfed him in a fury of malevolence; his blue eyes

dimmed to a menacing grey. The man I adored was just an illusion within my mind. At last, I had woken up to his dark, evil ways.

"Lucien!" I shouted. "I have done as instructed. In return, I beg of you my safe passage to freedom."

"No," he replied sternly. "You have to pay for what you have done!"

"But I was promised by the Lord."

"You only answer to me, wife," he roared, belittling me.

"No," I cried out. "Never, then I will take you down with me. I know your secret, Lucien; I have done for years. You will swing for murder!"

"Oh, will I," he replied venomously, walking towards me, "but not before I get my hands on you!" he roared.

With the pistol still in my hand, I fired a single bullet. Lucien's body slumped to the ground. Rubbing my fingerprints from the weapon with the scarf, I placed it into Lucien's hand, then retrieved my sapphire ring from his pocket. Quietly, I slid away into obscurity until it was safe for me to return to the House of De Vries. With only the sound of a woman's voice in the wind for comfort guiding me safely home, I was a fugitive running away from murder.

Chapter 42

My path back to freedom was fraught with many dangers. Clinging to life, I walked amongst the perils of crime. Going forward was my only hope, night and day; I trekked, for many months, tirelessly trying to forget my crime. My feet were red and sore, with blisters from my torn and tattered ill-fitting shoes. Every step took me further away from my past. Out of sight, blending effortlessly within the masses, I forged my way through the darkness that had engulfed me; every muscle in my body ached. I was exhausted, longing for warmth and love from Martha. I had to find my way back to the House of De Vries, but how? Finding a deserted hut, I took shelter from the prevailing wind. Hearing a familiar voice outside, I hid in the shadows of the night.

"Sophia, I know you are there; I am here to help you," he said calmly.

A strong aroma of patchouli hit my senses, lifting my spirit. I asked, "Is that you, Hooded Man?"

"Yes, my dear, come out of hiding; I need to take you back now; your time is nearly up," he replied assertively.

"The clock is ticking. Tick-tock! Sophia."

Emerging from the shelter, reluctantly, I accepted his offer of help.

"Who are you?" I inquired.

"One day in the future, you will know who I am, but for now, I cannot reveal myself to you," he urged, ushering me quickly into the safety of his carriage.

His hood concealed his identity, but I did not fear him. He was the voice of reason that I had come to trust. His brown-clothed gown cloaked him in a veil of mystery. I warmed myself next to him with the heavy scent of patchouli soothing my body.

"Sophia, do you have the ring?" he enquired.

"Yes," I replied, removing my dirty, threadbare glove.

"Good," he replied, "now hold on tightly."

As he held my hand, light emanated from our grasp. It constantly flickered as sharp bursts of pulsating energy spun furiously around the carriage, engulfing us in a golden glow. The horses gathered speed as lightning flashed before our eyes. A rush of adrenalin swept through my body, seeing timelines merging into each other. Light and dark blended as we raced through the night, chasing the stars back to the house that was my home. Time was irrelevant as I became an observer of myself. Drifting in and out of consciousness through the veils of life and death, seeing a vision of a smartly dressed woman, not the attire I was accustomed to. Her brown hair was neatly tied into a bun, and her dazzling blue eyes were reminiscent of Lucien's. She spoke softly to me in my subconscious whilst I journeyed with the Hooded Man through the many layers of time.

"Sophia, it's time to make amends; you know what you have to do," she constantly whispered in my mind.

Her words echoed my thoughts as we hastily sped from one reality to another, converging as one. Lucid memories from a distant life continually played out in my mind, consuming me with denial of the truth. They were strange and yet recognisable.

Eventually, we arrived at my destination. The House of De Vries stood out among the rest. With its gable ends protruding over the canal, I walked reluctantly to the imposing front door. Morning light filtered the skyline as daybreak broke. A passing crow swooped low, causing me to flinch.

"I can't go in yet. Please take me to the paddock where the old oak tree is," I begged the Hooded Man.

"Yes, but then I must leave you. It will be up to you to do the right thing."

Puzzling questions that I wanted answers to filled my mind, but I could not unravel my scattered thoughts. Tormented, my head ached, I so longed for inner peace.

The old oak tree stood tall and firm, with long deep roots sprouting outwards into the undergrowth. Walking around it, I felt the tree's energy gently comforting me. Dewdrops glistened on the grass verge as I ran my hands around the tree. The engraved heart was still there; my heart skipped a beat, seeing the carving which sealed my fate.

"I must now leave you, Sophia," said the Hooded Man. "Just rest for a while, then you must return to the house and hide your ring in your room. There is a secret panel under your bed. You will find a small box, place it there, and don't tell anyone that it's there, not even Martha. This is paramount for your future. Do you understand, Sophia?"

"Yes, I think so," I replied as he swiftly departed, leaving me alone by the tree.

The morning sun warmed my body as I rested under the branches of the old oak tree. Listening to the birds; a robin sang sweetly, lulling me into a restful sleep. I awoke abruptly as the sun beamed upon me, knowing it was time to return to the house. Silently I made my way along the canal path towards the House of De Vries. Apprehensively approaching the building, it glowed eerily, casting menacing shadows upon the canal. The big ominous black door was now in front of me; anxiety engulfed me, not wanting to enter, shivering uncontrollably as I reached for the brass doorknob. Courageously, I knocked hard as the delicate hazy light enshrouded the house, encapsulating me in time and space. I watched nervously as sinister energy spun up my arm. I gasped, horrified, seeing my hand and fingers change dramatically, becoming old and withered. I stared in disbelief as my sapphire ring hung loosely around my crinkled finger.

"Hello, Sophia. We have been expecting you! What took so much time?" asked Julian, eyeing my ring. "I knew you would return with it; now give it to me!" he demanded, pulling me into the house.

"No, let me have one more night with it. I promise you, it will be yours in the morning, dear brother."

"Very well, Sophia, you can play your silly games with me for one last night," he replied flippantly. "I've waited a long time for you to return. Where have you been?"

I stood apprehensively in the dark hallway, with its familiar smell of decay. Anxiety riddled me as Julian demanded answers. His emaciated body towered over me. Looking frail and gaunt, he clung to the wall for support whilst his other hand held his baggy breeches up. His brown leather belt hung freely around his thin waist; I flinched uncontrollably as violent images clouded my thoughts.

"You know where I have been, Julian; I've only been away a few months," I said, gawping at the old man before me.

"Scarlet's poison has really aged you," I said, perturbed.

"Sophia, that was years ago."

"What?" I yelled, not wanting to hear the truth.

"Yes, it was. Oh dear, I see you are not of sound mind. Come into the parlour; Martha is longing to see you."

Complex emotions tormented my soul. Confused, I cowardly followed him, pausing at the grand old clock in the hallway as it struck nine times; its sound was deeply embedded into my core. Entering the dark and dingy room, I became heavy with weakness. Shabby curtains stained with dampness barely fitted the small window, whilst the decaying wood was riddled with worms. I squirmed with disgust remembering the room just as it was. The round table took centre stage, a red linen cloth draped loosely over it, giving some warmth to the lifeless room. A single plant sat in the middle of the table, looking dead; its leaves crumbled as my body brushed past it. Martha stood quietly by the window; her face warmed my heart as she smiled affectionately at me. Age had been kind to Martha; she looked well but slightly thinner. Her brown hair with wisps of silver complemented her pale complexion.

"My dear Sophia, I knew you would return," said Martha, welcoming me in her arms.

Feeling safe in her warm embrace, I had an overwhelming sense of coming home.

"I have tried to keep the business going, but Julian has gambled away what profits we made," said Martha.

Julian kept quiet, staring vacantly out the window. Feeling the tension between them, I knew Martha was not telling me everything. The house felt hostile, cold and empty.

"What has happened, Martha?" I inquired.

"You don't need to know, Sophia; you are home now, and that's all that matters. The past years have been hard, but we have all survived. Now you are back, the light will return," said Martha.

"That's what you think, Martha; it's not over yet. Tomorrow my reign will be back once I have that ring in my possession," said Julian angrily.

"The ring belongs to me," I said calmly as the grand clock chimed loudly. Its sound echoed throughout the house. I held it tightly in my grasp, shivering uneasily. "Martha, I must retire to my room; I am exhausted."

"Yes, of course, madam, I will prepare a meal to celebrate your homecoming. You must rest now."

Her soft hazel eyes spoke an unwritten word of loyalty and love. Instantly, I knew I had to do the right thing and pay the ultimate price with my life.

Heavy-hearted, I made my way up the many stairs to my attic room, passing many chambers with ghostly images which haunted my dreams. Reaching the last few steps, and becoming aware of a woman's voice, strange sensations unnerved me. Worried, I retreated to my room as her voice became louder and louder.

"Sophia, Sophia, it's nearly time, tick-tock," she said repeatedly.

Closing the door behind me, I breathed a sigh of relief as a hazy glow filled the whole room, revealing a previously hidden mirror. Alarmingly, there was an old woman in my reflection. Mortified, examining my face, I tugged and pulled at my aged skin and sagging neck; reviewing my life with different eyes, I was now old and grey. How could this be so? Angrily, pulling away sharply from the mirror and throwing it to the floor where it smashed into tiny pieces, a deep sadness blackened my mood. Despairingly I gasped for air. Peering out of the small round window, nothing made sense anymore as I watched a flock of crows swarm over the murkiness of the canal. They flew in a circle towards my window; their menacing squawk prickled my subconscious.

"I know!" I shouted, exasperated at them.

Gone was my four-poster bed, and all the finery, just a simple mattress with a blanket was there to greet my body. Lying in silence, I listened to the sound of the crows until sleep came. Then I awoke startled, seeing a ghostly vision of my mother in a misty glow that lit up the room.

"Mother, is that you?" I inquired anxiously, sniffing the air as the sweet scent of jasmine lingered.

"Yes, my dear, it is Genevieve, your mother."

She looked serene as she gazed lovingly at me with her soft blue eyes. I stared in awe at her luminosity; her kindness engulfed me with her love. Her silver hair was neatly styled in tiny ringlets magnifying the roundness of her face.

"Sophia, my sweet child, it's time to do the right thing. Remember, you are a child of the light. The light is with you always. Now hide the ring and repent for your sins."

"Mother! Help me!" I pleaded.

"You are the light, now honour that," she replied softly as she faded into the darkness of my room, leaving a faint wispy trail of shimmering golden hues which melted my heart.

Guilt-ridden, I sat up rigid, knowing it was time to make amends from my past. Frantically, I moved the mattress, finding a small, crumpled piece of newspaper. The realisation hit me hard seeing my name in bold print.

"Wanted Madam De Jung for murder." Shamefully, I hid under the blanket, rocking back and forth, wrestling with my thoughts. Holding my ring for the last time, I reluctantly found the loose floorboard; placing it in the box, I surrendered to my fate.

Chapter 43

My time in the House of De Vries was coming to an end. So much had happened that I found it hard to take it all in. Many questions were still unanswered; perhaps I would never know. Staring out the small window towards the canal, I saw a woman looking towards me, uncannily similar to me but dressed in strange clothing. Moments later, a horse-drawn carriage drew up outside. Four burly men alighted and approached the house; they looked stern and fierce. I shrank deep into myself, knowing they had come for me.

They banged angrily at the door; there was nowhere to go but to give myself freely. Slowly I descended the flight of stairs, taking time to notice every detail of the house, the sights and smells of this sordid house that had kept me in prison, in the darkness of my mind.

"We have come to arrest Madam De Jung. We know she is here!" shouted a tall, dark-haired man.

The grand clock in the hall struck four times; I listened intently as the sound defied the moment. Courageously, I walked into the main lobby. Martha and Julian were standing next to the men. Martha tearfully hugged me for the last time. She whispered, "Sophia, it is time for you to return to the light."

"Yes, I know, my dear Martha. Thank you for being my constant companion. Until we meet again."

"Yes, madam, we will find each other; you have my word," replied Martha.

My eyes now turned to Julian, showing no remorse; he gloated at me, relishing my downfall, but I had already forgiven him. The ring is hidden; besides, he won't be in this world for much longer! His plight was far from over.

"Madam De Jung, we are arresting you for the murder of Princess Gabriella and Lucien De Vries," said the tall, dark-haired man. His deep masculine voice penetrated my soul; I could not run anymore.

"Do you understand, madam? The penalty is death."

"Yes, sir, I come willingly with you. Martha is not involved, but Julian is."

"We have only come for you; his time will come."

Grabbing me forcefully, they escorted me into the waiting carriage, taking one last look at the House of De Vries as it glowed eerily through the thick fog. Its toxic web had consumed me for many years. Now I will be free from its torment and repent for my sins. My mind raced lucidly, remembering all that I had witnessed. Hours later, we stopped abruptly.

Blindfolded, I was taken to a small derelict building; the stench was foul and putrid. I heaved, trembling with fear and reciting the Lord's Prayer.

"So, Sophia, do you think that will save you?"

Instantly I knew it was the Lord; my whole body crumbled inside.

"Take her away," he commanded. "Tomorrow, she will be no more."

"Please, my Lord, I beg of you, have mercy for me," I pleaded.

"Enough, Sophia, you were warned. Now tomorrow, you must pay the ultimate price."

"Yes, my Lord," I quivered fearfully.

"Lock her away until first light," ordered the Lord.

I was pushed into a tiny cell, bound and gagged; the sound of dripping water echoed in the chamber, amplifying my fate. Sleep did not come as I waited nervously until dawn, praying for forgiveness.

"Sophia, do not fear death; you will return to the light," said a distant voice.

Sniffing the air as fragrant patchouli oil filled the cell in a heavenly glow, I vowed never again to do any more harm.

My time had come; feeling cold and numb on the last day of January, the henchman escorted me to the plinth.

I shivered uncontrollably as he took the blindfold off. Dressed in a simple white cotton dress, I swayed nervously, as many had come to witness my death. Overcast light filled the sky with a sense of foreboding. Taking one last look amongst the crowd, I noticed the Lord standing prominently amongst the masses, his deathly eyes glared at me.

"Please, God, make this be a quick passing. I repent, I repent, I repent, please forgive me as I open my heart to the light," I mumbled quietly.

"Kneel," ordered the henchman. "I will make this quick, Madam Sophia," he whispered in my ear. "Remember the key; I have it here, hold it, Sophia, grab it tightly," he insisted.

"Yes," I stuttered as he placed it into my hand. "Who are you?" I inquired.

"The Hooded Man! Look at me, Sophia and remember my eyes," he said calmly.

His deep green eyes connected with mine; they reflected heaven and earth as one, giving me a sense of inner peace.

"Now read this, and then it will all be all over," he said calmly, handing me a prayer from the Bible.

Courageously I read Psalm 51 Verse 7, seeing the Lord fading into the hazy fog, my fear remarkably eased.

"Dear Lord, please purify my sins, and I will be clean; wash me, and I will be whiter than snow. Take me now, dear Lord of the Light." I knelt before my maker.

As the axe descended into my neck, severing an artery, deep pools of blood gushed into the waiting basket. Holding my breath for the last time, the pain was excruciating as I watched myself rise above the crowd, seeing my headless body, knowing I was free from years of torment and pain. The Lord cannot reach me now, for I am the light.

Chapter 44

The bright and expansive bubble of luminous light engulfed me in a vacuum of pure delight, noticing many colours. They swirled and danced around me, making patterns that awoke my soul. Soft and gentle, they guided me gracefully to a place of peace.

"Sophia, where are you now?" said a sweet-sounding voice.

"I'm in the empty space between heaven and earth," I replied calmly.

"Sophia, it's time to come back from your remarkable journey. Take your time and rest a little longer; breathe in the colours of the rainbow. Take another deep breath as the golden light will guide you through the realms of spirit, bringing you safely back into your body. The path you walk is now full of rich, vibrant energy. You feel lighter and brighter as you walk amongst the woodlands; stopping at the old oak tree, you smile warmly as the golden leaves surround you in a magical glow. The wise man of the tree offers you a gift of a small key. You hold it close to your heart as you walk through the valleys of new fertile land, leading you back through the path of light until you reach the stairs. Sophia, it's time to ascend; as I count backwards from ten to one, you will feel your body becoming heavier, the couch underneath you, and the warmth that resides within you. Ten, nine, eight, you are gently coming back. Seven, six, five, you are becoming aware of the sounds in the room. Four, three, two, one. You are now back in the here and now."

Feeling my body becoming solid, a deep sense of warmth radiated from my heart, giving me peace, knowing I was very much loved.

"Sophia, welcome back," said Anna. "Wow, you have been on an amazing epic journey. Can you remember any of it?"

"No, not really; it's all rather hazy, but I do feel so much better, thank you," I replied drowsily.

Anna was smartly dressed in a navy suit; her dark brown hair was neatly tied in a bun. She looked fondly at me through her crystal blue eyes; they seemed vaguely familiar to me, but I couldn't recall why.

"Thank you, Anna, you have helped me very much. I just wish I could remember it all," I replied, glancing at my finger and seeing the sapphire ring glowing radiantly. Stroking it gently for the last time, I was reluctant to return it to its rightful owner. The sharpness of the blue intensified the moment; it was a rare precious stone. I had seen it many times before at the National History Museum. Its magnetic energy compelled me as it engaged my soul on an unconscious level. Wearing the ring even for a short time was such an honour.

"Oh, can you please remind me how the ring came into your possession?" I enquired tentatively as I handed her ring back, regrettably.

"I inherited the house from my late great aunt. We are both distant descendants of Lucien De Vries. My aunt, many years ago, found it in this very room. It was hidden in a small box under a loose floorboard. She then passed it on to me. Since then, I have lent it to the museum until yesterday," said Anna.

My body suddenly stiffened as she mentioned Lucien De Vries. I gulped hard, trying to stop the tears from coming.

"It's OK, Sophia, it's over now."

"My dear, I have recorded your session for you. It will make an interesting article for the Sunday supplement; that's all I can say right now," she replied softly.

"Thank you, how long have I been on your therapy couch?"

"Two hours precisely, as instructed by Mr Hunter," she replied.

"Really, wow, how do you know my boss?" I enquired inquisitively.

"You will have to ask him that," she smiled warmly.

"Please drink plenty of water and give yourself time to heal. Your session was truly remarkable," said Anna.

"Thank you, Anna; yes, I will."

The small room was sparse with soft subtle lighting, painted in white with delicate pastel artwork, bringing a sense of calmness to the therapy room. A candle flickered gently as the grand clock in the hall downstairs chimed loudly. It echoed throughout the house, causing me to flinch. Above the door hung many beautifully coloured silk scarves. Instantly I was drawn to the delicate pink one, and strangely, I started to cough.

"I can't breathe, Anna," I said breathlessly.

Her dazzling blue eyes mesmerised me as she spoke. I felt safe in her company but also aware of how powerful she was. Hypnotised by her energy and words, I had somehow slipped through timelines bringing me face to face with my past. Do I want to revisit it? But I had a deadline to meet and an inner knowing I had to face my fears.

"Take a deep breath, Sophia. It's OK, remember your soul never forgets, but you have healed now," said Anna looking deeply into my eyes.

Standing by the small round window in the attic room, I looked towards the canal; all was quiet. I breathed a sigh of relief.

"Thank you for your kindness, Anna. I must head back to London now."

"You are very welcome; so pleased you enjoyed your stay at the House of De Vries," said Anna hugging me fondly.

Leaving the house behind, I stood by the canal, glancing up towards the attic room. My eyes fixated on the small round window; I gasped, shockingly seeing a lady waving at me. I froze, astonished, recognising it was me.

As I travelled back to London, my thoughts became my words as I made rough notes on my flight back to Gatwick, with an overriding urgency to listen to my recording. My home was still a few hours away. I sighed, frustrated, as I watched the clock tick minute by minute, knowing that Mr Hunter would promptly be phoning me at 7 pm. I have to get it right this time.

Home at last, relieved to be back relaxing on my comfy sofa, I poured myself a large glass of Sauvignon Blanc. With pen in hand, I pressed the play button, becoming increasingly alarmed by what transpired. Instantly I felt myself back in the House of De Vries, with vivid images captivating my imagination. Words effortlessly flowed, and I had an excellent story to tell.

At precisely 7 pm, Mr Hunter phones. "Good evening, Sophia. Have you got that article for me now?" he said brusquely.

"Yes, I have Mr Hunter."

"Good to hear this; I knew you wouldn't disappoint me. I expect to see your full typed article on my desk by 9 am sharp," said Mr Hunter.

Gulping another glass of wine, I sat at my computer as the words raced upon the screen, immersing myself in the world of Sophia De Jung. It catapulted me into another dimension, feeling and sensing her world. Anxiety gripped me as I raced to the climatic end. Shocked and traumatised, I retreated to my bed. Waking at dawn, I felt confident and self-assured; surely Mr Hunter would like my story?

Arriving early at the office, I prepared for my meeting. Glancing at my watch, it was 9 am, time to face Charles Hunter.

I approached Mr Hunter's office with butterflies in my tummy. Knocking on his door, I waited nervously.

"Enter," he replied.

His office as always was pristine, not a file out of place, but this time it felt different. A strong scent of patchouli oil overwhelmed me; instantly, it heightened my awareness. Charles Hunter sat comfortably in his chair; his crisp white shirt and bright blue tie contrasted against his conventional black suit. He looked relaxed as he smoothed his silvery hair from his brow.

"Good morning, Sophia. I'm looking forward to reading your manuscript," he said.

"Good morning, Mr Hunter; I feel you will find it an interesting read," I said, rubbing my neck briskly, trying to erase a sharp, sudden pain as I handed it to him.

"Thank you, I'm sure I will. What have you done to your neck?" he replied, concerned.

"I'm not sure, but it's rather painful," I replied, staring alarmingly at his emerald eyes.

"I have something for you," said Mr Hunter, making eye contact with me. His sea-green eyes sparkled radiantly, reflecting the light and darkness of the universe. Mesmerised and dumbfounded, I was engulfed in the intensity of his glare.

"Please do take a seat," he replied. "You are in shock," he said, smiling at me, as he produced a book from his desk drawer titled, *The Knowing*.

"I believe this is yours, Sophia," he said, handing me the book. "Now turn to page 212."

Turning the pages swiftly, I gasped in awe as a small key fell to the ground. Astonished and in disbelief, I sat pinching myself hard. Was this a dream, or is this my reality?

"But I don't understand."

"You will, Sophia. Time is all but an illusion of one's mind."

Speechless, I scrutinised it carefully, recognising the tiny silver patterns and the grooves within the key.

"But how?" I stuttered. "This is all rather weird. Am I dreaming?"

"Of course not," he replied.

"Sophia, there have been some changes whilst you've been away. We have a new managing director, Klaus Richter, and I have a new secretary, Martha," he said, shuffling in his chair, trying to avoid my stare.

My heartbeat quickened, hearing Klaus had returned. Still, I was somewhat perturbed remembering the recording of my deep hypnosis; it was fresh in my mind. Are they both from my sordid past? Surely not!

Moments later, there was a knock on the door.

"Enter," said Charles Hunter. "Sophia, please warmly welcome Klaus Richter back from his overseas travels, and let me introduce you to Martha."

Immediately my heart skipped a beat as they entered the room. My face turned a deathly white whilst brilliant sunlight beamed through the blinds bringing vivid images of the past and present into my vision.

Flabbergasted, I shrieked in a high-pitched tone, "Martha, is that really you?"

Her hazel eyes shone brightly at me. She looked exactly the same; her delicate features contrasted with her wavy brown long hair.

"Yes, Sophia, it is me," she said calmly.

My eyes then turned to Klaus, instantly recognising him by his distinctive blackened mole upon his forehead.

"Hello Sophia, we meet again," he smiled warmly. His kind cobalt blue eyes quickly energised my soul as he handed me a single red rose and a shiny pocket watch. Disconcertingly and shocked, immediately I was transported back to the House of De Vries. Examining the watch, I held it tightly, seeing timelines merging. Breathing deeply, I became aware of my past, present and future. In that brief moment, it all became clear.

"How could I forget, Klaus?"

"It doesn't matter, dear Sophia, you have remembered now, and that's enough. You have the key and watch back in your possession, a perfect match, don't you think? Now turn the key, Sophia," urged Klaus ...

Remember the fear and the darkness are all an illusion.
There is only light; when we remember that, we awake
to the truth of who we truly are. A pure being of light,
having an earthly experience in our physical body.

Truth.

There is only ever love.

Epilogue

And so the Prince of Dark was taken away ...
days, turned into months, and the months turned into
years. Princess of the Light was left alone but knowing
that one day in the distant future, their paths would cross again.

Now the time has come for us to rise once more and become our truth.
We had great power; many would seek our counsel.
We hid away in a cave until the day that dark was taken away and
the light became a distant star;
and through time and space, our journey had begun.

Many, many lives always knowing that we had an agreement
that we would meet in this lifetime,
to ignite one's soul upon the path of spirituality and love.

Yin and yang. Light and dark are why we are here
right now, to complete the journey of the Prince and the Princess,
for they have come full circle, and now it's time
to be that powerful light and dark again for the greater
good of mankind and for Mother Gaia.

Namaste.

Acknowledgements

Special thanks to my wonderful parents, who have always encouraged me to believe in my dreams and aspirations. Thank you.

Thanks also to my wonderful sons and their beautiful girlfriends for supporting me along this path of becoming a published author.

I also would like to thank my wonderful relatives, beautiful friends, and soul sisters who have patiently witnessed this process. They have listened and been there for me throughout this journey. Thank you all, from my heart to yours.

A big thank you to my mentor, Dawn G. Robinson. Without Dawn's help and guidance, there would be no book. Several years ago, I joined Dawn's writing group, and this book was born from a writing prompt, and so my story began. Dawn gave me the encouragement to keep writing and here I am, a published author.

Lastly, thank you to Spiffing Covers for your time and knowledge, helping me achieve my dream. Your attention to detail is brilliant. You've all made this process a wonderful experience.
www.spiffingcovers.com

House of De Vries A Book of Shadows by Susan Pfeiffer

House of De Vries is Susan's first novel, born from a writing prompt where she joined a creative writing group. She lives on the beautiful North Cornish Coast and is inspired daily by the ever-changing moving wallpaper, where light and dark embrace the rugged cliffs and the sweeping coastline.

Susan is also a professional Reiki/Spiritual and Transformational Healer with a vast knowledge of spirituality and is well-equipped to help her clients learn and heal from the inside out. She also has two wonderful grown-up sons.

Please refer to her website for more information regarding the healing Susan offers.

www.goldenhealinglight.com

"Everything is energy, and that is all there is to it."
Albert Einstein

Printed in Great Britain
by Amazon